Vaikom Muhammad Bash
varied and exciting as the
active participant in the f
he became a political pris
wandering through India and beyonu, ᴄ.ᴗᴗ
and meeting with adventures. His varied life experienceᴗ
have added depth and colour to his writing; the hardships
he has known have not quenched its irrepressible warmth
and humour.

Basheer began writing short stories in about 1937 and
his first novel *Balyakalasakhi* (Childhood Friend, 1943) was
an exciting event in the history of the Malayalam novel.
His book *Nduppoopakoranandarnnu* (My Grandfather had an
Elephant,1951) won the Central Sahitya Akademi Award,
and was selected for translation into fourteen Indian languages. Throughout, he has written stories both short and
long, on varied themes, and of great popular appeal, which
have earned him a legendary place in Malayalam literature.

V.Abdulla believes that creative writing in India has its
roots in the Indian languages and that it needs to be made
available to readers everywhere by translation into other
Indian languages and English. To this end, he himself has
from the early seventies been making available English
translations of modern classics in fiction in various Indian
languages through Sangam Books published by Orient
Longman with whom he was working.

He has to his credit half a dozen English publications
translated from his native Malayalam; Basheer,
M.T.Vasudevan Nair and Pottekkat being the more prominent writers whom he has translated. He retired when he
was Divisional Director of Orient Longman and lives in
Madras, translating and book-reviewing being his primary
interests.

Vaikom Muhammad Basheer

Poovan Banana

AND OTHER STORIES

Translated from the Malayalam by
V. Abdulla

വിവർത്തനം വി.അബ്ദുള്ള

പ്രസാധനം

Orient BlackSwan

POOVAN BANANA AND OTHER STORIES

ORIENT BLACKSWAN PRIVATE LIMITED

Registered Office
3-6-752 Himayatnagar, Hyderabad 500 029 (A.P.), INDIA
e-mail: centraloffice@orientblackswan.com

Other Offices
Bangalore, Bhopal, Bhubaneshwar, Chennai, Ernakulam, Guwahati,
Hyderabad, Jaipur, Kolkata, Lucknow, Mumbai, New Delhi, Patna

First published by Orient Longman Pvt. Ltd. under Disha Books imprint 1994
Reprinted 2005, 2007
First Orient Blackswan impression 2010

ISBN: 978 81 250 0323 6

Typeset by
Venture Graphic Pvt. Ltd.
Chennai

Printed in India at
Glorious Printers
Delhi

Published by
Orient Blackswan Private Limited
1/24 Asaf Ali Road,
New Delhi 110 002
e-mail: delhi@orientblackswan.com

Contents

	Introduction	1
	Translator's Introduction	9
1	Mother	15
2	The Love Letter	26
3	If War is to End	54
4	The Shore of Solitude	58
5	Tiger	67
6	Voices	73
7	Poovan Banana	109
8	A Man	123
9	Bully Panicker	127
10	The Blue Light	130
11	A Little Old Love Story	141
12	The World-Renowned Nose	148
13	The Walls	155
14	The Snake and the Mirror	181
15	The Gold Ring	185
16	Elephant Wool	198
	Glossary	217

Publisher's Note

In 1976, in an earlier paperback series, *Orient Longman* published *Voices/The Walls*, a book combining translations of Vaikom Muhammad Basheer's short novels *Shabdangal* (1947) and *Mathilukal* (1965).

In 1983, their associate company Sangam Books (India) Ltd. published a collection of Basheer's short stories under the title *The Love-Letter and Other Stories*.

Together these two books provided a view of nearly forty years of Basheer's writing.

In this new volume, the two books are combined, and the stories presented in chronological order, along with one more story, 'The Gold Ring', translated specially for this edition.

Also included are Professor G. Kumara Pillai's introduction to *The Love-Letter and Other Stories*, a fine study of Basheer's writing, and a Translator's Introduction by V. Abdulla. The translator of both the earlier volumes, V. Abdulla speaks with long-standing appreciation about Basheer, his writings and the experience of translating them.

Introduction

Vaikom Muhammed Basheer is one of the writers whom I love to read again and again. And every time I re-read him, I do so with immense relish because his stories never lose their freshness of appeal. I am sure that this is an experience which I share with thousands of Malayalam-speaking people who read fiction. A literary artist in the full sense of the term, Basheer strikes us by the range and intensity of his vision of life and the power and beauty of the inimitable style in which he communicates this vision. No anthology of a dozen of the best short stories in Malayalam can omit him, and any catalogue of a dozen of the best novels in the language is sure to contain the title name of one of his works. In the realm of shorter fiction his work compares favourably with the best work of his contemporaries not only in Kerala but anywhere else in the world.

Basheer is the kind of man who becomes a legend in his lifetime. Though he is popular with all sections of the reading public, very few of his readers have seen or heard him. This is especially strange in a land where every writer is expected to be a public speaker, and conferences, seminars, symposia and cultural meets are incredibly numerous. A warm-hearted person with a large circle of friends, Basheer is a brilliant conversationalist. But he shuns public appearance and is never seen on the platform. This has given him an aura of mystery which is reinforced by the glimpses of his life revealed by his stories, by reports of interviews with him and by the funny letters he sends to editors who publish them in their journals in lieu of his stories.

Abandonment of school and home in early youth, active participation in the fight for freedom and consequent police persecution and a few terms in jail, eight years of adventurous wandering throughout the length and breadth of India and even beyond, years of starvation as a struggling writer, spells of mental derangement, a late marriage and the evolution of an irresponsible bachelor into a devoted husband and a doting father—these are chapters of an eventful life which lend colour to the image of his personality. And besides all this, the character of the man leaves its imprint on the reader as a portrait of the artist as jesting prophet.

Basheer's literary output is comparatively small. Apart from a one-act play *Kathabheejam* (The Seed of a Story), an autobiographical fragment *Ormayude Arakal* (Chambers of Memory) and a volume of miscellaneous writings *Nerum Nunayum* (Fact and Fiction), he has produced only about a hundred short stories, and about a dozen short novels or longer tales in a writing career of more than forty years during which he had practically no other occupation. But what he lacks in quantity he gains in quality. A prefectionist by temperament, he has given us little that is slipshod. The only limitations or defects that can be pointed out are that he has not attempted the longer novel, and that once in a way he seems to delight in describing the sordid for its own sake as in some parts of his short novel *Shabdangal* (Voices). Except for these, he has given us a body of work which bears the indelible impress of an authentic master in the art of story-telling.

Prose fiction in Malayalam was born about a hundred years ago. Though we had fine writers, like Vengayil Kunhiraman Nayanar (1861-1915) and K. Sukumaran (1867-1956) in the first generation, and E.V. Krishna Pillai (1876-1938) in the second generation, who could spin out a humorous skit or contrive a well-made tale, the Malayalam short story came into its own only in the thirties of the present century. As for the novel, we were fortunate enough to have two giants at the beginning— O.Chandu Menon (1847-1900) whose *Indulekha* was published in 1889 and C.V. Raman Pillai (1858-1922) whose *Marthanda Varma* came out in 1891. But after their time the novel languished until a new life was given to it in the forties of this century. The same generation of writers who ushered in the golden age of the short story in the thirties also proceeded to inaugurate the second creative period in the history of the novel in the next decade. Vaikom Muhammed Basheer (b. 1910) belongs to this generation of highly gifted writers who made fiction one of the chief glories of our literature. The other major writers of this group are P. Kesava Dev, Thakazhi Sivasankara Pillai, S.K. Pottekkat, Lalithambika Antharjanam, Karur Nilakanta Pillai, Ponkunnam Varkey and P.C. Kuttikrishnan. They share a deep concern about contemporary social realities and their style is by and large based on conversational idiom. Beyond this no generalisation is possible about them. In fact any generalisation is misleading to a great extent because each of them has an invididual way of looking at life and a distinctive approach to the craft of fiction.

From the sociological point of view Basheer is of special significance to us. He was the first major writer to emerge from the large Muslim community in Kerala and thus he made a signal contribution to the evolution of Malayalam writing into the literature of the entire Malayalam-speaking people. His introduction into our literature of the Muslim background, imagery from Muslim religious lore and telling phrases and expressions peculiar to the community, is of more than sociological import. It adds a special colour to some of his works—especially, three of his novels. *Balyakalasakhi* (Childhood Friend, 1943), *Nduppoopakoranandarnnu* (My Grandfather Had an Elephant, 1951) and *Pathummade Aadu* (Pathumma's Goat, 1959). It should be emphasised that the abiding appeal of Basheer's writing comes from his deep humanity which transcends all partisan considerations and that the Muslim element is employed to give it a 'local habitation and a name'.

Balyakalasakhi was one of the earliest novels which heralded what I have called the second creative period in the history of the Malayalam novel. A simple story of passionate young love set against the background of a declining middle-class Muslim family, it was the first important literary work in Malayalam to portray Muslim customs and manners. But it is remembered mainly for the flaming intensity of the tragedy of Majid and Suhra. *Pathummade Aadu* is a moving tragicomedy woven out of the everyday life of a large impoverished Muslim family. Here too the appeal is universal because it comes from the alchemy of the author's art which transmutes the most trivial things of day-to-day occurrence into the stuff of exquisite art.

Nduppoopakoranandarnnu is perhaps the only work in which there is an obvious message for the Muslim community. The story is woven round the love of Nissar Ahmed for Kunjupathumma. But the dominant character is Kunjupathumma's mother who gloats over the glory that was, and the central theme is the conflict between the values she upholds and those of the educated, forward-looking Nissar Ahmed. The message of the need for modernisation is embodied in a story with the strange beauty of a myth. It is spiced with pleasant humour and coloured with images and anecdotes from Muslim religious lore.

Any student of Basheer's short stories and longer tales is struck by the variety of theme and tone in them. He has enshrined in them every kind of experience from the pangs of hunger and sex to the rapture of mystic vision. Its range includes stark realistic pictures of the material world as well as the realm of fantasy haunted by ghosts and spirits. He has written on love and hate, on politicians and pickpockets, on the foibles of woman and the mystery of the mind of man, on the fancies of childhood and the disillusionments of adult life. His vision of life is comprehensive enough to perceive everything from the sublime to the ridiculous. He has an intense sense of the tragedy of life and at the same time an irrepressible sense of humour. The present volume is a carefully prepared selection which represents as many facets of Basheer's art as possible.

As will be seen in this selection, one of the secrets of Basheer's success is the rare kind of intimacy he establishes with the reader. This kind of rapport arises from the fact that the writer creates the impression that he is revealing his own personal experience. In 'Mother' he writes : 'I am saying this about my mother; whatever I intend saying hereafter is about my mother.' 'The Blue Light' opens with the words: 'This is the story of one of the amazing incidents in my life'. Some kind of personal involvement on the part of the author is suggested in most of the stories. In a story like 'Mother' there is a genuine subjective element. In fact many of his stories have an autobiographical element in them and his stories are the richer for the unusual variety of experience he has actually gone through. But whether the 'I' of a story is the author or not, this device is very effective as a part of the narrative technique. In this respect he is the opposite of his famous contemporary, Thakazhi Sivasankara Pillai, whose approach is that of the impersonal narrator, of the uninvolved observer and objective analyst.

There is a vivid strain of realism in stories like 'Mother', 'Tiger' and 'Bully Panicker', but they are arresting for other qualities as well. Stories such as 'The Birthday' and 'Hunger' characterised mainly by stark realism have been excluded from this anthology probably because they are not uncommon. A piece like 'The Shore of Solitude' belongs to the other extreme of the spectrum of his art. It comes from a group which consists of pieces which are poems in prose rather than stories and which explore a level of experience akin to the mystical. It reminds us of the Sufi mystics, of Tagore and of Gibran. It portrays the luminous image of the love that is beyond the trammels of the flesh, beyond the bounds of time and space. It is the soulful yearning of the eternal lover for the immortal beloved. Basheer is endowed with a rare poetic gift and we get glimpses of it in many other stories as well. But it is in pieces such as 'The Shore of Solitude' that the poet in him finds the fullest expression.

Basheer has a flair for the portrayal of the unusual, the mysterious and the supernatural. In stories such as 'The Blue Light' and 'The Snake and the Mirror', he creates a world of fantasy which he makes absolutely convincing by his superb skill in the necessary 'willing supension of disbelief'. The weird experience of living for days and nights in a haunted house with no company except the ghost of a beautiful young woman; or the eerie encounter with a cobra which coils round one's left arm and from that position calmly enjoys the beauty of its own reflection in a mirror—Basheer can narrate such things with a sure touch of authenticity. The short piece 'A Man' shows how even a purely human story can be invested with a sense of mystery by the unexpected revelation of the enigma that man is. 'A Little Old Love Story' does not seem to belong to this category. And yet, in spite of its realistic framework, it deals with the unusual experience of a dream suddenly turning into a nightmare.

But not all of Basheer's stories are concerned with the supernatural and the unusual. The vast majority of his stories are rooted in earthy reality and are irradiated by his love for his fellow-beings. His imaginative sympathy is such that their joys and sorrows and all their problems become as much his as theirs. 'Elephant Wool' is a fascinating story that reveals an extraordinary insight into the psychology of a nine-year-old boy. The little jealousies, triumphs, humiliations and adventures of the age at which one cherishes a peacock feather or an elephant hair as a priceless treasure are described realistically and unsentimentally with an artless simplicity which defies analysis. It reminds us of the child Majid who declares in *Balyakalasakhi* that one plus one is a slightly bigger one and the naive Kunjupathumma in *Nduppoopakoranandarnnu* to whom marriage is just something which bestows on her the privilege of chewing betel. It is a far cry from the innocence of childhood to the complex mind of a criminal. But Basheer can depict both with equal understanding. His longer tales dealing with the characters of the underworld have the durability of folklore. In *Mucheettukalikkarente Makal* (The Cardsharper's Daughter), *Anavaarivum Ponkurisum* (The Elephant Lifter and the Gold Cross) and *Stthalathe Pradhana Divvan* (The Chief Local Celebrity) he has created a little world of petty thieves, pickpockets, small-time gamblers and two princes of their trade, Raman Nair the Elephant Lifter and Thoma of the Gold Cross, all of whom he has immortalised not as criminals but as colourful human beings with a different way of life.

Basheer's unbounded love for mankind made him a rebel in his youth. The uncompromising opposition to all kinds of tyranny, hypocrisy and superstition is a recurring theme in his writings. Sometimes this opposition took a negative turn as in the bitter anarchism and grim cynicism of the short novel *Shabdangal* (Voices, 1947). But very often his voice has been that of passionate idealism especially in the earlier stories. He is among the few writers who participated actively in the nationalist movement. He has written stories which recapture brilliantly the agony and the ecstasy of the stormy days of our struggle for freedom. 'Mother' is a powerful story of this group which includes other pieces such as 'Mother India' and 'The Policeman's Daughter'. By interweaving the pathos of an individual's situation with the general suffering of humanity and by juxtaposing the conflicting calls of the mother and the motherland, he has given a remarkable intesity to a straightforward, unadorned story in 'Mother'. 'Tiger' and 'Bully Panicker' deal with soulless tyranny, against the background of jail life, with which Basheer became familiar as a freedom-fighter and as a 'dangerous writer'. The effect of a strong indictment of oppression is conveyed to us without the use of rhetoric or sentimentalism.

Basheer views life as a tragicomedy. His sense of the comic is one of the most outstanding traits that contribute to the wider appeal of his writings. He has a fresh and delicious sense of humour and a brilliant mastery of wit, irony and satire. As he says in *Mathilukal* (The Walls), he never loses an opportunity to laugh and he regards laughter as 'God's special gift'. The hilarious humour of longer tales such as 'The Love Letter' and 'The Elephant Lifter and the Gold Cross' is one of the most delightful things in the whole range of our literature. In almost all his novels and longer tales the serious and the comic are interwoven in different ways.

In 'The Love Letter' (which is included in this volume) we have the youthful Basheer at his very best. The theme is obviously love and love thwarted by religion at that. It is the romantic love of a Nayar (Hindu) youth, Kesavan Nayar, for a Christian girl, Saramma. She is a damsel in distress—a burden on her father and step-mother, unemployed and without a dowry to offer a prospective Christian bridegroom. It is a serious situation which offers a great deal of scope for rhetoric, sentimentalism and melodrama. But Basheer tackles it with a rare lightness of touch and he does it without evading any of the numerous problems inherent in the complex situation. In fact one of his famous dictums on humour occurs in this story : 'Humour is the perfume of life'. Kesavan Nayar is a bank clerk lodging with Saramma's father and she approaches him for help in finding a job. After great deliberation, he offers her a regular salary and a permanent vacancy—in his own heart. She accepts the offer and continues to receive the salary for months on end without so much as allowing him to touch her. He is triumphant at the end, with his love's labours won, and she emerges as one of the merriest of the merry wives of Kerala.

Of the short stories that Basheer has written in a lighter vein, 'Poovan Banana' is perhaps the most amusing. It is a pity that philistine critics have accused the author of antifeminism in his writing this modern version of the taming of a shrew.

Even though a love of sheer fun is the most remarkable feature of Basheer's comic vision, he often employs an ironical or satirical tone. When he makes the famous writer reveal his original prescription to end all wars '... every man and woman living on this earth should get eczema like me' (If War is to End), he is not only having a comical dig at the futility of disarmament schemes, no-war pacts and peace offensives, but also poking fun at importunate journalists who expect every famous man to express his views on everything under the sun. The bizarre story 'The World-Renowned Nose' is a striking satire on the psychology of the masses whose curiosity is aroused by anything slightly unusual and the inveterate tendency of politicians to exploit everything for partisan ends.

For Shri V. Abdulla the translation of Basheer is a labour of love. It is the consummation of his life-long appreciation of Basheer, the man and his work. This translation of thirteen representative stories* is not Shri Abdulla's first work in this line. It is a sequel to his earlier volume, *Voices/The Walls*, a fine rendering of a short novel and a long tale by Basheer. Proficient in both languages and well-experienced in original writing as well as in translation, Shri Abdulla has done his work with steady competence and loving care. There are special difficulties that a translator of Basheer has to face. His language is very simple, but his style is terse and without any rhetorie. His writing is full of colloquial idioms and very often he produces a rare effect by a subtle turn of phrase. Above all he is a writer with a magic touch, and his artless art has an elusive charm. In spite of all this Shri Abdulla has succeeded in producing an English version which can communicate as much of the beauty and power of the original as is possible in any such version. I am sure this book will give the non-Malayalee reader an opportunity to share in the enjoyment of what we regard as one of the best and brightest achievements of Malayalam fiction.

G. Kumara Pillai

---

*   This refers to the volume, *The Love-Letter and other Stories* in which thirteen of
Basheer's stories appeared in translation.

Translator's Introduction

Vaikom Muhammad Basheer started writing late in life. His first book *Balyakalasakhi* (Childhood Friend, 1943) was published when he was about thrityfive. Few first books have made such an impact in Malayalam. The modest-looking 96-page paperback in the red and white covers went into three reprints within six months.

The son of a timber contractor whose business had fallen on bad days, Basheer was one of a large family. Living conditions at home were on the borderline between proverty and petty affluence. His formal education stopped with the fifth form when he ran away from school to take part in India's freedom struggle. He was beaten up by the police and jailed for defying the salt laws. On coming out of jail he organised a terrorist movement which again set the police on his trail with a warrant for his arrest. He then left Kerala and wandered round the country for almost seven years. On returning home he was picked up by the police of the tyrannical Dewan's regime of Travancore. He was kept as an 'under-trial' for more than six months and then received a sentence of rigorous imprisonment which he served. He came back to a family by then even more impoverished and he started his writing. There is no better account of the early conditions under which he wrote than in his foreword to *Vishappu* (Hunger, 1954), which reads as follows in translation:

> It is years since I have started writing stories. When did I start? I think it was from 1937. I have been living in Ernakulam since then. I was a writer by profession. I wrote a

great deal. I would get my writing published in newspapers and journals. No one paid me for it.

These stories were published between 1937 and 1941 in *Navajeevan*, a weekly published in Trivandrum in those days. What times! With four annas a day you could live a life of luxury. Four annas...! Let alone four annas, one couldn't get four pice in those days. Weeks, months, years...were spent in anxiety. I lived through them with a firm belief in a bright future.

'The ink with which I am writing this has been borrowed. I have borrowed the paper and the envelope. I am in want. I request you to send me something to help me.' So I wrote to editors. No one helped me with anything. I wrote all the same. I wrote a large number of stories. I lived on my writing.

The difficulty was not in writing the stories. I required four pice to send them by book-post to editors. That was the anchal postage. Four pice...four pice...God, how many persons have I begged for four pice!

And so I would beg and get four pice to buy stamps with which to send the story by book-post. Then came the burning anxiety of waiting; to see the coming week's journal...has the story come out? Oh, what a relief! The story has been published!

In those days half a glass of tea cost a quarter of an anna. I had no means to get that quarter of an anna. Without a quarter anna, without the means to buy half a glass of tea, I have sat and wept. I could not laugh then. Many years have gone by....

Today, smiling, I place these stories in book form before my kind readers. Please accept them.

I wish all my readers well.

During his long years of exile, Basheer travelled widely and lived by his wits which must have been sharpened by constant uncertainty about where he would get his next meal from or where he would find a roof over his head. Footloose and fancy-free, he read a great deal during his wanderings. This varied experience is reflected in Basheer's writing which is an amalgam of autobiography and imagination, difficult to unravel into separate strands.

Balyakalasakhi, a simple tale of love and friendship and tragedy, was written in the simplest possible Malayalam in the ordinary language of the people. 'Sanskritised' or 'bookish' Malayalam was deliberately discarded. Basheer was no poineer in adopting this style but his conscious adherence to it established it as the language of the Malayalam novel thereafter. Much more significant than the style itself was the content. There was no intricately woven plot and delineation of character and background moralising. Life as it was lived, sometimes raw, sometimes smooth and sentimental and perhaps slushy, unrolled itself in simple narrative and dialogue. *Balyakalasakhi* struck an emotional chord in the heart of every Malayalee in Kerala and outside.

Basheer has seen great hardship in his life and is familiar with the seamy side of humanity. But his pen is never dipped in gall. The essential humanist that he is, he can sense the goodness in every man and woman, that spark of divinity in the makeup of every being. He has a tremendous sense of humour and a capacity for laughter which he wants to share with his readers in full measure. And so out of everyday occurrence and experience he weaves tales with a magic simplicity that makes contact with readers' minds with instant impact.

The Muslim community of which Basheer is a part concerns him a great deal. He focuses on their shortcomings and lack of education and the way their women bring up their children. He preaches to them in the mantle of a prophet while speaking the language of the jester. To this group belong his three major novelettes—*Balyakalasakhi, Nduppoopakoranandarnnu* (My Grandfather had an Elephant, 1951) and *Pathummade Aadu* (Pathumma's Goat, 1959). No amount of discursive writing about these works can convey the artistry and wit in which they abound. You read and re-read them. You laugh till the tears blot your vision and then you get an uncomfortable feeling that you have been made to weep without your knowing. In *Pathummade Aadu* especially, the pendulum swings from laughter to tears and back again with an a-rhythmic compulsion all its own.

Fortunately for English readers, an excellent translation of these three major stories has been done by Prof R.E. Asher of the Edinburgh University as part of the UNESCO project on world classics. The book has been published by the Edinburgh University Press in 1980 under the lead title 'Me Grandad 'ad an

Elephant'. An Indian paperback edition has been brought out by Penguin India in 1991.

No doubt Basheer never forgets, nor lets his readers forget, that he is a Muslim but he has a catholicity of outlook which transcends the narrow confines of partisan faith. One often gets the feeling that his persistence in labelling himself a Muslim is to mock at the numerous Malayalees who label themselves by the faiths of their forefathers in caste and sub-caste ridden Kerala.

Basheer's other novels and short stories deal with love and marriage and beliefs and political attitudes. All these were written about not in the abstract but in terms of experiences and incidents. Human suffering is very much there in his writings but he puts it across in simple narrative and everyday speech in a way which touches one far more effectively than flights of florid prose.

Basheer has written on a variety of experiences and incidents and human foibles ranging from the supernatural to the taming of a 'wifely shrew'. Some were written in prison and there is a series of stories, hilarious and heartwarming, about the lives of some 'toughs' whom he met in prison and the lockup. Ettukali (Spider), Mammoonhi Ponkurisu (Golden Cross, since he tried to steal a gold cross from the local church), Thoma and Anavari(elephant-stealer) and Raman Nair have become immortals in the literary lore of Malayalam. Basheer has written one play Kathabheejam (The Seed of a Story, 1944) and a rambling, incomplete kind of autobiography, Ormayude Arakal (Chambers of Memory, 1973).

A faily long Basheer novel, Anuragathinte Dinangal (Days of Love), (perhaps even longer than 'My Grandfather had an Elephant') was brought out in 1981. The author reluctantly agreed to it at the insistence of some literary friends who had started a publishing house. The manuscript was rescued from a pile of unpublished material found in Basheer's house. It can be called an uncut diamond from Basheer's literary workshop.

Basheer is not a prolific writer. He has published 26 titles so far, averaging about a hundred pages each. This is not a large output over a writing age of about thirty years. The main reason for this relatively low output is that Basheer is a perfectionist. He writes and rewrites when he puts pen to paper and aims at achieving the maximum economy of words, preferably simple everyday words. He never permits anything shoddy or second-rate to come out in his name and is in fact extremely sensitive about it. Even the simple little postcards he writes to friends are a delight to read and editors have made use of them in lieu of articles in many a journal. Along with simplicity of language he makes abundant use of dialogue and weaves in subtle imagery which blends into a style that sets Basheer's writing apart.

This leads me to the problems of translating Basheer. His Malayalam is so artfully simple that the translator trips up in his choice of words. The very terseness of his writing brought to perfection by continuous writing and rewriting poses somewhat baffling problems to the translator. Much of this relates to his use of colloquial words whose nuances of meaning are difficult to convey in any language other than the original. This has been my peculiar problem in translating Basheer, something I have not had to contend with in translating many other modern writers in Malayalam whose very prolixity gives one more elbow-room. For a translator who gets fully absorbed in Basher's Malayalam it is difficult to judge how an English translation would appear to a non-Malayalee reader.

Something of this elusive quality of Basheer's writing is illustrated in the instance of the same process of translation into a different medium altogether—that of the film. Dialogue and background sketched in simple and colourful strokes play a great part in Basheer's writings. Despite these apparent aids, directors and screenplay writers have found it difficult to transform the stories into the medium of the film. Five of Basheer's stories have been filmed and two have been televised, all in Malayalam. To take the two bad films first, *Balyakalasakhi* (Childhood Friend) and *Mucheettukalikkarente Makal* (The Cardsharper's Daughter) were poor productions which hardly made an impact on audiences. The reason may have been that the screenplay was done by professionals familiar with the grammar of film but not conversant with Basheer's narrative nuances. *Prema Lekhanam*(The Love Letter), which is included here and was directed by a well-known maker of non-commercial movies (who is longer alive), is still in the cans and is not likely to be released.

One short story of Basheer's, *Neela Velicham* (The Blue Light) which also finds a place in this collection was made into a very successful film under the title *Bhargavi Nilayam* (The Abode of Bhargavi) now used freely in Malayalam to mean 'haunted house'. It is a fantasy where a ghost and living characters intermingle to present a poetic tale which is even now remembered by Malayalee cinema audiences. Basheer wrote the dialogues himself over a period of time under the advice of a talented cameraman-director. It was just a happy synchronization which has not been repeated. Basheer unsuccessfully tried to write the screenplay for *Nduppoopakoranandarnnu* but it has never seen the light of day.

The one film that made the grade among discerning cinema audiences in India and abroad is *Mathilukal* (The Walls), also included here. The screenplay and direction were by Adoor Gopalakrishnan, one of India's foremost contemporary film makers with many national and international awards to his credit. It was released in 1990 and won the President's Gold Medal for the best Indian picture made that year. In this well-known classic, Basheer dealt with the primordial male yearning for his mate with a winsome lightness of touch. The theme was interwoven into a simple account of a political prisoner languishing in a jail which was separated from the women's prison by a high wall. Adoor Gopalakrishnan transformed it into a great and sensitive film experience.

Mother

The mother writes to the son eking out his living amid the miseries of a distant city. She writes with pain in her heart.

'Son, I just want to see you.'

It didn't stop there. Many more words were strung together into sentences with no grammar and put down in a scrawling hand. And yet the sorrow in her heart is clear beyond doubt. It is a long time since they have seen each other.

The son knows that his mother is expecting him every day. But what can he do? He has no money to undertake the journey. Each day's living is a problem. Somehow I must leave tomorrow; I must go and see mother, so he consoles himself. But the days become weeks, the weeks turn into months and the months run into years.

The mother waits for the son every day.

I am saying this about my mother. Whatever I intend saying hereafter is about my mother. Every son would have similar things to say about his own mother in this India where we live. I am going to talk of the freedom struggle. It has no direct relationship with my mother. Except that I am the son of my mother. All over India there are mothers who have given birth to children like me. What did they do when their children were locked up in prison in the cause of the freedom of their motherland? The young women and men of India were persecuted and beaten up and had their bones broken by the lackeys of the foreign government. They were herded into prisons. What did their mothers in the thousands of homes outside do? I cannot say for certain. But I know well what my mother did.

I am jotting down what happened without any aim. When I read mother's letter some old memories come back to me. The story of how I went from Vaikom to Calicut to take part in the salt satyagraha.

I have to say something before I record that event. I am not revealing a secret when I say that I am writing this in 1937 or that India is still not free. I have however to reveal the secret that I received blows and was persecuted because of Gandhiji. Anyhow, if my mother had not given birth to me none of this would have happened. My mother would not have suffered any mental agony because of me. Why did my mother bring me into this land of slavery and poverty and untold misery? Perhaps this question is being asked of all mothers in India by their sons and daughters. Or else this question must be lying unasked in the minds of men and women. Why is India so poor? I cannot say with pride, 'I am an Indian.' I am but a slave. I detest the enslaved country that is India. But...is not India also my mother? Just as the mother who gave birth to me has expectations of me, does not India also expect something from me? The earth of India expects to receive my dead body just as my mother expects to see my living one.

Expectations!

I remember.

My mother gave birth to me. She fed me at her breast and brought me up. She made a man of me. Mother says I was born out of her longing. 'You were born to me after fond expectation and yearning.' Every mother says this to her offspring. I cannot record here the feelings that fill my heart. Like the chains that bind my hand, I see before me police lockup rooms, prisons, gallows and in front of them policemen, soldiers, jailors!

'India is a vast prison with high walls that confine the mind and body!' Gandhiji said this. I do not know when. I remember well the beating I received because of Gandhiji. I was beaten by a brahman called Venkateshwara Iyer. He was the headmaster of the Vaikom English High School. Seven sharp blows with a cane. That was during the days of the Vaikom satyagraha.

There was much excitement and commotion in the town because Gandhiji was coming.

There were large crowds on the banks of the canal and at the boat jetty. I pushed through the crowds with other students and reached the front line. We saw Gandhiji in the boat at a distance. A roar as if from the sea rose from a thousand throats. It rose like a challenge to foreign rule, 'Mahatma...Gandhi... ki...jai!'

The half-naked fakir bared his gums from where two teeth were missing and smiled as he landed at the jetty with hands folded in salutation. There was a great deal of noise all round. He got into an open car. The car moved forward slowly through the crowd, heading for the Satyagraha Ashram. A number of students hung on to the side of the car. I was among them. In all that confusion I had one wish! To touch the Mahatma, beloved of the world! I felt I would drop dead unless I touched him. Suppose someone among the hundreds of thousands of people there saw me? I was frightened and anxious. I shut out everything and lightly touched Gandhiji on the left shoulder!

No one knew of that.

That evening when I went home I told my mother with pride. 'Umma, I touched Gandhi.'

My mother who had no idea of the nature of this thing called Gandhi trembled in fright and consternation. 'Oh...my son...!' said mother, looking at me open-mouthed.

I remember.

Our headmaster was against satyagraha. He was against Gandhiji also. So he had prohibited the students from wearing rough homespun khadi. He had also ordered that they should not visit the ashram.

I wore khadi those days; and went to the ashram. One day, as I entered the class, the headmaster called me. He said with cruel laughter, 'My! Look at his clothes!'

I said nothing. Again he asked me,'You rascal has your father ever worn this?'

I said,'No.'

One day I went into the class some three minutes after the bell had rung. He was standing on the veranda with a cane. When he asked why I was late, I replied that I had gone to the ashram.

'Who have you got there?' He stood erect and gave me six blows on my palm with the cane.

'Don't go there again! Understand, you rascal?' He gave me one more blow on the back.

But I went again.

I remember.

In those days I owned one khadi shirt and one khadi dhoti. Just one shirt and dhoti. At that time khadi was a symbol of protest. I swore that I would not wear foreign cloth. I would say that if I died I should be buried wrapped in khadi cloth.

Mother would ask, 'Where did you get this coarse cloth which itches?' She believed that khadi next to the skin would make you itch!

I would say, 'This cloth is made in our own land, in India.'

And so—Gandhiji, the Ali brothers, self-government, British domination—these were the topics of conversation.

The old men in our town had only two youngsters whom they could ask to clear their doubts about England or China. One was Mr K.R. Narayanan. The indefatigable Mr Narayanan was the special correspondent of most of the newspapers. And if anyone asked me any question on any topic I hardly ever said, 'I don't know.' But once I was stumped for an answer.

Mother asked, 'Well, will this Kanthi put an end to our starvation?'

It was a big problem. It affected the entire country. I knew nothing about it. But I said, 'When India becomes free, our starvation will end!'

The year was 1930. I think it was that year that Gandhiji sent from the Sabarmati Ashram his letter containing his famous eleven-point programme to the Viceroy, Lord Irwin. I think it was a young Englishman named Reynolds who took the letter. But no satisfactory reply was received. As mentioned in the letter Gandhiji started his programme of satyagraha. Gandhiji set out with seventy followers to the sea near Dandi to break the salt laws. The British Government had levied a tax even on salt used by the millions of poor in the country. Before starting on the Dandi march which shook the entire country Gandhiji announced: 'Either I shall return to the ashram after having succeeded in achieving our demands, or my dead body will be found floating on the Arabian Sea.'

Gandhiji to die? The question echoed from the Himalayas to Kanyakumari and the whole country was in seething turmoil. The British Government used all its powers to oppose the unarmed Indians. The military, the police, jails—the Government was only these. Gandhiji and his followers were arrested on the seashore near Dandi.

Like other parts of the country Kerala was also agitated. The people who broke the salt laws on the seashore at Calicut were treated brutally under instructions from the Police Superintendent. They were kicked by heavy booted feet and beaten with lathis. And that too at the hands of Indian soldiers and policemen!

Kelappan, Muhammed Abdur Rahiman and other leaders were arrested. More people flouted the laws and there were more arrests. And police violence. The most heart-rending however, was the treatment meted out to the students on Calicut beach. Students so young! The future citizens of Kerala. They were beaten and felled to the ground by the policemen. Hundreds of students lay on the beach at Calicut bleeding, with heads broken. This is a statement made by one of the leaders, published in the *Mathrubhumi:*

'That policemen should have raised their hands and beaten up the poor students who had gathered in Calicut beach to do their duty by their motherland! They were mere boys, unarmed and innocent. Their heads and their arms and legs were broken by policemen who claim to be born of Malayali women! When I find that the so-called men of status and wealth in this town remain silent about such goings-on, why should I blame the ignorant policemen who blindly obey the orders of their superior officers?'

Those were days when men of status kept silent. But the common man was not silent. Men and women marched in protest singing songs of defiance.

I went too. Without asking anyone. I gave up my studies and went to Calicut with a companion named Bavo. Bavo took a gold ornament from his house. We sold it at Vaikom. That evening my mother was cooking in the kitchen. Mother knew nothing. I asked for a glass of water from my mother as a kind of farewell. I drank it, looked at her and left.

We were afraid someone would follow us. We got off at Ernakulam and walked to the Edapalli railway station. It was dark, well past sunset. The train was very late. Then some policemen came in. We were trembling in fear. They called each person and questioned him. We pretended to be sleeping. One of them jabbed me in the belly with a lathi and called me. He shone a light in my face and asked, 'Where are you going, you rascal?'

What was I to say? I was afraid to tell him that I was going to Calicut to join the Congress. I lied, 'I'm going to Shoranur.'

'Why?'

One more lie. 'My uncle has a tea shop there.'

Luckily he did not ask any more questions. They were in search of a thief. We bought tickets to Shoranur, got off there, walked up to Pattambi and again took the train to Calicut. There we stayed at the Al-Ameen Lodge. The first thing I did was to write to a person who had come from near my village. He was Syed Mohamed who was then in Bellary Jail. I wrote to him saying that I had made up my mind to dedicate myself to the service of the motherland. I would use all my powers to break the chain of slavery which bound her. I would court arrest immediately.

He replied, 'I have just a few more days left. Then I will be released. You may join the Congress only after we meet and talk.' He was at that time the joint editor of the newspaper *Al-Ameen* and an important leader. He, along with E. Moidu Moulavi and others, had received a severe beating from the Superintendent of Police, Amu. I did not have the patience to wait till his return. India was going to be free the next day; I must also have a part in fighting for that freedom! Many who belonged to my religion had not joined the freedom struggle. I had to redress that imbalance.

But my companion did not wish to join the Congress. He tried in many ways to dissuade me. His father came down and abused me a great deal for inducing his son to run away from home. I gathered that the incident had caused a great commotion back home. I felt despondent. It was not I who had run away from home with his son. But no one would believe me, for I was older. I was in a sad plight. At that time my father also came. Again I lied. 'I'm not joining the Congress. Nor am I going back to school. I'm looking for a job. I'll get it soon.' I managed to soothe my father's feelings and send him back. I then went straight to the Congress office. There again I was to be disappointed. They suspected me to be in the pay of the C.I.D! Their doubts were strengthened by my diary. I had jotted down things in it in different languages—English, Malayalam, Tamil, Hindi and Arabic. I left it on a bench while I went to the toilet. When I returned I found that the Secretary had picked it up and was reading it. He could not have understood much of it. But it gave him reason to doubt me. I showed him Syed Mohamed's letter. Even then his doubts were not cleared. They tried to assess me from my appearance and my general demeanour. Photographs of national leaders hung on the walls of the office. I saw the picture of a man with a thin moustache on his upper lip and a look of quiet dignity. He wore a felt hat at a rakish angle and a white shirt with broad collars. I felt contemptuous of this leader dressed in foreign clothes and I asked who it was.

The Secretary said, 'Bhagat Singh.'

My heart missed a beat when I heard that. The great adventurous Bhagat Singh! He had not been hanged then. I had read in the papers about the three revolutionaries involved in the Punjab Conspiracy Case—Bhagat Singh, Rajguru and Sukhdev. I had heard of their attempts to throw a bomb in the Assembly and to blow up the Viceroy's train. I looked at the photograph intently. The Secretary said, 'You have Bhagat Singh's features. Your moustache and shirt collar are identical. All you need is a felt hat!'

I said nothing. I was also thinking of the similarity of features between Bhagat Singh and myself. The Secretary again asked me, 'Are you really a Muslim?'

I said, 'Why do you doubt that?' I told him my life story until then. Finally he asked me, 'Are you ready to go to the beach tomorrow and make salt?'

'Ready!' I agreed.

And so we got up early the next morning. We were getting ready to start with the mud pots and flags and other things when we heard a *thud – thud* on the stairs. We were surprised to see some six or seven policemen walking in with an Inspector in charge. All eleven of us were arrested and taken away.

That was a Sunday morning. None of us had eaten anything. I was weak with loss of sleep. A crowd followed us. When we reached the police station all my courage evaporated. It was my first visit to such a place. Swords, bayonets and handcuffs hung from the wall and gleamed balefully at me. I was thoroughly intimidated by the shining weapons and the cruel faces of the policemen. The place reminded me of my conception of hell.

We were lined up on the veranda. The Inspector with the narrow grey eyes went in. A hefty policeman with long arms marched up and down in front of us. His bulging red eyes looked at each of us in turn. His number was 270. He caught hold of our volunteer captain by the neck and pushed him into the office room. We heard the sounds of blows and kicks and loud cries. I trembled. I was standing fourth in row. Ten minutes later the second man was taken in.

I shivered as I heard his heart-rending cries. I decided I would ask for pardon. But only for a minute. For again I thought to myself, why ask for pardon? I have done no wrong. How many young men and women have courted death in the cause of freedom. I thought of Bhagat Singh and his comrades. Let me die. It is my duty!

Constable No. 270 was asking each one of us where we came from. The others replied, 'Cannanore. Tellicherry. Ponani.'

He asked me, 'Yours?'

I said, 'Vaikom!'

Vaikom. He looked at me with surprise. 'Name?'

I gave my name. No. 270 raised his head and asked me,

'Does Travancore have self-government?'

I replied, 'No. Gandhiji has said there need not be any struggle in the Indian states.'

'Hm.' He grunted fiercely. *Phut – phut*! Two violent blows fell on the nape of my neck! Then he caught me by the shoulders and made me bend down. He began beating me. It sounded as if he were beating upon a copper pot. I counted up to seventeen, or perhaps it was twentyseven. After this I stopped counting. Why keep count?

Badly beaten up, I was finally escorted inside with the help of two policemen. Seeing the state I was in, the Inspector asked, 'Hm?'

A policeman said, 'Nambiar had a small go— '

The Inspector grunted as if it was nothing, 'Hm.'

Another policeman took off my shirt and other clothing and called out my height, girth and identifying marks.

Finally the eleven of us were sent to the lockup.

It was a small cemented room. In the corner was a pot full of urine giving out a powerful stench. We did not get any food that day. The night was extremely chilly. There were no mats to lie on. In the morning all our faces were bloated. We could hardly walk. We were handcuffed and made to walk through the bazaar to the court with a police escort carrying bayonets.

We were remanded for fourteen days and sent to the Calicut Sub-Jail. There, my companions later told me, that when No. 270 got tired of hitting me with his closed fist he used his folded elbows on me. One volunteer massaged me with oil. He told me that there were nine places, each the size of a rupee coin, where blood had congealed and where the oil had no effect.

I received nine months' rigorous imprisonment. I was taken to Cannanore Central Jail. There were six hundred political prisoners there, including T. Prakasam and Batliwala.

The food in the jail was very bad. In the rice gruel they served us, there would appear a floating layer of worms. We removed these before eating it. We had news of the outside world only when new prisoners came in. When we learnt that Bhagat Singh and his comrades had been hanged we went on a three-day hunger strike.

There were prisoners there from all parts of India. There were people of different ideologies—revolutionaries, anarchists, socialists and communists. However all of them had one objective in common, freedom for India. After some months we were released as a result of the Gandhi–Irwin Pact. I did not know where to go. There were many volunteers like me. Most of us did not even have a railway pass.

I had two wishes. One was to possess a shawl. Mr Achuthan bought me a khadi shawl with a grapevine border. However, my very first wish was to kill No. 270! But I had no weapons. If only I could get a revolver! I longed for one. I saw him standing on traffic duty at Palayam junction. A demon of a man six foot tall. If I hit him with bare hands he would hardly feel it. I must stab him in the chest with a knife! I stole a penknife from Al-Ameen Lodge. As I was taking it away I saw Mr Achuthan. He was surprised to see me.

'Haven't you gone yet?'

I said, 'No.'

'Don't you want to go home and see your father and mother?'

I said, 'I have something to do before that.' I told him everything. He led me to a place near Mananchira tank speaking to me very gently. 'Are you a satyagrahi...?' He told me the story of how Gandhiji lost his two front teeth. 'And if you want to kill, remember there is not a single policeman who deserves to live. The policeman is an indispensable part of the government. The poor creatures are mere instruments. What is the use of blaming them? Have patience. Go and see your father and mother.'

Mr Achuthan put me on the train. At Ernakulam I stayed for a month at the Muslim Hostel. I was filled with disappointment, sorrow and unwillingness! Finally one night I reached Vaikom. From there I walked to Thalayolaparambu. It was past midnight, about three in the morning. At home, when I entered the yard my mother asked, 'Who is it?' I stepped onto the veranda. Mother lit a lamp, and asked as if nothing had happened, 'Son, have you eaten anything?'

I said nothing. I was shaken, unable to breathe. The whole

world was asleep! My mother alone was awake! Mother brought a vessel of water and asked me to wash my hands and feet. Then she placed a plate of rice before me.

She asked me nothing.

I was amazed. 'How did you know, Umma, that I was coming today?'

Mother replied, 'Oh...I cook rice and wait every night.'

It was a simple statement. Every night I did not turn up, but mother had kept awake waiting for me.

The years have passed Many things have happened.

But mothers still wait for their sons.

'Son, I just want to see you....'

Original title 'Umma'; from the collection Ormakkurippukal *(1937).*

The Love Letter*

My dear Saramma,

How does my dear comrade spend this all too brief phase of existence when life is bubbling with youth and the heart is fragrant with love?

As for me, my life passes moment by moment in the love for Saramma. And you, Saramma?

Begging of you to think it over well and reward me with a sweet, kind reply,

Saramma's own
Kesavan Nayar

So wrote Kesavan Nayar. He looked round. He had a pleasant feeling that Saramma was standing behind him with a sweet smile. Just a feeling. He read through the letter. It had poetry in it. There was philosophy and mysticism too. Why, did it not contain the entire secret of Kesavan Nayar's heart? The letter had come out better than he had planned. He folded it, put it in his pocket, left the bank and walked along the road. There was a sudden doubt whether Saramma would make fun of him if he gave her the letter. Or would she reply? What would

---

*In the original Malayalam version, this note by Basheer prefaces the story: 'This story was written in 1942 in Trivandrum Central Jail as my fellow prisoners wanted some stories to read. It was published in 1943 as a book, but was banned in Travancore State in 1944, and copies were confiscated.'

the reply be? Saramma had a great sense of humour and loved making fun of others. He recalled one incident. He had been deep in conversation with her. They were exchanging jokes about women. Saramma said that a great poet had sung of women as the noble creations of God. Kesavan Nayar could not help laughing, and said in repartee, 'Women's heads are full of moonshine.' He told the story of an eminent man who had married seven times. The gentleman's seventh life companion had fallen on her head down the granite steps of the staircase. After taking her to the hospital he visited his bachelor friend to tell him about it.

'The accident is not so serious.'

'Isn't the skull split open?'

'That's right.'

'Has the brain been exposed?'

'Oh, that's nothing!' said the eminent gentleman who had known seven women intimately. 'Even if the skull is split wide open, how can one see any brains—with women?'

'What I guess from that is,' Kesavan Nayar concluded, 'the insides of women's heads contain only moonshine.'

When Saramma heard that she only chuckled. She never said anything about it afterwards. Even then would she not have resented the suggestion that the inside of her head, too, contained only moonshine? When she received the love letter would she mock at him with talk of moonshine? She might have forgotten it—after all, she was a woman.

With all this in his mind Kesavan Nayar went into the restaurant. He did not want coffee. All the same, he drank a cup of coffee, lit a cigarette and sat there for a long time, thinking. Would Saramma make fun of him when he gave her the love letter? Saramma had remained untouched by love. Kesavan Nayar had tried a hundred thousand times. But when he tried to uncork the perfume bottle of love, she would hold her nose! What's this bad odour? Haven't you been bathing recently? These unasked questions were expressed by her gaze! How should he make her love him?

Distraught with love he went home, and when he looked up at the first-floor room he occupied, Kesavan Nayar was aghast—Saramma! She was on the landing intent on taking something out of the room with a long stick she was manipulating through the window!

Kesavan Nayar stood on the ground floor in surprise, and did not go up. What was Saramma about to steal? If it was his wallet, that was in his pocket. Could it be a shirt or a dhoti? Or some book? But then, what book was there which she had not read? This was not necessary, Saramma! Don't I love you more than my life itself? If only you had asked me wouldn't I have given you anything, anything you wanted? Let her come down with her loot. As she descended he would say all this to her sadly and pull out the letter, saying, 'Look at this. It's the love letter I have written to you, Saramma.' He would then give her the letter. She would read it and weep at the thought that she had murdered such love. Then Kesavan Nayar would console her, 'Oh, it's nothing. I have forgiven everything.'

And so heart and heart would merge one into the other. As he stood there imagining these things, she spoke. 'I saw you sneaking in and waiting down there. I suppose the bank staff must have been working today till sunset.'

'Oh!' Kesavan Nayar's very soul groaned inwardly. He went up the stairs.

Saramma was sweating. She smiled and said, 'I must have been engaged in this futile task for half an hour! Whatever I do, it doesn't hook on to this stick! Anyhow, I've decided to get a duplicate key made tomorrow!'

'Is it for opening the door when I'm not there?'

She looked out into the crowded road and smiled.

Kesavan Nayar asked, 'What was it that wouldn't hook on to the stick?'

'Didn't I tell you that?' Saramma asked. 'What were you thinking when you stood down there?'

'I thought....' Kesavan Nayar stopped. What was he to say? 'I thought that Saramma was trying to take something from my room. What were you trying to fish out?'

'The magazine that came addressed to Mr Kesavan Nayar! I saw the postman throwing it in through the window. I was bored, with nothing to do!'

In that case, can't you love me? he thought, as he put his hand in his coat pocket, took out his keys and the love letter which he gave Saramma.

She read it, crumpled it up and threw it down, saying, 'What's the news?'

Kesavan Nayar said nothing. He opened the door to the room, picked up the magazine and gave it to Saramma. Then he took off his coat and hung it up. Saramma, looking as if she had swallowed something sweet and warm, tore off the wrapper of the magazine and stood there turning the pages.

Taking care to hide the pallor on his face, and pretending to ignore the matter of the love letter, Kesavan Nayar asked, 'Well, what's your news, Saramma? Didn't you quarrel with your stepmother today?'

Saramma replied, 'I think my father and stepmother are going to demand some room rent from me.'

'Has it come to that?'

'Why not? The room I occupy could be given on rent, and....'

'And then, Saramma?'

'And let Saramma live in a corner of the kitchen—that seems stepmother's way of thinking.'

'And your father?'

'What opinion has father got, other than what stepmother thinks?'

'What was it like before father married stepmother?'

'Whose attitude? Stepmother's?'

'No, father's.'

'Then he was my father. I feel that men have nothing inside their heads.'

Kesavan Nayar said nothing. After a pause, he asked, 'But, Saramma, haven't you got some right over this building?'

'What right do I have?' she said. 'It was with the dowry brought in by stepmother that the debt on this building was cleared. Father says all that debt was incurred for mother's illness and for the ceremonies after her death. If only my poor mother had lived for another two years, I could have passed my B.A. Then I could have easily found a job.'

'There are any number of unemployed women who have

completed their B.A.,' Kesavan Nayar said. 'Anyhow, it's a pity you don't have a job, Saramma.'

Saramma looked up from the magazine and asked with humility, 'Is there any vacancy in the bank where you work? Some job for me somewhere?'

Kesavan Nayar looked at Saramma's clear eyes, at the golden skin of her neck, at her firm, shapely breasts, and thought to himself, what is a woman's job except to love a man? God created women to love and be loved. Not to strut around as officers! All the same he said, 'I'll try.'

'Do you know of any vacancies anywhere?'

I do know! Kesavan Nayar thought. There is a large vacancy in my heart. It requires no bribes or recommendations. He gently massaged the region of his heart and said, 'There is a vacancy.'

'Where?'

'I'll tell you tomorrow.'

'The work?'

'That—' Kesavan Nayar smiled. Look at her! Crumple up my love letter and throw it away, will you ? And not a word about it, eh? Am I a person who writes love letters to women every day? Hm, a job. I'll create a job. Kesavan Nayar felt proud that he had been born a man. He lifted his left hand and fondled his bare upper lip. I must grow at least a half-moustache. His eyes gleaming with good humour, he declared, 'I'll tell you definitely tomorrow.'

'Telling me isn't enough! Will I get the job?'

'Certainly.'

'I feel so relieved.'

Without saying a word about the love letter, she picked up the stick and the magazine, and went down the stairs to the front yard. As she went to her room, she turned round at the half-door leading in and cried out, 'Don't forget that other matter.'

He kept still, saying nothing. He did not dare to look out at the crumpled love letter that had been thrown away in the yard. He controlled his anger and said, 'N – n – no!'

II

Here's the key to my heart! said Kesavan Nayar to himself as the next day he dropped the key of his room on Saramma's lap and went to the bank.

Saramma gave the key back when he returned from the bank in the evening. He also took back the previous day's magazine and went up to his room. He drew the chair upto the door, sat down and started looking at the magazine. He was full of happiness, thinking of what was going to happen. When Saramma knew the kind of job he had found for her, would she tear him to bits ? Kesavan Nayar thought over it and laughed to himself. As he sat there, Saramma came up. Although he knew Saramma would be very anxious to know the details of the job, he pretended not to be aware of any such thing and asked her the usual question, 'What's the news, Saramma?'

'Oh, nothing.' Saramma smiled as usual, then asked, 'Has anything been stolen from your room?'

Kesavan Nayar said, 'I haven't searched it.'

'Then take a look.'

He pretended to be absorbed in the magazine, as his mind rehearsed what he was about to say, the rare secret he would disclose to her. The secret in his heart was seething to come out, like perfume from a bottle.

Saramma stood leaning against the window seat facing Kesavan Nayar. She looked in turn at the shine on the curly hair on his head neatly parted down the middle, at the rosy hue round his brows which moved ever so slowly, at his broad chest which heaved up and down. She said in a low tone, 'You didn't tell me anything about that job.'

'I don't think you'd be interested in it, Saramma.'

Saramma said, 'If the pay is low, it does not matter. I'll accept it. I'm a burden on everyone here. I am fed up with this life. To tell you the truth, do you know the kind of things I feel sometimes?'

'What kind of things? Let me hear!'

'Oh, you're always making fun of me! I am speaking seriously. Whatever the job, I shall accept it.'

'Saramma, do you know how to cook?'

Saramma was surprised. 'Why?'

'Just a question.'

Saramma said, 'Well, I do know some cooking. I can make rice and curry. I can make snacks. I can make tea. I can make coffee. I know how to make cocoa. I can make ovaltine— '

'In short, if you're given some rice, you can cook a rice meal and serve it?'

'Why, do you intend to appoint me as a cook somewhere?'

'Oh no, nothing like that, I just asked. Educated women sometimes don't know how to cook. Their clothes are not meant for the smoke and cinders of the kitchen. They know how to dress up, put on powder, redden their lips and arrange their hair in a hundred and sixtyfive ways. They dress up and decorate themselves and carry shoulder bags.'

'Shoulder bags?'

'Handbags.'

'Oh!'

'"She walks along with a handbag. She's a lady!" I wanted to find out whether Saramma was a lady.'

'I have no handbag.'

'Even then, Saramma, tell me what they carry in that thing.'

'A small mirror, a tiny powder box, a little comb.'

'Would it contain love letters?'

'Love letters?'

'Yes, the love letters they get hour after hour would be kept inside. At the end of the day, when the bag is full, the letters would be transferred to a big trunk!'

'I don't know all that. What's this job you have found for me?'

'You wouldn't like it, Saramma.'

'I would.'

'Are you sure?'

'A thousand times, yes.'

'Then...,' Kesavan Nayar hesitated. How could he say it?

'Saramma, you won't like it.'

'Didn't I say I would?'

'Suppose you regret your decision afterwards?'

THE LOVE LETTER 33

Saramma was firm. 'No I'm prepared to bear any hardship and make any sacrifice. Do you know a secret? It happened before you came to stay here, Kesavan Nayar. There were three enquiries about my marriage. They came bang – bang – bang in quick succession last year. I was happy on all three occasions. Not because I dreamt of living a life of comfort with a man whom I had neither heard of nor seen. But because I thought I could escape from this hell. But all three enquiries came to nothing. No one would marry me without a dowry! My father and stepmother say that I am to blame. I'm always the one to blame if anything goes wrong. If there's no rain in these parts, it's my fault. I have looked for jobs everywhere. But, but for me alone, there's no vacancy.'

'There is a vacancy.'

'Where?'

'I shall tell you. What's this dowry?'

'It's the hire paid to a man to keep a woman.'

'I don't understand.

'Suppose someone wants to marry me— '

'All right, let it be me.'

'Oh! If you marry me and take me away—won't money be required to feed me and clothe me, to bathe me and provide me with oil and powder and perfume, to look after my confinement and the birth of my child, to nurse me when I am dying and to see that proper obsequies are performed after I die? Well, all this money must be provided in advance—then only can I be accepted in marriage!'

'All this is because no one loves Saramma. Suppose someone loved you— '

'Even then, dowry must be provided. That is our religious custom.'

Kesavan Nayar felt very happy about this custom of dowry. A delightful arrangement, he thought. If such a custom had not existed—my God!

Saramma said, 'I detest the dowry system.'

Kesavan Nayar retorted, 'I love this dowry system.'

'Why?'

'I shall tell you. This dowry system exists among the

Nambudiris.'

'It's there in the Muslim community also.'

Kesavan Nayar said, 'Those who find it difficult to provide a dowry, must be prepared to marry men of other communities who do not want a dowry.'

'A fine thing indeed!'

'Yes. A Nayar should marry a Christian, a Christian should marry a Nayar or Muslim, the Muslim should marry a Nayar or Nambudiri— '

'May I interrupt you with a question?'

'Ask away!'

'You haven't told me about the job you have found for me.'

'Oh.... But, Saramma, you will turn it down.'

'Didn't I say I won't? I'll never, never turn it down.'

'Then...' Kesavan Nayar suddenly opened the perfume bottle in his heart, the cork came out with a pop! 'Saramma, you have to love me as much as I love you. That is the job I have found for you, Saramma.'

Saramma was startled. For a moment only. All of a sudden her face was flushed. Her eyelids drooped heavily. Not just that. She stood there beautiful and calm, with a smile that exuded an inner awareness.

The dam inside Kesavan Nayar's heart burst. He said, 'I have loved you for a long time, Saramma. More than my heart, more than my life, more than my country, more than my— !'

She laughed. Her cheeks took on a new colour. Her eyes became brighter.

Kesavan Nayar asked, 'Saramma, what do you say now about the job?'

Saramma smiled and said in a low voice, 'The job is not bad; what is the pay you've fixed?'

Pay? Oh, you're ready for a fight? War is all right by me. The hot blood of gallant warriors flows through my veins.... If it's a fight you want, a fight you shall have.... To victory or death! Long live revolution! With grave dignity Kesavan Nayar asked, 'What pay do you want?'

'You may decide that yourself!'

After considerable thought Kesavan Nayar decided. 'Twenty

rupees.'

Saramma said, 'That is very low.'

'I can't give you a paise more. After working nine hours six days a week for one month, I get a mere forty rupees. Out of this, I have to pay the rent to your father, pay for food at the restaurant, meet the laundry charges and a host of other expenses. If I economise, if I practically starve, these expenses can be kept down to twenty rupees. It's the balance of twenty that I intend to give you, Saramma. On the other hand, your job is not a hard one. Think of that.'

Saramma said, 'The work is hard. Kesavan Nayar has to work only nine hours out of twentyfour. Don't you rest for fifteen hours every day? In my job there will not be a moment of rest. I must think of Kesavan Nayar day and night, while I eat and while I sleep mustn't I? I must weep when Kesavan Nayar weeps, laugh when he laughs. I must not eat till he eats and I must keep awake and love him while he sleeps.'

Saramma looked at Kesavan Nayar as if she had swallowed some bitter medicine. Then she asked, 'Is the job permanent or only for some time?'

He said, 'Permanent! Forever!'

'Oh, good! So even if something happens to Kesavan Nayar I shall have this job?'

'What do you mean?'

'Do I keep the job even if Kesavan Nayar dies?'

'Without doubt. Even if I pop off you must continue to love me.'

Saramma raised a doubt. 'When you die who will pay me?'

Kesavan Nayar was silent. What could he say?

Saramma laughed at Kesavan Nayar's silence. She said mockingly, 'Even if my head is full of moonshine, I can point out that the job has this drawback. After your death who is there to pay me?'

What could he say? Kesavan Nayar thought deeply. Finally he found a way out. He smiled.

'Suppose we die together?'

'Aha! Selfishness, naked and shameless! When Kesavan Nayar dies, I must also die—is that so?'

'Saramma, are you making fun of me?'

'Not at all. Is it making fun to point out facts? Am I not a woman? Where would you find brains even if the skull is broken open?'

'Forgive me. I do not have Saramma's intelligence or knowledge or beauty.'

'Look, you're making fun of me now!'

'I'll never, never, make fun of you, Saramma.'

'Oh, make as much fun of me as you want to.'

A nerve within Kesavan Nayar snapped. 'Would I mock at my life partner? Would I make fun of the goddess of my life? Would I make fun of my own heart, of my own soul? How can I make fun of the divinity in my life?'

Saramma interrupted, 'Please stop! I have to ask you something.'

'You can ask, you can command.'

'Am I to be your life partner?'

'You are.'

'Since when have you thought this?'

'For a long time.'

'For how long?'

'A long, long time.'

'Then why didn't you tell me all this while?'

'Didn't I tell you? I would think of you every day. And every day I'd write you a love letter, Saramma.'

'And then?'

'And then I would tear it up!'

'Is that so?'

'Yes.'

'To put it briefly, I'm to be your life partner. Then you will listen to whatever I tell you, will you not?'

Kesavan Nayar was thrilled. 'Anything you say! Do you want someone murdered? He shall be killed. You want me to swim across the ocean? I shall do so. I shall juggle with mountains. I am ready to die for you, Saramma.'

'For the present you need not die—just stand on your head. Let's see.'

'Do you really want me to stand on my head?'

'Oh, there's something called "really" in all this, is there?'

'No!' Kesavan Nayar stood up happily. 'Is it enough just to stand on my head?'

'For the present, yes.'

'Right!'

He pulled off his shirt and put it on the chair. Then he folded his dhoti up to the knees and tied it up securely between his thighs. He stood on his head, his legs straight up in the air.

She stood there happily, looking down on him from toe to head. She commented, 'Very good!'

Kesavan Nayar asked from the same position, 'Does Saramma love me?'

Saramma was silent.

Kesavan Nayar asked again, 'Saramma, have you accepted the job?'

Slowly and carefully, without making any noise, she descended the stairs and called out from below, 'I shall tell you tomorrow.'

III

'Saramma, have you accepted the job?' Kesavan Nayar asked the next day.

Saramma said, 'I'll tell you tomorrow.'

The next day again Kesavan Nayar asked and Saramma had the same reply. 'I'll tell you tomorrow!'

When Kesavan Nayar asked the same question again the next day, Saramma again replied, 'I'll tell you tomorrow!'

Kesavan Nayar asked the question again the next day and Saramma replied, 'I'll tell you tomorrow!'

Kesavan Nayar did not ask the question the next day. He made a declaration. 'I am going to commit suicide! What's the use of living?'

'A very good idea! And someone can write an elegy!'

Kesavan Nayar said nothing.

Saramma asked, 'So you've decided to commit suicide?'
'Yes.'
'When is the auspicious event?'
Kesavan Nayar said nothing.
Saramma asked, 'What type of suicide is it to be ?'
'I haven't yet come to a decision. I'm thinking.'
Saramma advised, 'You can lay your head on the railway track and die. Or you can hang yourself. Which of these would you prefer?'
Kesavan Nayar said nothing. What a cruel heart!
Saramma advised again, 'There is another way. No one would know either. Take a small boat, put a heavy stone and some rope inside. Row across quietly to the middle of the lake at dusk. Then tie one end of the rope to the stone, at the other end tie a running knot and put it round your neck. You must manipulate the boat with your feet and let it sink.'
What a terribly cruel heart!
Kesavan Nayar said, 'I've discovered another way. I'll hang myself here. As I hang, there will be a large piece of paper tied to my legs. It will proclaim: Oh world! There is no connection between Saramma and my death! It is true that I love Saramma and that Saramma does not love me! It is also true that she crumpled up the love letter I gave her and threw it away. Even so, there's no connection between my death and Saramma— signed the late Kesavan Nayar.'
'Will it say anything else ?'
'No!'
Saramma said, 'I did not throw away that love letter. I picked it up and used it to wrap up my toothpowder!'
'My love letter?'
'Yes!'
The hardness of women's hearts! Kesavan Nayar said nothing. Aimless days passed by without count. He went about with a downcast face, talking to no one, looking at no one.
He could not stand the sight of women! Bloody fools! With hearts of stone! Saramma was a bloody fool. And cruel-hearted. Kesavan Nayar was also a bloody fool. But he was not hard-hearted. Every man and woman in this world was a

bloody fool, every single one of them! As Kesavan Nayar's opinions took shape one evening Saramma stepped out into the yard, stood before him and stretched out her hand as if she was expecting something. Kesavan Nayar did not know what all this was about.

Saramma said, 'My salary?'

'Salary? Salary for what?' Kesavan Nayar was bewildered. Seeing his confusion, Saramma explained. She said in an aggrieved tone, as if she had been insulted by his breaking his word, 'Oh, so this is what it has come to! I deserve this. Is it for nothing that people say my head is full of moonshine? Fifteen days have passed since I took up that exacting job.'

'Oh.' Kesavan Nayar's face cleared, his eyes shone. In sudden happiness his heart swelled like a football, pressing against his left ribs. 'Darling , why didn't you tell me?'

Saramma said in a hurt, complaining voice, 'In this all too brief phase of existence, when life is bubbling with youth and the heart is fragrant with love—if people go about with sad faces, muttering about suicide, seeing nothing and hearing nothing—what am I to do?'

'There is nothing else, is there?'

'No!

Kesavan Nayar commanded: 'Come!'

He went ahead. Saramma followed. They climbed up the stairs. Kesavan Nayar went inside, opened his suitcase, took out two ten-rupee notes with a thudding heart, put them into an envelope and wrote 'To Madame Saramma' on it, and handed it over.

Saramma asked, 'Is this a love letter?'

Kesavan Nayar said nothing. Love letter? Let her wonder!

But Saramma showed no sign of anxiety. She took the notes out of the envelope and like a seasoned trader she held the notes against the light and examined them gravely.

'They are not fake notes, are they?'

Kesavan Nayar said nothing.

'Good,' she said in a warning tone. 'Don't delay like this from now on. My salary must be ready without fail on the first of the month.'

Kesavan Nayar wanted to embrace Saramma and cover her with a hundred thousand kisses. He moved closer to her.

Saramma said, 'It's enough if you stand four feet away

'I want to kiss you.'

'Me?'

'Yes.'

'But, that's not in the contract, is it?'

Kesavan Nayar said nothing.

Five months passed in the same way. A hundred rupees changed hands. He never enquired what she was doing with it. But Saramma told him in the third month that she had won a raffle for a thousand rupees. It was the luck of one rupee from the salary Kesavan Nayar paid her! But Kesavan Nayar did not pay any particular attention to this. How could he give any attention to mundane money matters? He was basking in the moonlight of love. He believed what his beloved told him. It did not matter if he got nothing in return. He would carry on according to her behests; go the way she set forth. He was not capable of doing anything else. According to her wishes Kesavan Nayar sent applications for many jobs at far-away places. Why? Merely because Saramma asked him to do so. But Kesavan Nayar also did things which Saramma had not asked for. Like calling the doctor in when Saramma was ill, buying medicine for her, trying to bring about an understanding between Saramma and her stepmother, talking to her father about the responsibilities of a parent and so on. But she never thanked him for these services nor did it appear that she was grateful. Kesavan Nayar bore this with fortitude. But what he found insufferable was her prefacing every conversation with the words: 'In this all too brief phase of existence, when life is bubbling with youth and the heart is fragrant with love...'Kesavan Nayar would turn pale whenever he heard them. Whenever Saramma was about to say something, he would anxiously wait for her to start with those words. If she didn't say them, he would sigh with relief. In spite of all this, did his love decrease? Not one whit. It increased from day to day. He always wanted to see Saramma! He wanted to embrace and kiss her and—there were no limits to his desires.

And Saramma? She showed no signs of love for Kesavan Nayar. She betrayed not a sign by word or deed.

Then came a time when parting became imminent. Kesavan Nayar got a job in a distant city. The salary was two hundred and fifty rupees. On Saramma's advice Kesavan Nayar wrote and accepted the job. She said, 'So my salary is going to be one hundred and twentyfive rupees now.'

That was all. She had nothing else to say. Even so, she reminded him, 'You must send a money-order on the first of every month. You know the address, don't you?'

Kesavan Nayar said nothing.

Saramma asked, 'When are you leaving?'

Kesavan Nayar said, 'You know I have to start work in ten days. I plan to leave the day after tomorrow. So I have resigned my bank job.'

'You've decided to go, haven't you?'

'What kind of a question is that?'

'I'm still your goddess, am I not?'

'Yes.'

'Are you prepared to court death for my sake?'

'I am.'

'You swear to it?'

'I swear to it!'

Saramma said, 'You don't have to die though. Will you agree not to take up this job if I ask you?'

Not go for the job? He would really be in trouble! He would be unable to pay the rent. Or to feed and clothe himself. He would be on the streets, a mere loafer! Chin in hand, Kesavan Nayar looked at the ground throughtfully.

Saramma got up and walked towards the stairs. Kesavan Nayar sadly called out, 'Saramma, I have to tell you something.'

Saramma returned.

'If you want to talk about love, I'm heartily sick of hearing about it!'

Kesavan Nayar said nothing.

She said, 'Speak ! I am on a salary. How can I refuse to hear you?'

'Saramma, everything seems funny to you.'

'Is that what you wanted to say?'

'No.'

'Then what is it?'

'Saramma must also come with me. I cannot live there alone.'

Saramma looked as if she would burst out laughing. She asked, 'Are you afraid?'

'No Saramma, I love....

'I love...Saramma! Haven't I heard this a hundred thousand times? What is this love?'

That was not difficult to answer! Kesavan Nayar knew very well what love was. But he felt a certain sense of shame in saying it aloud.

'Affection, love...are a kind of moonshine...love is a sort of fragrant moonshine....'

'Moonshine!' Saramma was surprised. 'Isn't that what you said was inside women's heads?'

Kesavan Nayar nodded in agreement. A little later he said, 'Will you come, Saramma?'

'What shall I do after coming?'

'You must live as my wife.'

'Don't we belong to two different religions?'

'What of it? We can have a registered marriage.'

'Don't you want any dowry?'

'Saramma is my dowry. Saramma is my—'

'Please stop! I have other doubts also!'

'What are they?'

'I see many difficulties in the way of our living as husband and wife. When one goes to the temple, the other goes to the church! Can we do anything together? The temple and the church will always be between us, will they not ?'

Kesavan Nayar was all happiness. 'Nothing to it,' he said. 'Why can't we do away with the temple and the church? If church and temple do not want Saramma and Kesavan Nayar, then Saramma and Kesavan Nayar do not need church and temple either! Saramma, think of it. Think of the hardships you've been through! Didn't your father and stepmother treat you most harshly? What did the church do then? What did God do? The temple hasn't done me any good! In short, if God and church and temple want us, let them come and fall at our feet!'

'Quite right,' Saramma said. 'But I have some other doubts as well!'

He said, 'Tell me, Saramma. This Kesavan Nayar of yours has the answers to all your doubts!'

She became shy. She said, 'There's another thing.'

'Ask, ask!'

She asked, 'Wouldn't we have children? What religion will they belong to? I wouldn't like to bring them up as Hindus. To bring them up as Christians, my – my – husband may not like that. Then what would their religion be?'

Kesavan Nayar broke into a sweat. He had not thought about this. It was a good question—what would be the children's religion? Kesavan Nayar thought about it. He thought deeply, intensely. Veins stood out on either side of his forehead. Sweat glistened on his brow. There was no solution in sight! He groped in the dark. There was no light anywhere! And then an idea crossed his mind like a streak of lightning! As if a lighted door had opened and he could see a beautiful garden beyond. He declared with excitement: 'I have it!'

'What?'

'I'll tell you,' Kesavan Nayar said. 'We will not bring up our children according to any religion. Let them grow up without religion!'

'And then?'

'Why, as they grow up we will educate them impartially about all religions. And when they are some twenty years old, if they want a religion, let them adopt the one they like.'

Saramma said happily, without looking at Kesavan Nayar's face, 'Quite reasonable.... And the name? Assuming that my first-born is a boy. What name will the little darling have?'

Kesavan Nayar was troubled. 'Really, what would we name the darling boy? We can't give him a Hindu name. Nor a Christian name.' Kesavan Nayar thought a little and then he got excited. He said, 'You know we could pick a smart name from-some other community and call him that!'

'Then won't that community think my child is one of them?'

'Right!' Kesavan Nayar agreed. 'If it's a Muslim name people will think he is a Muslim. The same with a Parsi name. A Chinese or Russian or any other name will create the same confusion.'

What name would they give the boy? It should be a name no one had used before. The name should give no indication of either faith or religion. Where would one get such a name?

Then Saramma asked, 'How would a Chinese name sound?'

Kesavan Nayar tried a sample. 'Sing Lee Fo.'

'Sing Lee Fo?' Saramma mouthed the name of her first-born to come, a darling boy. 'Hey son Sing Lee Fo, where are you you brat—Sing Lee Fo?'

'Doesn't it have style?'

Saramma didn't like it. 'I don't want that name for my son!'

'Then there are Russian names. You just have to add *ski* to any name.'

Saramma asked, 'What *ski*?'

'...to any name.'

'*Ski...skkee*....No!'

'I've got it—names with style!' Kesavan Nayar's imagination broke loose. He repeated names one after another. 'India. Love Letter. Short Story. Hurricane. Sahara. Sky. Moonlight. Pearlspot. Symbolism. Areca Palm. Toffee. Drama. Ocean. Shrimp Eyes. Prose Poem. Sapphire. Fire Flame. Mysticism. Star—'

'Please stop! Let me try out the names—hey son, Shrimp Eyes! Mother's own Shrimp Eyes...! No!'

She tried calling out other names. 'Hey son, Prose Poem! You little brat, Short Story! You mischievous little Moonlight!'

He said, 'Let's write each name and pick lots—two of them. No quarrels! Double names are in fashion!'

Saramma agreed.

They wrote out the names on small bits of paper, rolled them up and jumbled the lot. Saramma picked up a paper and Kesavan Nayar another. Kesavan Nayar unrolled his paper and declared, 'Toffee!'

Saramma also unrolled her bit of paper and said in a low voice, 'Sky!'

Each looked at the other's face.

Saramma boldly called out their son's name, 'Toffee Sky! Hey, you little urchin, Toffee Sky...! My son, Toffee Sky...!'

'Wrong!' Kesavan Nayar rearranged the name of their offspring and called in a dignified voice, 'Sky Toffee!'

Saramma liked it. She called affectionately, 'Sky Toffee...! Hey son, Sky Toffee...! Where are you, little Sky Toffee?'

'Simply grand!' Kesavan Nayar gave his verdict. 'Mister Sky Toffee! Sriyut Sky Toffee! Comrade Sky Toffee!'

Saramma was troubled by a monstrous doubt. 'Is my darling son a communist?'

Kesavan Nayar laughed. 'What a question! If he wants to be a thingummy, let him be one!

'That's his pleasure, isn't it?'

'Yes, let my son join any party he fancies.'

My son? Saramma's son? Kesavan Nayar became angry. Such selfishness!

He reminded her, 'Saramma, all this while you've been saying "my son", "my son"—do you realise that? Such selfishness is not good. If people heard you they'd think I have no rights at all over Sky Toffee! From now on you must say "our son"! Understand, woman?'

Saramma also became angry. 'Good thing you reminded me!' Her face took on the expression of someone who has swallowed something bitter. 'I just asked about all these things that's all! But don't think I've become your wife. Do you understand, Mr Kesavan Nayar?'

Kesavan Nayar's face fell. He asked in a contrite voice, 'But Saramma, what did you say at first?'

'What did I say?'

'That you would be my wife!'

'And after that?'

'Oh Saramma, you're always making fun of me!'

'Ah, fun! Do you know what humour is to life?'

'I don't want to know.'

'That's fine! You don't listen to me. I am just "woman" to

you. I'm your "life mate"! I'm your "goddess"!'

'Tell me Saramma, what is it?'

'What is what?'

'Humour to life?'

'Ah, smile like that.... She got up, went down the stairs and added, 'The perfume of life.'

Humour is the perfume of life. Not bad at all!

IV

'Saramma, I have to leave very early tomorrow morning.' Kesavan Nayar said this at the approach of dusk. 'Have you anything to tell me finally Saramma?'

Saramma said, 'In this all too brief phase of existence, when life is bubbling with youth and the heart is fragrant with love—some questions!'

Kesavan Nayar felt depressed all of a sudden.

Saramma continued, 'Question one, have you cleared the arrears of rent due to father?'

'Cleared!'

'Good. Question two, have you settled the restaurant man's accounts?'

'Settled!'

'Question three, have you got money for your travel expenses?'

'Yes!'

'Then a supplementary question—where did you get the money?'

'I sold my wristwatch and gold ring.'

'Good! Now that the honourable Kesavan Nayar will not be remembered once he leaves this place, I extend all good wishes to him!'

So saying, Saramma went down the stairs shaking with laughter.

With pain in his heart Kesavan Nayar called out, 'Saramma!'

Who was there to hear him? Woman must be the very essence of hard-heartedness; woman is just *dukkudukku*. *Dukkudukku* is all she is!

V

Kesavan Nayar sat there like a living corpse. Night came. The moon rose in the sky. Kesavan Nayar sat on. Finally he got up and lit the lamp. The alarm clock showed eleven o' clock.

He set the alarm for four, shut the door and lay down on his bed, exhausted. This was his very last night! He felt neither hunger nor thirst. Kesavan Nayar lay with his eyes open. He thought of nothing but his eyes brimmed over with tears. Women were cruel beasts. How good men were! Why did God create women? Had there been any reason? He was close to bursting into tears.

Suddenly there came a voice from outside...soft and musical.

'Are you asleep?'

She! Despicable! Cruel! Hard-heartedness personified!

Kesavan Nayar kept quiet.

Again the same voice. 'Open! It's me!'

Kesavan Nayar got up and opened the door.

Saramma entered the room. Kesavan Nayar stood at the door.

Saramma said softly, 'Please come near; I've to say something.'

Kesavan Nayar retraced his steps and sat on the bed. Saramma stood near the door and looked out for some time. The coast was clear. She closed the door, drew the chair near the bed and sat down. Her hair hung loose and her elbows were on the bed. Her chin was supported on her palms and her breasts touched the mattress.

Kesavan Nayar wanted to kiss those breasts. But he hardened his heart and leaned back on the pillow. His eyes were still brimming.

She asked, 'Why are you weeping?'

He did not speak. She got up, sat down on the bed, bent her face towards Kesavan Nayar and suddenly planted a monstrously sweet kiss right on his lips!

'Have you taken an aversion to me?' she asked softly.

'Yes.' He pulled her onto his lap. He had lost his sadness but the tears were still flowing as he smiled.

She said, 'It looks like the sun shining through the rain, your thinking is so colourful!'

'You must come with me on the train at four-thirty in the morning!'

'Where to?'

'Where I go.'

'And if I do come?'

'Oh, Saramma always makes fun of things.'

'Do you know what humour is to life?'

'I know. It's what my dear girl has on her lips.'

'Hm! So you make fun of me!' She took out a fat envelope from under her blouse and put it in Kesavan Nayar's hand with reverence. 'You must open it and take a look only after the train leaves.'

'It's quite heavy, isn't it?' Kesavan Nayar asked. 'Is it a love letter?'

'Yes, a love letter!' Saramma smiled. 'It must not be opened until the train leaves the station. You must swear to that!'

He said, 'I swear!'

'Not enough. You must swear by something in which you have faith and which you hold in reverence.'

Kesavan Nayar looked at Saramma and took the oath. 'By my Saramma in whom I have great faith and whom I love and revere, I will look at this only after I get into the train!'

Saramma got up and opened the door. 'Before you go early in the morning you must wake me up. Sleep in peace now.'

She left. Kesavan Nayar is alone..., the whiff of her fragrance....

VI

Kesavan Nayar woke with a start. The time was exactly 4 a.m. He got up, had a wash and prepared for the journey. He dressed and rolled up his bedding. His other belongings were packed in trunks. He went out, found a cart and a cart-man, put his luggage into the cart, and returned. He switched on his torch and focused it through the window into Saramma's room and softly called, 'Saramma! Saramma!' But there was no movement. He pushed at the door.

It opened!

He flashed the torch around. There was no one inside...! Neither Saramma, nor her suitcase...! What had happened? Where could she have gone? The light fell on an envelope on the table. With a thumping heart he opened and read it.

> Saramma is writing this to her dear father and stepmother :
> In this all too brief phase of existence when life is bubbling with youth and the heart is fragrant with love—at this time when I have a job with a high salary, I am leaving for my place of work. I have also found a man who is prepared to marry me in my everyday clothes and without a dowry! As I love him and he loves me, I would like you to bestow deep thought on the situation. Begging of you both to give us your sweet, kind blessings,
>
> father's and stepmother's own
Saramma

Kesavan Nayar replaced the letter on the table, closed the door, left the house, climbed into the cart and quickly reached the railway station. Saramma was standing there smiling.

She asked, 'How did you know I had come?'

'Divine prescience! Male wisdom for sure!'

'Male wisdom! Fiddlesticks! Not by surreptitiously reading the letter meant for my father and stepmother?'

'I shall tell you! I shall tell you everything, woman.'

He bought two tickets. The two of them entered the train with their luggage. The train left the station with a joyful whistle. They sat shoulder to shoulder without talking. The train halted at three stations before the two of them were alone.

The train stopped at another station. Kesavan Nayar ordered some tea. Saramma declared that both of them would have coffee. Kesavan Nayar said they would both have tea. They both became angry. Finally Kesavan Nayar drank a cup of coffee and Saramma drank tea. The sun rose. The train passed slowly over a bridge under which a golden river flowed. They forgot their recent quarrel over tea and coffee. Kesavan Nayar softly said to Saramma with unmixed delight, 'My sweet perfume, my honey, my golden one!'

Saramma moved closer and asked, 'What is it, father of my Sky Toffee?'

'My darling Moonshine!'

Saramma pinched Kesavan Nayar. He said, 'I'll beat you to a pulp!'

Saramma's eyes brimmed over. Being a woman, there was no lack of tears. She wept for no reason at all. When he saw her crying, the man in Kesavan Nayar felt sorry. He kissed her on the eyes.

'No!' Saramma said. 'Don't touch me!'

'Why not?'

'After all the sacrifices I have made, you're still behaving like this to me!'

'Behaving like what? And what was your sacrifice, Saramma?'

'Am I not coming with you, leaving behind my dear father and stepmother?'

'You're coming with me. So what?'

'Have coffee, at least for my sake...make just a tiny, little, wee sacrifice for me...and now you want to beat me to pulp!'

'O goddess of sacrifice! O woman, mother of Sky Toffee!'

'Yes, my lord!'

'Today we will go to the Civil Registrar and get ourselves married. The public should know. Don't you agree?'

Saramma said nothing.

Kesavan Nayar pinched her thighs and asked, 'Do you agree?'

'Didn't I say yes? Silence is consent!'

'You'll have complete freedom in three matters!'

'Only in three insignificant matters?'

'Yes. Food, clothes and faith.'

'Then will our house have two kitchens?'

'One, tiny, little kitchen!'

'Will I have to cook two types of food?'

'Only one type.'

'According to whose taste?'

'The taste of the mistress of my kitchen.'

She smiled. 'I'll make only coffee in the morning!'

'Oh...afterwards, I'll have tea outside!'

'I'll not permit it. Your entire pay, the whole of it, mind you, will be entrusted to me, me alone!'

'My dear woman, how will I get my tea then?'

'Give up tea! Look at a woman who has sacrificed so much for you."

'Didn't I stand on my head for your sake?'

'Is that a great thing? Aren't there those who have sacrificed great empires for the sake of love? Those who have battled with dragons for love?'

'My dear pearl among women! You moonshine! If I want, I can sit back in my armchair and sacrifice ten great empires! Or fight a thousand dragons! On the other hand, try and stand on your head for your beloved! Who has ever done such a thing, woman? Kesavan Nayar stands on his head before Saramma! History has yet to record a parallel to this! Is there a sacrifice to beat that?'

'O father of Sky Toffee!'

'What is it, woman?'

'I'll show you!'

She bent down and touched his feet. Kesavan Nayar pulled her up and embraced her. The train rumbled on. Who was there to see them?

She put her hand inside Kesavan Nayar's pocket.

'What are you searching for, you perfumed moonshine?'

'The envelope I gave you!'

'The love letter? My goodness! I forgot to read it!'

Kesavan Nayar took out the envelope and opened it. He removed the contents and looked at them, stunned—notes, currency notes, a bundle of currency notes!

He counted them. One thousand and ninetynine rupees!

'Listen,you will have to buy a wristwatch and a gold ring with this. Understand?'

Although Kesavan Nayar was happy at seeing the money, he was anxious to see the love letter. He asked, 'Where's the other thing?'

'What other thing?'

'The love letter!'

'Are you anxious to read it?'

'Just to look at it woman, you precious gem!'

'Then look!' She straightened up coyly and looked Kesavan Nayar in the eye with a smile. 'Don't you see? I am the love letter. Young man, young woman—that is the love letter!'

Kesavan Nayar liked that immensely. 'You and me! Fine! Where's the love letter? Show it to me!'

She put her hand deep inside her blouse and took out a paper much crumpled by days of sweat, and handed it over to him. He unfolded it, smoothed it out and looked at it in the light. It was a letter he had seen before, a letter out of the infinite past. As he started reading it out she threw her arms round his neck and kissed him. She said, 'In this all too brief phase of existence when life is bubbling with youth and the heart is fragrant with love—didn't I tell you? We are the love letter!'

'Woman, I understand. I'm convinced. Let go of my ears. Let me hear it read out!'

'You shall not hear it!' She held him in close embrace and showered kisses on his neck and face. The train gave a gleeful whistle and thundered on. Kesavan Nayar had a difficult time trying to read the paper which Saramma had taken out from between her breasts. He read it out slowly:

My dear Saramma,

How does my dear comrade spend this all too brief phase of existence when life is bubbling with youth and the heart is fragrant with love?

As for me, my life passes moment by moment in the love for Saramma. And you Saramma?

Begging of you to think it over well and bless me with a sweet, kind reply,

Saramma's own
Kesavan Nayar

Original title 'Prema Lekhanam'; published as a novelette in 1943.

If War is to End

'If war is to end,' muttered the well-built figure reclining in the easy chair. He was a famous writer and a great thinker. He had also a reputation for shortness of temper. He was scratching away at his dry eczema with a look of delight on his face. He let out a *shush* of relief through the left side of his mouth which he kept open above his clenched teeth. The writer asked the young newspaper reporter who had come to see him, 'What is it you say that I should do if the war is to end?'

'Sir, there is nothing you need do,' the reporter clarified. 'It's your opinion we want to know. What should the people do if war is to end forever?'

'There's nothing to be done! It's enough if you go away from here. Fool!'

'Sir, you must say something. The world is in a bad way. Great destruction is taking place. All this must end. We must achieve peace and goodwill. What we want is your valuable advice on how to attain this. If war is to end...?'

'You stupid oaf, did they start the war after asking me? Weren't there wars from ancient times? If the present war ends, there'll be another one again. Go away!'

'Alas, that's not enough! There should be no more war! If war is to end forever...?'

'Go and ask other thinkers. Don't bother me!'

'We've got everyone's opinion,' the reporter said with some

trepidation. 'Don't we all know about your short temper? We thought we'd come to you last. We realize that your opinion has more weight than that of the others.'

'What are the opinions of the others? If war is to end?'

'The world must accept the religion of Zoroaster. The world must observe the principles of Confucius. The world must listen to the music of Sri Krishna's flute. The world must follow Buddha. The world must follow Jesus. The world must believe in Muhammad. Nanak has set the way and so on.... '

'Is that all!' The short-tempered one scratched with relish and abandon as he asked, 'Didn't the other lot say anything?'

'They did. One group said the world should adopt communism if war is to end. Another group says we should accept anarchism. Another sage says that fascism is the only hope. Still another says the world should believe in the principles of non-violence. Sir, what do you say—if war is to end?'

'You must accept me as the prophet of this age!'

'I will accept you. But will the rest of the world?'

'You must persuade the rest of the world to accept me. Publish it in your paper! Announce that you are my first disciple!'

'But, sir, have you had any divine call... revelation?'

'Yes, fellow,' he said as his eyes bulged out and his lips twisted. He scratched away with a grating sound.

The newspaper reporter thought that the great man had forgotten the entire world the way he sat there. He cleared his throat loudly. The short-tempered one turned and looked at him.

'Stupid blighter! Haven't you gone?'

'No, sir. You have not yet given me your message to the world. If war is to end...?'

'I suppose you know the secret—that one has to beat one's wife and children. Hey you, it's one and a half years since I have beaten my wife and children. I forgot. Yes, just forgetfulness!'

'What sir! Forgetfulness has affected you for the last year

and a half?'

'Fool, no! Ecstasy! Ecstasy!'

'I don't understand.'

'I say, have I beaten up any editors or reviewers or publishers for one and a half years?'

'No!'

'Have I got any new book published in the last year and a half?'

'No!'

'Has there been any police case against me during the last year and a half?'

'I haven't heard of any.'

'Why you fool, why?'

'I don't know why.'

'Why didn't you find out why? Am I not news?'

'Yes, it was wrong on the part of my paper. Excuse us, sir. If war is to end...?'

'Go and pray!'

'Ayyo, people have prayed for a long time. Nothing came of it. You must tell us of your revelation. If war is to end...?'

'You have eyes but you do not see! You have ears but you do not hear! Fool, go away!'

'Ayyo, that's not enough! Sir, we await that revelation from you. If war is to end...?

'If war does not end? Who cares? Does the circulation of your paper drop?'

'No....'

'Do my books sell less?'

'No....'

'Then you can go.'

'Ayyo! Sir, you must give some advice. On your words rest the future peace and wellbeing of the world. If war is to end...?'

'If war is to end!' The great writer scratched and scratched with a grating sound, his face suffused with pleasure and relief. He declared: 'All the political leaders of the world today, all religious heads, all thinkers, all members of the armed forces—in fact every man and woman living on this earth—must get eczema like me. They must get eczema which bothers them day and night with itching!'

Original title 'Yudham Avasanikkanamengil'; from the collection Anarganimisham *(1944).*

The Shore of Solitude

The cold light of a dying moon washed the garden. A vanished fragrance lingered in the air. As of old a formless dream hung over it all.

I, just I, on this shore of solitude.

I do not know where you are.

Once on a night like this when we had sat together in this garden I had thought of the unknown end to come and sighed.

You had asked me with concern, 'Why do you sigh in sadness?'

I had asked, 'When I sink into the darkness of dead memories, who will remember me?'

'I will!' you had said. 'My girl, thoughts of you will come to me with the silver light of the morning star, through the golden rays of the rising sun, borne on the fresh fragrance of spring. When I hear the clouds bursting into mighty peals of thunder, when I see the blinding flash of lightning, my soul will come running to you.'

That moment is long past.

Now remains only this living moment of time!

Between the two the vast ocean that is time undulates, wave upon wave. All hope is ended. The wings of thought have weakened. I am descending. Moment...by...moment. I am merging with the darkness of memories that are no more. And yet tender leaves sprout. Buds blossom. Spring comes in its freshness. A formless dream hangs over the garden bathed in moonlight. In the silence that fills the world my heart blossoms into thought.

'My girl, why did you not come?' I remember that precious moment when your call came joyously floating to my ears.

'This night of a spring is coming to an end. This loneliness is burning me up. My girl, why have you not come yet?'

'When the tender leaves move to the rhythm of your soft heartbeats;

When the soothing moonlight peeps out through your sweet smile;

When the breeze of the night caresses me with the cool fragrance of your tender body;

My girl, I hear the sound of your impatient footfalls. She's coming! She's coming! My princess so full of love is coming! My heart has known no rest. Why do you make it beat so fast?'

'My girl, why have you not come?'

II

O passer-by on the road! Why did you put that flower into my hands, into my hands alone? What is so special about me? My companions asked me—they lifted up my face and asked me again and again—who you were. I said I did not know!

'You sly liar, you don't know, do you?' They teased me. They made fun of me all the time. They asked each other,

'What does he see in her?'

III

'Girl, it was from your eyes that the first rays of awareness came and kissed my heart awake. In your presence other faces pale into formlessness.'

IV

'What did you do with that flower?'
'Which flower?'
'That flower, red like blood!'
'Oh...that...?'
'Yes! What did you do with it?'
'Why are you so eager to hear about it?'
'I was wondering if you had crushed it underfoot.'
'What if I had?'
'Oh...nothing. It was my heart.'

V

'Why are your eyes red as if with weeping? Why does your face look crestfallen? Oh...no, I have not crushed it underfoot. I will never, never, destroy it. For a little while I stuck it in my hair. But then I did not want to show that, of all things, to the world. If you ask me where it is, I will not tell you! I have kept it somewhere. Do you want to know where it is? I will tell no one, no one!'

VI

The flower buds bowed their heads to guard their enchanting secrets. The evening breeze gently stirred the leaves. I lay on my back, stretched on the grass in the garden. My companion came and asked me petulantly,
'You've forgotten all of us, haven't you?'
I said, 'I have forgotten no one.'
'Then why is it you don't come out with us?'
'I do not want to see the same things over again.'
'Why not?' She made me sit up. She loosened my hair and

spread it, lock by lock and curl by curl, on my breast. Then she
looked deep into my eyes. Softly, very softly, with a sly glance
she asked me, 'Won't you tell me the secret?'
    I said nothing. Unknown to me, my head sank on my breast.
After a long while, she asked me, 'The thief, who is he?'
    I said, 'I do not know.'
    She gurgled with laughter. 'His name?'
    'I do not know.'
    'His faith?'
    'I do not know.'
    'What does he do?'
    'I do not know.'
    'Ssh, you sly thief!' She called me so. What had I stolen? I
spoke but the truth.
    'I know nothing.'
    'Tell me this wonderful secret of yours.'
    'That secret...! I will tell it to no one, no one!'

VII

'O bud that is about to blossom, what is the secret?'
'I will not tell.'
'My princess! What is the secret?'
'Did I not say that I will not tell?'
'My ocean of love...!'
'My beloved...well...I...you!'
'Say it.'
'Hmm...hmm....'

VIII

When you went away mother asked, 'Who is he?' I said, 'My...
my friend.' She demanded that I tell her everything about you.

I said, 'I know nothing.' Mother ground her teeth in anger. Something unfamiliar stared at me through her eyes. She asked softly, very softly, as if the whole world would hear, 'Who is he?'

'My friend.'

'How did you come to know him?'

I said nothing. Mother threw me down on the bed. She dragged the door shut with a noise that echoed through heaven and earth. The heady fragrance of that flower pervaded my bedroom and the inmost centre of my heart glowed. How I came to know you.... I refuse to tell anyone, anyone. I will not share the sweet sorrow with anyone.... For,

When my thoughts were like homeless birds which flew into the endless skies,

When my aimless days and nights drifted about in darkness and in light,

When all my virginity was a silent prayer in deep darkness;

I saw—

In the distance, through the window of light, your face.... In the glow of that moment my inmost being burst forth into song. This morning the tender rays of sunlight shine on the dewdrops on the flowers and transform them into veritable rubies that sparkle.

The song is taken up by the lone bird that flies over the seas. And the bird sings,

'Who are you, who are you, flawless gem,

Who are you, who are you, beauteous star,

Who are you, who are you, lovely light,

Who are you, who are you, auspicious brightness!'

IX

'I am alone!' As the moonlight filtered through the leaves and fell on my face you whispered into my ear, 'I have no companions.'

'And who am I?'

'There was a time when you were not there. Then I was on the great shore of solitude.'

The great shore of solitude! That is my mind, my very being. That day as you were about to go I asked, 'When you go away, will you forget me?'

'I will never forget. When I go from here let us go together. You must be ready and waiting....'

'When will you go?'

'I will come when it is time.'

'How did you come here?'

'Following a hope.'

'What hope?'

'In search...!'

'Of whom?'

'You...!'

'Where did you search?'

'In millions of eyes, in thousands of hearts, along the streets, in land after land...,'

'Where else?'

'Through the wondrous calm of sandy wastes bathed in moonlight, across the mighty peaks of vast mountains embedded in golden sands...,'

'Where else?'

'Through primeval forests where light had not entered, in the heart of the great city, in the garden as I stood at the gate...,'

'As you stood there?'

'My ocean of love...my beloved...."

'My...beloved....'

X

I want to sing at the top of my voice. As I try to capture the ecstasy of meeting you with the sweetness of my melody it breaks into tremulous gasps. All my attempts turn to humming sorrow. As I sit near the light and read I see you in every letter

I scan. The hand that carries food to my mouth stops halfway. I see signs of you everywhere. My heart bursts with awareness of you. The links between my nights and days have been broken. Everything has disappeared in the flow of silent tears. Like the crystal glass, in which you took water from me last time, everything has been shattered to pieces. No one else will drink from the glass. I say your name endlessly. Each breath of mine is your name. I may be no one to you. And yet, and yet, I wanted to make you beg, 'My beloved, come...my ocean of love come....' I wanted to make you call me once again. But I did not realise the intensity of parting to come. At a moment when I was totally unaware I made a senseless excuse. 'My parents. My home. My city.'

'True!' you sighed. 'Dear heart, I am going. I shall come again.'

You walked away...I stood dazed. My companion came and asked, 'Who was he who went away?'

'Oh...! just a passer-by....' Overcome, I ran inside and fell on my bed. Even then I thought you would come back. How could you go away without me...? I opened the window and looked out. The path was deserted. The mark of wheels stretched into the distance....The tired sun had left a yellow path of light in its track and was sinking in the deep blue waves of the sea. The rays of the sun formed a gilt border round a vast black cloud which came up and engulfed the sun. Gradually I became calm like the sea and sank into the blackness.

XI

In the profound depth of my being, like a point of uncertain light, I saw—the memory of you!...of you alone.

I feared it would also be wiped out in the onward march of time. Like the sharp cold sigh of the all-pervasive darkness...a vaporous smoke enveloped my heart. A fearful cyclone blew incessantly. The earth trembled. The mountains shook and crumbled. Flames of fire billowed up to the skies. Everything was burnt to ashes. In the vast darkness, like a tiny ball of snow, a point of light...finally it became an all-pervasive, benevolent luminosity...that alone remained.... The earth was vast tracts of sand laid upon sand like the petals of a flower. You walked step by step towards that light. I was sinking. My eyes followed your footsteps into the infinite distance. My consciousness was slipping away. You disappeared like a shadow into that mighty presence. Suddenly a voice, like the reverberation of creation itself, resounded.

'Girl! Why did you not come?'

'Beloved!'

I woke up with a start. Through the open window, from the dark sky, two bright stars stared at me!

XII

I eagerly await your coming. Every day, every moment. I make myself beautiful from dawn to the onset of night. Every day fresh flowers are strewn on the silken white bed. There is a heady fragrance in my bedroom ever ready to receive you. In the evening crowds on the seaside I look at every face in search of you. Footsteps approach my door with steady tread and then, without stopping, they fade away. When all the world sleeps I lie awake listening. Nights and days thus pass me by. When the end of a day comes I fear that the end of my life is coming. When neighbouring houses light their lamps and I see within them love at play, my house is dark and I am desolate. I cannot bear the burden of this life. I am but the dust of varied hues and moods. That it should be fashioned into this form that is me and kept alive! I must escape forever from the great shore of this crushing loneliness. O clouds! Destroy me by your mighty roar...! O lightning! Split me open with your blaze...! I am finished. I am letting go my hold on consciousness.

In the whiteness of this cold moonlight, in this fragrance which scatters my last breath,
Beloved! May I...once...kiss your presence.

Original title 'Ekanthathayude Mahatheeram'; from the collection Anarganimisham *(1944).*

✦

Tiger

Tiger was a fortunate dog. Although the common people all over the countryside had been reduced to mere skeletons by the prevailing famine, Tiger looked far from famished. When he sat he looked like a fat bundle wrapped up in a black blanket. His body was black, his legs and tail were white. His eyes were brown with a tinge of red. Tiger's eyes looked cruel, like those of a policeman.

Tiger was the pup of a stray bitch. He was littered in the city gutter. He did not know this. From the days he could remember he had been in the police station. His world was confined to the four walls of the police station yard, the building and the square piece of sky above.

The prisoners and policemen were his only companions. He could identify each one of them. He was most attached to the Police Inspector. The prisoners used to say that the expression in the eyes of the Inspector and in those of Tiger were the same.

Tiger did not make any distinction between the prisoners. The murderer, the thief, the political agitator. There were two classes of human beings—policemen and prisoners. To the dog the fortyfive prisoners looked alike. Tiger never paid attention to the fact that the four prisoners herded together in one lockup were political agitators. To him all lockup rooms were alike. Neither air nor light entered any of the rooms. Pale beings with overgrown beards resembling human figures wrapped up in old rags lived in the dank darkness of those rooms. They had to bear the stench of human urine and excreta and the bites of innumerable bugs.

The stench emanating from the lockup rooms was enough to burn up all hope in the human heart. But the inmates were not affected by this at all. Their predominant thought was of food. The overwhelming desire for food eclipsed everything else. They went to sleep at night with the thought of the rice gruel they would get in the morning. By the time they finished their rice gruel they thought of the noon meal. And with the noon meal they thought of the food they would get in the evening. There was turmoil in their hearts as their gnawing hunger was never appeased. All of them looked forward to getting convicted and sentenced to jail. Everyone knew there was no prospect of an acquittal in cases where the charge had been brought by the police. Once they were sentenced they would be taken to jail. The jail was paradise for the prisoner. The lockup was his hell.

The prisoners in the lockup seethed with anger which blazed through their eyes at Tiger. Supremely indifferent to this, Tiger would pace up and down in front of the lockup rooms. Or he would lie down in front of one of the rooms. At lunch time he would be guarding the door to the Inspector's room. After finishing his lunch the Inspector would belch and put the leaf containing the remnants of his meal before Tiger. There would be enough food there for a man, and the dog would snap it up. The prisoners would feel their mouths water when they saw the dog eating it.

After his noon meal Tiger would go into the garden and rest in the shade of the shrubs. After a short nap he would again make his appearance in front of the rooms. There would be the semblance of a smile in his eyes as if he knew the secrets of everyone there. Most of them were there on fake charges. False cases brought against them by the Inspector and the policemen after receiving bribes! Some of the prisoners may have stolen something maybe once in their lives. After that they were considered responsible for all the thefts in the town. The inmates of the lockup would confess to any crime they were accused of. They would confess it before magistrates; for they were always accompanied by policemen.

The Government had fixed a daily allowance of food for every undertrial prisoner. Thirty times that was more than a policeman's monthly salary. That is to say the total daily allowance worked out to much more than a policeman's pay. A policeman had to eat and dress and provide for his family. He had no income other than his pay. How could he manage?

The prisoners would stretch out their hands through the bars towards Tiger's body with ill-concealed anger. 'All that you eat is our food!'

Tiger would wag his tail. 'Yes! That is life—no one can change that!' The dog seemed to be saying just that with his eyes. Was it in fact possible to change such a state of affairs? There had been prisoners who had complained. 'Our hunger has not been satisfied. We must get the amount of food allowed for each of us.'

What they received however, were blows from policemen and kicks from the booted feet of the Inspector. The Inspector was even heard to mutter with contempt, 'What the Government has fixed! As if the Government is your grandfather!'

Could the Government be anyone's grandfather? They said: 'Tiger is the Government!'

Was that a correct comparison?

It was a hotelkeeper who had been taken on contract to give every prisoner food according to the daily allowance fixed. He had started his business in a humble way. Now he was a rich man because of the prisoners. He was fat and sported twirling moustachios and had a pot belly. He and the Police Inspector were hand-in-glove. The Inspector and the Station Writer ate food from his hotel. They did not have to pay for their meals or coffee. Further, the hotelkeeper paid the Inspector and the Station Writer a fixed amount every month. All this the hotelkeeper recovered from the prisoners. Daily there would be some fifty or sixty prisoners to be fed. Who was to ask even if no food was given to them? If they thought of complaining to the Magistrate when they were taken to court, they had to keep in mind that they would be returning to the lockup in the evening. The Inspector would ask with a laugh—and what a laugh! 'Did you tell him, you rascal?'

After that they would be beaten till they were unconscious. After a while the prisoners had no complaints to make! They would try to take their revenge on the dog. Everyone knew that the prisoners did not like Tiger. The Inspector would wonder why they could not love that poor animal.

But the prisoners continued to dislike Tiger. They would try and hurt him whenever they could. Tiger would start moaning the moment he sensed that someone was about to hurt him.

The Inspector would come out of his room cane in hand. 'Who is hurting that dog?'

When nobody answered, he would continue, 'You curs, haven't I told not to touch Tiger? Come on, whoever has hurt him, stretch out your hand!'

A hand would slowly come out through the iron bars. The Inspector would grip the hand firmly by the fingers and slash it with the cane, again and again. The atmosphere would sizzle. The skin on the wrist and palm would break and blood would drip, drop by drop. The dog would lick the floor clean.

The punishment only put up the backs of the prisoners and they repeated the offence. Every prisoner there had suffered more than once for hurting the dog. As for the dog, he was always prepared to make them commit the offence over and over again.

Tiger seldom went out of the station premises. He was a great coward. He would bark with the ferocity of a tiger if any dog came into the station yard. But when he went outside and saw even a mangy street cur, he would run back to the station quietly, with the tail between his legs. A political prisoner saw this one day and said laughing, 'Look at the return of our Inspector!'

A philosopher among the prisoners said, 'There exists such an Inspector in each one of us.'

That remark gave rise to a lively discussion. Three of the prisoners took one side while one was against them. When the discussion was at its loudest the Inspector came out. 'What's the excitement about?'

No one replied.

'Open the cell,' the Inspector ordered the sentry. The doors were opened and all of them filed out. The Inspector said, 'You have some visitors.'

When they went to the Inspector's room they found that some friends of the young man who had set off the discussion had come to see him. They had brought some oranges and other things to eat. The Inspector ate two of the oranges. They ate what was left of the oranges and the other food. They talked about happenings in the country. The news they heard did not surprise them. There was acute poverty everywhere and many people had died of starvation. The war still raged and prices went up every day. There was severe famine everywhere.

'We are also experiencing it,' the young man who had started the discussion said.

'What do you have to complain about? You are fed well. You have no worries, lucky fellows!' remarked one of the visitors.

Just then Tiger came ambling to the door and the young man who had started the discussion pointed to the dog and said,'If only the prisoners were as fortunate as he is!'

The Inspector laughed. The visitors laughed. The prisoners laughed. They returned to the lockup. The four of them were contented. They had eaten their fill; and so there was rice and curry left uneaten from their evening meal. They pushed this before the door of the lockup next to theirs. The twentytwo who were inside came to the door and looked out greedily. One of them pulled in the leaves containing rice and curry. Some of the rice spilt outside. Tiger stood there ready to lick it up. Twentyone men sat down in a circle to eat. One man got ready to serve them. Each of them would get hardly a handful. All the same, they were ready to eat it up. The man scooped out rice into the hands of five and then ladled out some curry. Some of it splashed onto the bars of the door and on the floor outside. Tiger licked up the floor and then stretched out his tongue to lick the bars. One of the prisoners gave him a well-aimed kick on the face. The dog let out a yell in agony. The sentry came running. So did a few policemen and the Inspector. The Inspector made the prisoners put back the rice onto the leaf which he had pulled out of the cell. The hearts of twentytwo people were being plucked out. The leaf with the food was placed before the dog. As if this was not enough, the Inspector had the lockup opened. He entered the cell and showered kicks and blows on the prisoners.

The incident ended in the afternoon. That night, long and agonised moans of pain were heard. The police station reverberated with the cries. When the sentry came running to the scene he found that two prisoners were pulling the dog by its head into the cell through the bars. It was clear that there were two prisoners but the sentry could recognize only one.

The Inspector had the identified prisoner brought out of the lockup. He had been accused in a case of theft. To begin with the Inspector gave him a resounding blow on the face. This was followed by a kick. The man fell down on his face. He was repeatedly kicked on the back. He was lifted up. His mouth was full of blood. On the floor was a circular patch of blood and a broken tooth.

The scene was witnessed by fortyfive prisoners, nine policemen and the dog Tiger. Tiger licked the floor clean of the blood.

'You rascals, who is the other fellow?'

The prisoner, already beaten up, would not say anything. So he would refuse, would he? His legs were pulled out through the bars of the door and tied together. He was given hard blows in quick succession on the exposed soles of his feet. He would not say anything even though the skin split. His blood oozed out. He lost consciousness. That was why he lay still even when Tiger licked the blood from the soles of his feet with his rough tongue.

Original title 'Tiger'; from the collection Janmadinam *(1944).*

✦

Voices

I : The Midnight Visitor

'Once upon a time there was a young man who had no known father or mother. He committed a large number of murders. In his twenty-fourth year he—'

'Let me interrupt with a question. Are you starting the story?'

'Yes!'

'Who are you talking about?'

'About myself, of course.'

'I see.'

'Didn't you ask me to begin my story somewhere?'

'Yes...yes.... I didn't mean it so seriously. I thought...you were....'

'Mad? Isn't that so?'

'What's your illness?'

'Insanity!'

'Even if that is true can't you clean your teeth or take a bath? Look at your hair, your beard, those foul-smelling clothes.... Can't you take a bath at least and go about clean?'

'I believe that water is the blood of the earth.'

'I see.... Can't you think of another excuse?'

'I've no other clothes to change into, no towel for a bath.'

'Who sent you to me in the middle of the night?'

'No one sent me. I saw you during the day. I heard your name being mentioned. You were pointed out to me; I followed you. Other people joined you on the way. All of you came to this room and were talking till now. When I saw them leave after the argument and talk and laughter and noise, I came in.'

'So you were waiting in that dark alley till now?'

'Yes.'

'How do you know me?'

'I have read your books.'

'Where did you get them?'

'I bought them.'

'Where did the money come from?'

'I was in the army.'

'Is that how you became a murderer?'

'Yes. But it is not only the enemy whom I've killed!'

'So you say you're an admirer of mine?'

'Yes.'

'What have you brought for me?'

'I've brought nothing.'

'Well?'

'What do you think of killing and murder?'

'You mean whether I think it's good or bad?'

'Yes.'

'What am I to say?'

'You've nothing to say?'

'Don't be annoyed! I shall tell you something. I don't wish to be murdered by anyone. What I usually do is...I try and gauge whether the person who is coming to kill me is stronger than me. If he is not, I fight him bravely! If he is stronger, I run away as fast as I can!'

'Are you making fun of me?'

'What is it you want?'

'I have no philosophy of life. I want to tell you some stories.'

'Can't we do that tomorrow? I'm so tired listening to so much talk. I want to eat something and go to sleep. You may come tomorrow. Don't come too early. It's enough if you come about eleven or twelve. I wake up only then.'

'Where will I go till then?'

'Haven't you a place to go to?'
'....no.'
'No one you know here?'
'I don't know if I do.'
'Have you eaten?'
'No.'
'Got any money with you?'
'No.'
'How nice!'
'What do you want me to do?'
'What do I want?'
'Yes, tell me.'
'I want only that you shouldn't get angry. Two, you shouldn't stare at me with those fierce big eyes. Three, you should clean your teeth and take a bath. Four, you should wear the laundered clothes I am giving you. Five, if you want to comb your hair and beard I have no comb with me. Six, I have only food enough for one. Seven, both of us can share that...O.K?'
'Yes.'
'Then go that way into the next room without touching my bed. Take a towel and some tooth powder from the packet in the corner. Pick up the torch on your way into the bathroom and have a bath. Wait! I'll give you laundered clothes. Don't bring back what you are wearing. The bed in the next room is for you. When it is time to sleep I'll close the door and you can use the other room. You can go out when you want to. You are perfectly free. Now go and have a bath. Then we'll eat. We'll do all the talking tomorrow. Is that all right?'
'That's O.K.'
'Let me ask you something. Were you discharged from the army?'
'Yes'
'What was the reason?'
'We won the war!'
'How many soldiers were demobbed?'
'Must be about four or five hundred thousand'
'Are you their representative?'

'I represent myself! Have I no right to speak for myself?'

'You've every right.'

'I have no special preferences for anything in particular. I love this whole world of ours. I was born on this earth. Everyone here of any belief, of any religion is related to me.... I love them all. I became a soldier. What is supposed to be the duty of a soldier? To kill as many people as possible...and so I killed. In order that some despicable scum could rule this country. I am speaking of the leaders of the war. None of them were on the battlefield. A people's war! People armed with destructive weapons were ranged on opposite sides and asked to kill one another. People's war! Which people?'

'Didn't I tell you not to get angry? And...I have to remind you of one thing. I didn't send you into the army. Why are you angry with me?'

'I have to be angry with somebody. It has hurt me so much.'

'That's wonderful!'

'What do you want?'

'Go and have your bath; let's eat and go to sleep.'

II : AT THE CROSSROADS

'It's a long time since I slept in peace. No place to stay, no food, no work.'

'You have a father and a mother...?'

'No.'

'Then how did you come into this world?'

'Just like anyone else!'

'But I have a legitimate father and mother, brother and sisters.'

'I have none.'

'Where were you born?'

'At the crossroads, where four roads meet!'

'What do you mean?'

I know only what my foster-father told me. He found me early one morning as a new-born baby in a bundle of rags.'

'What did he do?'

'He took me away. He informed the police. He informed the government authorities also.'

'And what happened.'

'What could they do? No one wanted me! So he took me along and gave me a bath. I yelled furiously. He laid me down on a clean white sheet. He put me in a little box and carried me away. He gave me a name. Thus I grew up in his religion. He gave me a fairly good education.'

'So you grew up as a member of his community.'

'That is right. I do not believe in any religion now. All religions are more or less the same—they all try to make man better.'

'Which religion were you born into?'

'How would I know? It could have been any religion. Christian, Muslim, Hindu, Jew, Parsi or perhaps from a union of any two of them...whichever way it is, I have never fed at a mother's breast!'

'What did you do once your foster-father died?'

'I had to give up my studies and go looking for a job. Finally I became a soldier. I can't tell you the story of my life systematically, in order of events. I can only talk haphazardly from here and there.'

'Who was your foster-father?'

'A priest. By which I mean a pujari in a temple, an old man. He had no family. He was a kind man. His thoughts were always of God. May I ask something? Is there a God?'

'If you want one...yes.'

'Why do you say, if you want one?'

'I am thirtyfour years old, that's how I feel now. How old are you?'

'Twentynine.'

'Didn't you ever want to find out who your real father and mother were?'

'Yes, I did.'

'Did you try?'

'We asked around. We made enquiries many times. My foster-father and I came here and asked many people.'

'Here?'

'Yes, it was at a crossroads at this place that I was found as a new-born baby.'

III : THE BLOOD OF THE EARTH

'Why do you say that water is the earth's blood?'

'I become pale all over when I think of that event. Didn't I tell you I killed many people. Every soldier has killed thousands of men. Who is responsible for all this?'

'Who do you think is responsible?'

'Emperors, kings, presidents, dictators—aren't they all murderers?'

'Do you think so?'

'Yes, their thrones are bathed in human blood. What they drink is the people's blood. They—'

'Stop. Let me ask you something. In a war, isn't there one side at fault?'

'Maybe. But what if you look at it from the other's point of view?'

'Can we survive if you look at things that way?'

'From the point of view of animals and birds and foodgrains and trees and fishes all men are murderers. What do you say to that?'

'Oh...is that a proper reply? Anyhow, let me tell you my love story.'

'What about the earth's blood?'

'I will not talk about that.'

'Why?'

'I'll talk about a person whom I killed.'

'Tell me about the earth's blood before that. Why do you feel that way about it?'

'I can't explain this properly. I find it difficult to recall every event. One night some five hundred of us soldiers drank what we thought was water. In the morning when we looked at what remained in the vessels it was blood. It was a place where a small battle had taken place. Countless men lay dead; but not entirely.

I'll talk about the other matter. That stands out clearly in my mind. The death of a friend of mine. It was I who killed him; *tup, tup, tup!* I fired two or three shots. It was broad daylight; during summer. One can't describe the heat of the battlefield; the loud sounds, echoes, explosions; bombs that whizzed past you, stunned you and exploded with shattering impact, blazing into your eyes; the heat and the sweat; the continuous roar of bomber planes; tremendous explosions that tore at your eardrums. People taking flight, loud cries. Everywhere there's a fearful alertness and lassitude. So many nights and days of this. In the midst of this, one ate. One slept. One did everything. Everything was like a nightmare. Once I found in the food I was eating a human eye. All around were human beings in bits and pieces; decaying corpses. Death was always next to you. Bullets kept flying past you!

I do not know why I did not die. This was not my experience alone; every soldier will tell you the same thing. My friend and I were next to each other. A bomb that exploded forty feet away did not kill him. The crater it formed buried me in the earth. It was noon. Earth filled my eyes and nose and mouth. I crawled out. All kinds of things had caught fire. I could hear the sound of flames and of burning. Just then I heard the voice of my friend full of deep pain and fear. He was right next to me.

"Please, in the name of God kill me. I can't bear it." Those were his words. I saw him. It's a sight I will remember to my dying day. I was shaking with fear, bathed in sweat. Think of yourself being skinned alive from the soles of your feet to the top of your head. Blood oozed out from every pore.... I thought he had caught fire. A naked blood-red man. Those eyes! From his fingers and his penis blood oozed out like molten steel rods! He was dripping and every drop made a sound as it fell on to the uniform of a dead soldier.'

IV : THE BELOVED

'Let me hear the love story!'

'All soldiers have their loves. One love for many of them. Or one of them would have many. It is a confusing situation. The ordinary soldier gets an ordinary prostitute. As his military rank rises the women he gets also rise in social stature. What have you to say about prostitution?'

'Whether I think it is good or bad?'

'That's right.'

'I have heard it said that prostitution is the world's oldest profession. Many follow the profession even today; from beggars to queens. Anyhow I wouldn't like my mother or sisters to practice it.'

'Do you have a wife?'

'Openly, no.'

'In secret...?'

'Let's say that secretly also I have none. Even if I did I wouldn't like her to be a prostitute. Go on with your story.'

'Have you felt that there is always an economic problem behind the practice of prostitution?'

'There has to be something of the sort.'

'Why do women become prostitutes?'

'Probably because there are men.'

'Is that any kind of reply?'

'Why should men go to them? Let us not waste time in pointless discussion. From the point of view of the male the fault is always that of the woman. Looked at from the woman's point of view the fault lies with the man. Either the fault is on both sides or on neither. On what basis will you decide about right and wrong?'

'On the basis of morality.'

'Morality of which part of the earth, of which people?'

'I don't know about that. Isn't there something that we ordinarily call morality? Not to covet other women, monogamy, chastity and so on?'

'Morality is different for different religions. Take monogamy.

Some religions allow polygamy. Some allow polyandry too. There have been kings and people among whom mothers and sisters could be taken as wives. That was their morality. Among animals and reptiles and birds, mothers and sisters become mates. Among humans too, even today such practices go on. A sister could conceive through a brother, a mother through her son, a daughter through her father.'

'Isn't that terrible?'

'Why?'

'Well, I don't know why!'

'I'll tell you why. You have a philosophy of life. You were wrong in saying you had no such thing. You have had it since you were a child. Wasn't your foster-father a priest in a temple? He has taught you about good and bad. That is your philosophy of life.'

'You may be right. Let me ask something. Is it possible to maintain mutual honesty in relationships between man and woman?'

'In sexual matters?'

'Yes.'

'How can I say? How can I speak for all the men and women in the world, other than myself? I only wish honesty could be maintained—it's just a hope. Generally speaking can anyone be said to be consistently honest or truthful in anything? We may try to be good and honest before others but are we so before ourselves?'

'What would you say of the future of the human race?'

'Nothing bad. Why do you ask?'

'Among the people in this world, seven out of ten have gonorrhoea or syphilis.'

'Who said this?'

'An eminent military doctor.'

'He must have said it to frighten the soldiers.'

'Among soldiers nine out of ten have the disease. This is a fact. They are next door to death. What about the others? Workers, farmers, officials, lawyers, kings, political workers, artists, journalists, writers, poets, prostitutes, reviewers, beggars, presidents—in this varied population of the world seven out of ten have syphilis or gonorrhoea!'

'I do not know whether they have it or not. Anyhow aren't there medicines?'

'Only the rich can afford them. Even then it cannot be completely cured. It is rather like a smouldering ember hidden among the ashes. Doctors say there are instances of gonorrhoea being transmitted through the blood and semen for three generations. Perhaps it is more terrible than leprosy. Anyhow I am terrified of going near prostitutes. I haven't gone to them. When I was discharged from the army and stayed in the city I had a woman. Till then, as long as I was a soldier my love was just the photograph I had of a film star. That picture was the beloved for many of us.'

'Meaning?'

'The picture had lips, eyes, breasts, navel and thighs....'

V : The Lover

'I became a lover when I was staying with a prominent person of the city. It happened soon after I was discharged from the army. Demobbed soldiers loafed around jobless. There was a famine with many epidemics. That is nothing unusual, is it? Whatever it was, for a man to live without a woman was—'

'Wait! How did you come to stay with a VIP of the city?'

'The reason was some popular upheaval either communal or political. I was standing on the first floor of a hotel. There was a beautiful sunset. But the sun had not set.... Do you think these riots and violence will ever end?'

'So long as there continues to be more than one view about anything....'

'Who is in the right?'

'Think for yourself and decide. If you can't do that accept the more convincing opinion.'

'What's the meaning of these opinions?'

'I do not understand the meaning of your question.'

'Don't you have religions now? And political organisations. Everyone is kicking up a row. What do all of them want?'

'Their main demands are for authority, power.'

'To what purpose?'

'To rule over humanity and every living being in this world! Religions want to do it in the name of God. Those who do not believe in God want to do it in their own name.'

'Why?'

'Each person has a philosophy of life. Each tries to do things his own way.'

'I alone have no philosphy of living. Is that because I have no bonds with anyone?'

'You do have a philosophy of life. I explained that to you before. As for your bonds, you are bound to everyone.'

'With what bonds?'

'Have you got a navel?'

'Navel...? What sort of bond is that?'

'You were bound to your unknown mother.'

'What about it?'

'Your unknown father was bound to his mother. In short everyone in this world must have bonds with each other.'

'I do not have any feelings about that.'

'If you feel nothing, then accept there is nothing in it. We are wasting our time talking of this and that. Tell me how you became a lover. You were standing on the first floor of a hotel in the city, a beautiful sunset—'

'Yes but the sun had not set. Think of the city as a large forest. But is it a forest? It is a city. Roaring, groaning, hooting, whispering, the city was reverberating with life. The noise of vehicles, machines. The vast flow of humanity going in every direction. The roar of racing vehicles. What a variety of buildings. Mills, banks, workshops, hospitals, government buildings...every one of them displayed pieces of cloth dipped in different colours.'

'What do you mean?'

'Flags!'

'Oh.'

'Aren't each of those pieces of cloth a symbol for the people?'

'Yes'

'Doesn't each of them have a programme of action?'

'Probably.'

'Doesn't each of them speak for the people?'

'Do they?'

'A big gunpowder dump belonging to some people caught fire. A procession by one group of people clashed with the procession of another group. Soda-water bottles were thrown. Chunks of granite flew. Knives sank deep into human breasts!

Slogans! Counter slogans! Abusive language! Obscenities! A festival of blood! The dance of death! Blows! Fisticuffs! Cries! Tumult every where!

The police came. The military came. Machine guns started rattling—*rat – tat – tat – tat – tat – tat!*

An endless roaring din and noise everywhere overhead, planes kept circling. *Br – r – r! Br – r – r!*

Below, human beings had fallen with broken heads and gashed chests. Buildings were in flames; a hot breeze blew. There was the stink of blood and gunpowder. And then the lights of the city started burning. Songs rose from cinema houses. The darkened sky lit up with signs that showed up red with the colour of blood. Oh, what a wonderful city!

Six-storeyed buildings burnt in the sky like heaps of dried leaves. How many thousand pairs of eyes reflected those flames. Men in their thousands were burnt to ashes. Vehicles ran continuously clanging their bells. The sound of fire engines. Somewhere a huge water pipe had broken and jets of water rose into the sky with a terrific noise!

The hotel I was staying in was enveloped in smoke. Soon it was burning. Everyone was blindly groping and running, coughing in the smoke. I also got out and ran. I ran aimlessly, half-consciously; for the sake of self-preservation. I jumped into the fire and I ran with clothes already in flames.

The VIP said I had rescued many people from the fire. I don't remember. When I gained full consciousness I was in his mansion. His wife and children liked me. I was considered a brave young man; a man the country should be proud of. There was need for thousands of young men like me!

I think he got my picture published in some paper along with a statement from him. Then for some time one kept having press statements. All the readers issued statements; which were followed by counter-statements. Large numbers owing allegiance to different flags had died. The people loyal to one flag held the people following other flags responsible for the killing. The accusations chased each other in a vicious cycle. Then came the statistics, an account of those who died. They made speeches. They wrote in the papers. Only the slogans of each were different; otherwise they were all the same. Bombs and gunpowder dipped in brotherliness and those pieces of cloth of different hues.'

'And what about your becoming a lover?'

'I'll talk about that. I was staying in the mansion of that VIP. The garage had two good rooms on either side. I was in one. The driver was in the other.

I ate there. I had the full freedom of the house. When I was sitting in that room one evening in the twilight and the city lights came on all of a sudden, I became a lover.'

VI : In the Image of Love

'A dreamy-eyed smile. Firm upstanding breasts; that gait, that look.

Daily at sundown she would go past my room. She would look at me. She would smile specially for me.

I too tried to smile but I didn't have the courage. All this was without knowing who I was. She must have thought I was a member of that household. Once my position was known all this might change. Even then I wondered—who and what she was I didn't know. A student or a working woman.... Whoever it was...she was a sweet poem fashioned in loveliness. I didn't know her name. My heart was captive. A storm had blown into my life.

How I longed for a kiss, for a passionate embrace! How would a woman look without her clothes on? I didn't know. I must see. I must touch. I must kiss. I must embrace. Full of the smell of woman, my nostrils would flare; I lived with a suppressed strength that could reduce granite into powder. I would stand at the window full of expectation, looking at the crowded street. She would come when the sun was just setting. Each day the dress was a different colour; with matching chappals and handbag. And then one evening.... The lights became brighter as the darkness grew. The noises of the city became louder. My heart thumped faster. There she came! With a look full of love! Then she walked on. I locked my room and walked out into the road. She saw me approaching. She slowed down. I went near. She looked at me. A smiling endearing look. Then she asked a question as if her throat was choked but still with the sweetness of a song!

"Where are you going?"

'In reply I attempted to smile. I was sweating.

My mouth was parched. A sweet fragrance... a face as fair as the jasmine. Rose-red lips. Hair as black as the night. I felt a desire to kiss her all over. Firm breasts that stood up through the bodice, through the thin material of the sari and blouse. In her left hand was a handbag and a little umbrella. In the right hand was a tiny handkerchief. I walked with a sinking feeling, looking at her hungrily. I could not talk. Just then a car came towards us, noisily. In the car was the wife of the VIP with whom I was staying. I slid into the shadows to avoid being seen. The car sped past. I was alone. At my feet lay that handkerchief. I bent down and picked it up. It had touched that face and those lips. It had soaked in her sweat. I kissed it. I kissed it a thousand times. I kept it under my shirt, beneath my vest next to my heart.'

VII : THE PERFUMED HANDKERCHIEF

'And then?'

'I'll tell you. Oh... there, look at that over that tree!'

'The moon, isn't it?'

'What a wonderfully perfect circle, like incandescent white powder—a hazy day without warmth.... Why does the moon have this haziness—look, the thick green foliage shines bright...ah, now on the mountains and in the deserts and on the oceans....'

'Let the moon be. Go on with your story of the perfumed handkerchief.'

'Have you ever received gifts from your beloved?'

'Plenty of them.'

'How much do you value them?'

'Why do you ask?'

'I just asked.'

'But love is not a new concept. Take a look at that moon. Ages and aeons ago and ages and aeons before that also—that is ever since man inhabited the face of this earth, whatever it is that the male feels for the female and the moon... what I am trying to say is that the idea of love is an old, old thing. From ancient times man has loved woman and written love letters. How does one value them?'

'It is all so wonderful!'

'So is life and the earth and the moon and the stars....'

'I remember that perfumed handkerchief. Do you know how many times I kissed it that night? What dreams I dreamt! My love flew out over that mansion, over that city.'

'What was your work in that house?'

'Nothing very important. I was expected to teach four or five children. It would be more correct to say that I was to look after them.'

'Did that household know everything about you?'

'Some things. Generally they all liked me very much. What a strange creature is man!'

'What doubt is there? You are yourself a strange creature!'

'Somehow I am full of a great sadness. You could call it sadness full of a delicate poetic fragrance. I would feel that of the moon. Do you?'

'Perhaps...sometimes all living beings may feel that way.'

'Are there living creatures on the moon?'

'Scientists say there is nothing on the moon. It is a dead world.'

'In the stars?'

'They say there may be life on some. When ages pass...in the distant future who knows what may happen! There was nothing in the distant past.'

'Nothing?'

'That is to say, the earth and the moon—'

'Then how did they come into being?'

'Religions say that God created them. Scientists say that they were pieces that fell out of explosions in the sun.'

'Who is right?'

'What can one say.... In some religious scriptures the earth is flat. Scientists prove that the earth is round. Which of them is right? You don't believe in religions therefore believe in what the scientists say.'

'In religious lore the stars and the sun and the moon are lamps lit by God. In your opinion how did man come into being?'

'I have no opinion on that. What I mean is that I do not know anything and I have discovered nothing. I know what scientists say. They say different things. I will summarise it briefly. It's not interesting. Take your imagination back to the beginning of the world...ten million years. Look back ten years, hundred years. Before you and I were born, before man came into being, before any life came into being, before earth and water were found, millions of ages ago.... Think of the earth as a ball of white-hot fire melting, boiling, perpetually revolving... before that this white ball of fire that was the earth was a tiny drop in a fiercely burning sun.'

'After that?'

'It fell out of the sun and went round and round for millions of years of days and nights.'

'Then?'

'It cooled down—ages pass. Water and earth form. Again ages pass. Creatures living in water come into being, plants and trees come up, during millions of years. Birds and reptiles and animals come into being. Time goes on. Ages pass. Man comes into being—men and women in their nakedness. Human life passes through millions of years of days and nights. There may be some mistakes here and there in what I have said. Broadly this is what happened. Among living things man alone progressed. Hunting, cultivation, religions, places of worship, towns, cities, machines, vehicles—that is how we progressed.'

'Now what is our future?'

'...of the human race?'

'That's right.'

'Brave and beautiful! We have terrible diseases but we have the medicines and the means to fight them. We have electricity, we have transport. The means for going on land, in the sky, on water and under water.'

'What is there inside the earth?'

'The stuff that flows out of a live volcano, the molten mass of metals and other elements. There must be something inside the earth in constant flow, melting and boiling in the fierce heat.'

'Will the earth become a dead world at some future time?'

'It is a fact that you and I will not be there at some future time. Then why think of the future of the earth?'

'They say that the moon is a dead world, don't they?'

'It is not known whether there was anything before that. Why should we think of something which is far beyond our comprehension? Accept that everything was created by God. Think of the sun, moon and stars as lamps lit by God for us.'

'When it comes to that, one has to believe in religion and heaven and hell.'

'Believe that too! Who told you not to?'

'Do you believe it?'

'What I believe...why do you want to know about that?'

'Just in order to know.'

'No, that's not necessary for you to know. We have wasted a lot of time talking of all sorts of things. Tell me what you have to say. I have a great deal of writing to do.'

'Will you write my story?'

'After I hear everything.'

'Do you remember all that I have told you?'

'Every word of it.'

'How is it possible to remember like that?'

'I can't tell you. Go on with what you have to say.'

'Where did I stop?'

'The perfumed handkerchief. Then you saw the moon yes, then you kissed that handkerchief, you kept it beside you in bed and dreamt.'

'That's right. It was covered with perfume. A very costly perfume. The same type of perfume that my host's wife used. I learnt that through the servant. "Master, you smell like madam." I asked, "Which madam?" and she replied, "Our madam!" This was when she brought me coffee. I did not pay attention to her talk. I was thinking of my loved one.'

'Then what happened?'

'One day there was a wedding. One of the girls in the house where I was staying was getting married. It was a big affair, fireworks, grand dinner. All the important people had come. Each of them was served what they wanted. Liquor for those who wanted it. I was quite tipsy even before nightfall.

That evening also my beloved came. I went with her.

I was taken in a car.

She smiled with dreamy eyes. She made me get down from the car, took me inside a room opening out into the street. She closed the door. She embraced me. She made me sit on the bed. The room became enveloped in darkness; a heavenly fragrance. I kissed her on the face and on those eyes. I kissed her on the blouse. We were locked in each other's arms. I...I was a river that had sprung forth from a mountain top. For ages the water had been locked up in the mountain without flow, without movement. And now by my strength the mountain had rent asunder...split into many pieces. I was running at tremendous speed. I was losing myself in a boundless ocean. Finally...finally I surfaced from the ecstasy. I opened my eyes. The light was on. My head cleared. I felt very happy, contented...but the surroundings were so unpleasant! There was a wall from which the plaster had fallen like so many sores. I saw a clothesline from which hung dirty-smelling dresses. An iron trunk stood on a dusty platform. Pictures of film stars, male and female, were on the wall. The entire room had an odour of decay wrapped up in fragrance.

"Would you like to drink something?" came a question. I shuddered. What kind of a voice was that? Like that of a king crow. There was no womanliness in it. I saw black hair peeping out from under the blouse! I was surprised and afraid.

I stood up and caught hold of those breasts. They were bags filled with cotton wool...! Bags of cotton wool.... I just sat there. Many hours must have passed. Or perhaps only some minutes. I slowly placed those breasts along with the blouse and cotton breasts on the bed. I did not know whether I felt anger or surprise or sorrow. I lit a cigarette and inhaled the smoke. Smoke...! I could hear the sound of fireworks clearly above the noise of the city.

VIII : A Male Prostitute

'She, it, he—came near me and took the cotton breasts and bodice and tied them on. Then he put on the blouse. Then the rest of the clothes. He asked me, "Haven't you seen people like me?"

"People like you?"

"Aren't they everywhere?"

"Everywhere!"...everyone in women's clothes like this? I sat and stared. I did not know any women. I had not seen any women without clothes. In the dark under the influence of lust and intoxication and passionate love I had done all sorts of things. I broke out into a sweat. I felt miserable. I felt sympathy as well as anger. I was nauseated. He was a male like me!

I asked, "How many persons like you are there in this place?"

"Quite a large number."

"How do you become like this?"

He...turned his face away. I persisted.

That—it, painted its lips red and said, "We have a society. Before joining it we have to sit on a sharp spike, something like a nilavilakku, a brass oil lamp. Then we have a marriage ceremony. Everyone belonging to the society would attend. There is singing and celebration. Then hair is plucked out from the face with tweezers. There is a christening with a woman's name; skirt and sari are worn; the hair is grown long."

"Who are the persons who come to you?"

"Women as well as men."

"You can't like a man...?"

"...not for the last two or three years."

"Then why do women come to you?"

"Don't you know why?"

"No...tell me your story."

"I have no story to tell."

"...about your childhood. Don't you have a father and mother?"

"Yes. They do not know I am like this. I have stayed in the house you are now staying in. Today is his daughter's wedding, is it not?"

"Yes."

"That girl's mother was very fond of me."

I said, "I have no father or mother or anyone."

"No one?"

"No."

"Are they dead?"

"I don't know. I haven't seen them."

"That's a lie."

He could not believe what I told him about myself. He told me his story.

"Do you want me to tell you?"

"Yes, do tell me."

That story was about how he became a male prostitute. His school master, his classmates; they had a part in it at the beginning. He was born in a village about fifty miles from the city. In his fourteenth year his master made use of him homosexually. He also introduced him to the pleasures of masturbation. After a while he realised it was practically a daily routine among such persons. In schools, colleges, convents, seminaries,he learnt all the perversions practised in these places. In his sixteenth year he became a servant in a hotel in the city. There he contracted gonorrhoea from a colleague. Servants in all hotels have either gonorrhoea or syphilis. He loafed around and stayed for a time with my host's driver. From there he moved into the main house. At first he was just the servant. Later on he had to massage the legs and feet of the master of the house. The massaging of the legs didn't stop there. As for the mistress of the house she was not satisfied with mere massaging either...in those days he was not an impotent male. Finally he became an acknowledged male prostitute. That was a street full of male prostitutes. There are a large number. There are as many male prostitutes as there are women prostitutes. I caught syphilis and gonorrohoea from him.'

'You have both?'

'Yes.'

'Even now?'

'Yes...I thought you had already realised that.'

'Why do you think that?'

'What about your instructions about the towel and the bed?'

'I usually never allow another person to use my bed. And I never give my towel to anyone. The reasons are different. When a person has a bath he would wipe himself all over with the towel...a bed would have absorbed someone else's sweat... people come visiting me at all times and all hours. So I keep a bed and towel in the other room. That's all.'

'I thought there was another reason!'

'Is this infectious?'

'You can contract it even through the sweat!'

'It is a good thing that you spent all your time in that room.'

'I am now going to tell you the story of a mother and son.'

'How did you leave the house of the VIP?'

'I was ill. I felt ashamed to look at any of them in the face. I left. I had no means of getting food. I had no money for treatment. I had no place to live. As I was wandering about thus I met a mother and son. The mother struck me on the chest—'

'We will talk about that afterwards. What did that male prostitute tell you when you left?'

'He looked at me with unsatisfied lust and said, "Do you know what passionate desire I feel when I look at strong and handsome men?"

"I'll come tomorrow," I said and left. All the money in my pocket had been taken by it—him.'

'So that's how you caught the disease, is it?'

'Yes.'

'Is it very painful?'

'It's impossible to piss. You feel like urinating a whole sea of water...but not a drop will come out. It's terrible. You feel a burning sensation as if chilli paste had been smeared on...as if a bundle of thorns is being drawn through you.... I piss grinding my teeth and with my eyes popping out...your insides melt and come out as pus. The inner skin has become septic and it is raw flesh. Through that, you feel only the heat and the burning.'

'Is all this because of syphilis or gonorrhoea?'

'Gonorrhoea. With syphilis you have sores. Red spots...like blood...like fire...they burn painfully and become bigger.'

'Did you see that male prostitute again?'

'I saw him; not only him, I saw many others. Before that I burnt that perfumed handkerchief. He—it, asked me sadly, "Why didn't I see you again? Have you forgotten me? I know why, you are going to someone else, aren't you."'

IX : MOTHER AND SON

'Sad at heart and weak in body, I sat beneath a tree. Behind me was a ruined temple. On the left lay the city. And before me an open waste land. On the right at some distance was a graveyard. I was feeling weak. I had eaten nothing. I had no money with me. I lay down on a stone slab, probably one of the steps to the temple. The sun was still up in the sky. I dozed off. The cool of the granite soothed me. I fell asleep. The sun set and night came. I was aware of nothing.

I felt someone calling me. Was I in the midst of some commotion...? I woke up. I was sweating profusely. I opened my eyes. There was no frightening darkness. Everything was bathed in moonlight. The moon peeped through the foliage. Amidst the noise came the clear voice of a woman, a very petulant voice which said, "Who is that intruder lying there?"

It was directed at me. I kept still and didn't move. Though I was no believer in ghosts and spirits I was still afraid. From the distance came the voice of an old man, "What does it matter if I've lost the sight of both my eyes?"

Gluck – gluck – gluck. Was it the sound of a dog lapping water? Was it now the voice of a little child I heard?

"Didn't your mother feed you? You slut. You animal with breasts!" It was a man's voice to which a woman's voice answered, "I am pissing."

I didn't hear the sound of urinating. There was a hubbub all round of people talking. Of men and women; and children. Where was I? When things became a little clearer in my mind, I got a little more frightened. There was a bad odour about. All kinds of things were burning. There were some pleasant smells also.

"Get up and go!" Again it was the first woman. She was next to me. I kept still. Leaves stirred in the breeze. Shadows moved about on my body. White fleecy clouds sped past. They came between the moon and the ground.

"Will it rain?" came the voice of a man from a distance. Someone answered back. It was a woman's voice. "God

Almighty won't let it rain."

"Why were you lying in the path?" This was asked by way of greeting from a man. A woman answered, "I fell unconscious as I was walking."

"How did that happen?"

"I...I gave birth to a baby...yesterday."

"Who is the father?"

"Who knows!"

"Stupid woman!" someone said. There was laughter all round including the laughter of a few women. Now voices came from another direction. An old man told the woman, "We need to ask a hundred men!"

"That's true all right!" said another woman.

Gluck – gluck – gluck.

"Get away, you dog!"

The dog barked.

"People here are God-fearing. Some feed five hundred people, some hundred, some ten."

"But those who eat the food have to say they belong to the same caste as the donor."

"That means you shouldn't tell the truth."

"They'll kill you if you tell the truth."

"It's eleven years since I came here."

"And what did you get out of it?" a woman asked.

"Sh – Shit!"

"Shit?"

"Get along, you dirty slut!"

"Why do you stretch out your dirty septic foot on my face?"

"It's your cunt that's septic, that's what!"

"Get up and go!" Again came the voice of the woman standing beside me. "Haven't I been lying down here every day?"

She touched my body. I froze like a piece of ice.

"Are you dead?" She was asking me. I was still. A whiff of perfume assailed me. Was it the smell of soap? Or of talcum powder? Some cheap scent; rather strong. I slowly turned my head to the right. I could see her clearly. A woman; with a baby on her hip.

She stood aside and started feeding the child at her breast. Large breasts. The baby sucked away.

I have never fed at a mother's breast. The baby was trying to hold the other breast in its hands.

"Son...mother's little darling...drink your fill, son...and sleep...someone is coming to mother.... He...he will give us money...son, go to sleep."

She kissed the baby and laid it on the ground on a piece of rag. She tidied her dress. She tied up her breasts keeping them partly jutting out. She loosened her hair and knotted it up again. And then she stood leaning on the broken wall.

Who was coming? My heart beats quickened. I felt hot all over.

"That's nothing to be proud of." It was the voice of a woman from amid the commotion. It was in answer to something. "My mother gave birth to me in a gutter. Even then I have had two husbands and nine children."

"My mother says my father was a soldier!"

"Today I rode in a car!" It was the voice of a young woman. Another asked, "Who took you in a car?"

"*Ra...ra...roo,*" a mother was singing her child to sleep. In the midst of it there was a fight between fanatics.

"What is their business over here? Even though the place is ruined it is ours."

"Shut up you dog ! It is ours!"

"It's neither yours nor theirs. It is ours. And there is proof for that!"

"Ay! You want to quarrel about this? Give me a whiff of ganja and then quarrel if you like!"

"What if I am blind?"

"You can see nothing."

"What is there to see? I can hear everything!"

"There's the moon and the stars to see!"

"Shall I tell you a story?"

"The blind man is going to tell a story!"

"In a wayside shrine without money or friend or food... Give me a whiff of ganja beedi."

"Is that your story! Here comes the ganja beedi, catch!"

"Ouch!" came a woman's wail, "a spark fell on my breast! May a thunderbolt strike you!"

"That serves you right, you slut!"

Suddenly there was a woman's cry full of love, "There he comes! Roaring drunk."

"*Yesh*, my honey!"

"Yes, what do you want?"

"*A kish!*"

"You're reeking of toddy!"

"You *shlut*, it *ishn't* toddy, *it'sh frandy!*"

"It's toddy!"

"If you call *frandy* toddy I'll kill you!"

A command comes from someone: "Shut up and lie down!"

"My wife's mother gave birth to me!"

"Is that so?"

"O.K. I am your son?"

"No, you aren't!"

"Am I your daughter, then?"

"No!"

"Am I your wife?"

"No!"

"Your father?"

"Not father. Not mother. Not even God!"

"Then whom do you need?"

"*Mishter* ganja!"

There is sad news from a distant corner. "A person laid his head on the railway track and died; the head was severed; and it lay gaping into the skies with open eyes."

"Must be a beggar or a sick man or a blind man."

"What else could it be."

"In the forest there are big trees and small trees. Snakes and tigers and leopards and lions and bison and deer and rabbits and rats. And in the cities there are kings and emperors and mill owners and ministers and presidents and generals."

"Is our blood and their's the same?"

"All blood is red!"

"The blood of dogs and pigs even."

"Dogs and pigs can eat anything!"

"Do you want to hear a piece of news?" This was from another corner. "Someone thought one man had money and strangled him in the corner of the street. In the pocket there was only one fake rupee."

"Then what did you do?" The question came from a woman.

"Son, here he comes." It was the woman standing near me. Who was coming? Steps approached. They reached the woman. They were talking in low tones. She was reprimanding him. "Now, wait a minute. Pay the money before you start pawing!"

"Oh, you only think of money. Haven't I come all this distance because I like you?"

A choking laugh. "Affection can't satisfy my son's hunger and mine."

"How much do you want?"

"One rupee...in advance,in my hands—put it in my hand!"

"Here's one rupee.... You slut, have you any disease?"

"Go on...! disease indeed!"

"Haven't you had anything to eat today?"

"Forget the fine talk. Do what you want to do and go."

"Is it all right if I stand against this wall and take my dhoti off?"

I was not shocked. I didn't turn a hair. That man must have seen me just then. He asked in a hesitant voice, "Who's that? Your...?"

"Nonsense. No one of mine. Came and lay down there uninvited. I think he is dead!"

"Is it a corpse?" A small pebble fell on my body.

"It looks like it! Come on, finish quickly and go."

"Let us go in."

"Don't you have a house?"

"Good lord, you can't come there. There's my father and mother and my wife."

"You've got a wife?"

"She's pregnant."

"How many months gone?"

"Five or six months. Leave that child somewhere and come along."

"I'll not leave the child and come anywhere."

"Sweetheart! I'll give you half a rupee more!"

"Ooh that hurts! Haven't you seen breasts before?"

"Come darling."

"My child?"

"Put it down somewhere!"

"Near the corpse?"

"Will the corpse eat up the baby?"

"That's true, it won't."

She spread a rag on the floor at a little distance and laid the child on it. She covered it with another piece of rag. She did not realise there were ants there.

"Mother will be back in no time!"

She went away. Both of them went inside the ruined temple.'

X : A Citizen of the Future

'The child was alone.

I got up. What a sight—in the distance lay little improvised hearths made up of stones put together and from each of them tongues of fire leapt out. There were a great many of them. How many of them? The fuel consisted of rubbish, old paper, dried leaves and old rags.The place was full of smoke and a bad odour and there came a constant noisy rumble. There were men,women, children and a few dogs. Faces lit up by the glow of fire. Nothing was distinct; red eyes, sweating faces,whiskers and beards; beggars' cloth bags; women with breasts uncovered; many communities; many fashions in dress.

It was all commotion there. Eating. Talking. Smoking. Praying. Playing. Laughing.Weeping.Quarrelling.Embracing.

"Listen, everybody!" said a fellow from one corner. "I'm setting off some crackers! A garland of them!"

Tat – tat – tat – tat – tat – tat!

Faces that lit up;bodies that crouched in calm silence.They
had no specified programme of activity.No village or town of
their own. No home. They had nothing.But they had all that
was needed by men. In that community childbirth is not a
private happening. Nor is copulation. And the children grow
up.

I went to that lonely orphaned child.

A citizen of tomorrow. What did he know of things? He was
born just like everyone else. He would grow up with passions
and desires like everyone else.Whiskers and beard would
appear as he grew into manhood.He would lose his semen in
many ways,drop by drop. Some of it would turn into babies.
His hair would go grey with age and he would die. Or he
would.come to an untimely end. If he were to grow up what
faith would he follow? Whatever the mother told him would
be imprinted on his young mind. But as he grew up he would
attach more importance to what he believed than what others
told him.Now he is neither Hindu nor Christian nor Muslim
nor Jew nor Parsi.

He was just a child born of man and woman.

I was also a child born of man and woman. Now I have
turned out this way. What would be the future of this child?
Would he go through experiences similar to mine? Would he
have any disease, I wondered. Perhaps he would become a
beggar. Or a thief. He could become a poet. Or a writer of
stories. He could become a political worker. Or the future
President. He could be a scientist. Or perhaps the prophet of a
new religion.

There was a sound in the sky.A tearing vibrating rumble!

$Br - r - r - Br - r - r.$

"Aeroplane!" shouted a hundred voices, "plane,plane!"

Two green stars.They came nearer and nearer. One red star
slowly moving forward. They passed overhead with a majestic
rumble.

Silence. The noise all around which had stopped started up
again. Voices.

Suddenly the child which was lying near me started to
scream loudly. When the cries became unbearable I picked it

up. A hundred thousand ants bit into my arms. I laid the child on my lap and started picking out the ants.

"Oh lord,my baby!" Hearing the screams of the child its mother came running and panting full of anxiety and sorrow. She grabbed the child and gave me a kick on the chest! I said nothing. I went and sat down where I had been lying down. My head was reeling. She offered her breast for the child to suck. When ants started biting into her breasts she must have realised that the baby was being bitten by ants.

"Lie quiet!" came a call from amidst the noise.

"So what if I can't see with either eye? Can't I remember things?"

"What do you remember ?"

"I was once sitting at a wayside shrine with neither money nor company. It was the day our country became independent. I was twenty years old then.I remember that day."

"Did the bad ants bite and try to kill my little darling?"

The baby stopped crying and began to suck from her breast. From the distance came the voice of the blind man: "That day I asked, why should one live? I asked this question of myself. There was no answer. Yesterday I was fortyfive years old. Last night when all of you were asleep I got up and asked—"

"Beggar man!" she came near me with the child. "I thought you were dead!"

"Yes"

"Did it hurt when I kicked you?"

I said nothing.My eyes brimmed with tears.

"Did you pick up the baby when it was bitten by ants?"

"Yes."

"I thought you were stealing it!"

She took out a quarter-rupee from a knot in her dress and dropped it on my lap. "Lie down there."

She lay down on a stone step a little distance away. I asked no questions. I said nothing. My eyes continued to brim over with tears. I felt as if my heart had broken into a thousand little pieces. I lay there. I felt a humming in my head. When I opened my eyes there was bright sunlight. Silence all round. There was not a single person. Only the ruined temple;

that was all. There was a quarter-rupee lying near me. I sat up. The entire area was empty except for a number of hearth stones; like burnt-out sores. One could hear only the rumble of the city. I picked up that quarter-rupee. It was hot to the touch, probably because of the sunlight.I walked towards the city.'

XI : At the Edge of Infinity

'I reached the seashore when it was well into the night. There was bright moonlight. I walked aimlessly along the crowded streets. The electric lights were far brighter than stars. A city as vast as the sky. Hundreds of thousands of people. Cars and vehicles. But all the same I was alone. I entered a street which smelt good. Well-dressed woman stayed in the houses that faced the street. Hair that was well-oiled and combed; decorated with jasmine flowers. Faces made fair with powder. Painted lips. Glowing eyes blackened by mascara. Women dressed in thin materials that showed off their near-nude bodies. A smell of perfumed oil and flowers—jasmine, champak, rose. A promise for suppressed desire; beckoning hands; waist, thighs, breasts, lips.

What a commotion in that street! Laughter, singing, fun. You could select anyone after paying in cash. It was the marketplace for female flesh. They were the houses that quenched lust.

Every type of person walked in and out of this street. Some came nonchalantly. Others timidly, casting anxious looks around. I just walked on. I was feeling an inexplicable sense of solitude. That was how I reached the seashore.

There were many men and women on the white sands. On the roadside near the shore stood their cars. They had came to enjoy the fresh air. All kinds of people. Bank managers, army officers, mill owners, government officers, advocates, journalists, politicians, writers, hotel owners, cinema actresses and so on. I could tell their vocation from their speech. They, were spending time arguing and talking and joking. After some time they would all get into their cars and go home. I left them behind and walked along the shore. As I walked on I came across some boats; evidently fishing boats. Dilapidated broken-down boats. I got into one and sat down. The milky ocean stretched in front of me.

It was as if a heavy vapour was rising up. Everything was still. I felt very tired. I lay down. I was thinking about my fate. There was not a living being either to love or hate me. How many millions of people this earth held, how many kinds of men and women. What was the difference between others and myself? None of them meant anything to me. Or else they were all a part of me. But this thought gave me no modicum of courage. You can say anything in poems and stories and speeches. But for life in real each person is an isolated being, an orphan. If someone dies what does it matter? What does it matter if someone lives? It may be that all men and women are part of the human community. If this is so, bacteria, worms, reptiles, birds, aquatic creatures, animals, grass, trees all these must be distant relatives of mankind. Didn't I tell you neither my life nor my thoughts had ever any coherence or pattern.

I am an isolated creature. Just that. In this vast machinery that is mankind I am not even a tiny cog in the wheel. Why would anyone do anything for me?

The one thing that remains is that no one has showed any kindness to me. Even if they have....

It is doubtful if I had shown enough love towards my foster-father when he was alive. After his death now I revere his memory. I was full of an overpowering sense of sadness. I contemplated suicide. I thought of the railway track. I wept profusely. Slowly I fell asleep.

An infinite silence; bitter cold. I opened my eyes. Darkness. Not pitch darkness. Something mixed with light, something...

which one would call primeval darkness found before the dawn of history...something like that. That was what suggested itself to me. The stars were dim. Where was I? Suddenly I remembered.... I wondered how much longer it was for sunrise. Nothing was distinct. My clothes were wet. I stepped on the sand. The soles of my feet shrank in the bitter chill. The entire top surface was wet. I pushed aside the wet sand with my feet. Inside, it was dry and still warm. I sat down.

The sea is a thick carpet of darkness.

There was a frightening sense of solitude. It went through my veins and reached the innermost core of my heart. Then it came to me! God is the last refuge of the lonely.

I sat immersed in that thought. I do not know how or why my eyes brimmed over. It would not be right to say I thought of all the men and women in this world. How can one think of people one has neither seen nor heard? And is my heart so big that it can contain the thought of everyone in this world?

Perhaps it would be more correct to say that I sat there thinking of nothing. As I sat there a feeling of liveliness began creeping into me. It was soon clear why. There was a change of colour in the horizon. Dawn was about to break. One could hear indistinct sounds of the living world.

I thought, what will this day be like? I couldn't imagine however much I thought about it. Noises, sirens from factories; loud empty whistles from ships. They were summoning the workers.

There was no one to call me. Neither man nor machine. One more day was to dawn on life. There was a change of colour on the visible bounds of the limitless horizon—from the deep blue edges of the sea rose a lighted golden orb!

For a moment it was a sea of blood. Then it turned into a wide splash of molten gold. A little later it gleamed and glistened like glass.

I stood up.

My shadow lengthened out beyond the limits of the city.'

XII : THE VIBRATION OF THE RAILWAY TRACK

'And then what happened?'

'The railway track thundered and reverberated! That's what I have to talk about next. Are you feeling sleepy?'

'No. I am listening.'

'I don't have much more to say. What's your opinion about all that I have said?'

'Opinion? I have recorded all that you have said. In my mind. Now it has to be put down on paper. I will have to go somewhere else to do that.'

'Where will you go?'

'I must go somewhere or the other and write it down in peace.'

'What is your opinion about suicide?'

'About whether it is good or bad?' ·

'Yes. That's right.'.

'I have not so far felt like committing suicide.... Life in its ultimate analysis is a failure. I say this with one fact in mind, that one has to die if one is born. But one must live till one dies; live with courage. Live consciously, fully, like a man....This has been my attitude.'

'Live to do what?'

'You can do anything.... Isn't the whole world before you...? There may be a number of things you can do. Make up a programme, a plan of action.... Suppose you want to become the president of the country then try for that. You need not worry whether you will succeed or fail. You can at least try!'

'Didn't I tell you? I have no philosophy of life or living. What is the programme I can draw up? This house that is me is in ruins; no mother, no father, no one. I am alone in this world. There is no living being to love me or hate me. That was why I asked you about suicide.'

'Haven't you so far experienced what is called wellbeing in this life?'

'Only like a dream.'

'What do you mean?'

'To eat food when one is hungry, to drink when one is thirsty, to warm oneself when one is feeling cold, to sleep when one is sleepy—I have experienced the comfort of doing these things.'

'What else have you experienced?'

'The rising of the moon, sunrise, fragrant flowers, beautiful women, music—all these have given me happiness.'

'Anything else?'

'Drinking—I have enjoyed that also.'

'What else?'

'When one scratches where it itches it brings relief! If you look at it like that is not life full of happiness?'

'Have you ever done anything all by yourself and derived happiness from it? Growing things... plant at least one seedling and see it bloom and bring forth fruit. Make something new.'

'You know, don't you, that the only thing I have done by myself is to shoot and kill people. I have even drunk human blood. And once I have attempted to commit suicide.'

'What else?'

'Let me tell you about that also. I am leaving tonight.'

'Where are you going?'

'Is this not the land of my birth? I can search for my father and mother. I will walk into every home. I will ask each woman, "Are you my mother? Are you the woman who gave birth to me, then wrapped me up in old rags and left me at the crossroads?" Even if I die I will be a horrible ghost which will go to every house and knock on the door—'

'Please stop! Tell me about your suicide.'

'Yes I decided to commit suicide. I decided I would stretch out my neck on the railway track. The train would come. The wheels would crush my neck and pass on. My head would be severed from my body. Everything would be over. It would be an end to all pain and difficulty.

It was a moonlit night; the lonely unfrequented railway track in a corner of the city. It always reverberated with noise. There was a train every half hour. I sat beneath a tree. One train went past thundering and shaking. I crossed the wire fence and lay down with my neck on one of the many lines that went criss-cross. My neck felt unbearably chilly. I lay like that. Tomorrow I would be an unclaimed corpse in the true sense of that word. It was time for another train to come by.

Br – ṛr – rr – Brr – rr!

It was an aeroplane. At the same time a train also came along. A sensation of burning as well as of cold fear went through my limbs. The rails vibrated. I was all excited and confused. It is a feeling you can understand only if you have lain with your head on a railway track. Two or three times I felt like getting up and running away.

I kept still. My ear drums were near bursting. A whistle crashed through the earth and sky. The train was coming fast. I closed my eyes. I stopped breathing. I was sweating all over. The inside of my head was afire. I lay and waited for the moment of time when my neck would be crushed. Crashing and thundering, the train went past! It passed by on the track next to where I lay!'

'What happened then?'

'Mangalam.'

Original title 'Shabdangal'; published as a novelette in 1947.

Poovan Banana

I am not writing this story of the poovan banana because I want to do so. I am writing it because Abdul Khader Sahib insisted that I should. He thinks it has a moral. The story is about his wife Jameela Bibi.

Jameela Bibi has a university degree, a B.A. As for Abdul Khader Sahib, he has studied only upto the school finals. According to custom was it proper for such a person to marry a woman with a degree? But Abdul Khader Sahib proudly says he acquired his bride as a conquest of war. In ancient days men would steal women. They would even make running knots on ropes and lasso women into captivity. Men inflicted many indignities on women. Men used to to force women into submission. But as Abdul Khader Sahib was a civilised person he did not resort to such tactics. He was a well-known strongman of the village in addition to being the secretary of the local Beedi Workers' Union and a good football player. Abdul Khader Sahib says he studied from class four till the final year in the same school as Jameela Bibi and right from the beginning he was in love with her. Jameela Bibi says that this is a lie.

Be that as it may Jameel Bibi passed her B.A. With money from her father's beedi factory she went about as a very fashionable woman. All the eligible young men of the place were in love with her. The amateur poets of the village wrote verses about her ranging from mere sonnets to epic pieces. An army of young men lined up in military formation laid siege to Jameela Bibi's heart. In other words, there was a regular queue for it. Abdul Khader Sahib was not one in the queue. He did not attempt to write verses or love letters. Abdul Khader Sahib says he did not know how to write either. Jameela Bibi says that he composed a ballad about her. Abdul Khader Sahib totally denies this. What he says he did was this. One day he stopped Jameela Bibi as she was walking along the country lane. He asked her, 'Your name is Jameela, isn't it?'

Jameela Bibi did not care for the question. Was there any young man in that village who did not know her? She put on the dignified air of a fashionable woman and asked haughtily, 'And if it is?'

Abdul Khader Sahib laughed. It was an attractive laugh. Jameela Bibi had heard him and seen him laugh before. And she had liked it. But that abominable attitude of his! As though he were sizing her up! Jameela Bibi did not care for that.

'What do you want?'

'Oh, nothing very important!' Abdul Khader Sahib said. 'Your father's beedi factory has one hundred and twenty workers. I am the secretary of their trade union. My name is Abdul Khader!'

'Well, well,' Jameela Bibi replied. 'I have heard that you are the village bully.'

'The beedi workers are thinking of going on strike. We will make you close down your factory.'

Jameela Bibi asked, 'Why do you tell me this? Go and tell it to my father.'

'I have a reason for telling you this, Jameela Bibi.'

'What is that?'

Abdul Khader Sahib said, 'I love you, Jameela Bibi!'

Jameela felt a thrill of satisfaction. But she felt that he should be put to shame. So Jameela Bibi laughed. A very sarcastic laugh.

'That's fine,' she said. 'What else is new in the village?'

A question like that would have stunned the ordinary young men in the queue. But Abdul Khader Sahib took it as a challenge and replied, 'Jameela if you don't marry me!—'

Jameela Bibi also took it as a challenge. 'What will you do if I don't marry you?'

I'll hang myself! thought Abdul Khader Sahib, but he did not say it. He said instead, 'Jameela, I will break every bone in your body!'

Jameela Bibi said nothing in reply.

Abdul Khader Sahib continued, 'Jameela, don't throw away my life. I love you. I love your dress. I love every inch of you. I love even the roads and lanes you walk on!'

Jameela Bibi was happy in her heart. But could she show her feelings? How could she talk about them? She asked, 'Are you in the habit of stopping all young women passing by and talking like this?'

'No my Jameela, I have talked to no woman other than you. I have not even looked at any other woman. You are the very sight of my eyes!'

She asked with an attempt at dignity, 'And what else?'

He replied, 'You and I, we are for each other.'

'Oh, very good,' said Jameela Bibi and walked away.

Then the war started. The two families opposed the connection. The people were against their getting together. There was conflict. There was a strike. Why prolong the tale? Finally Abdul Khader Sahib married Jameela Bibi and they lived happily for a while until the incident of the poovan banana.

II

The time was five-thirty in the evening.

It was during the monsoons. Sunshine and rain followed each other without warning. The water rose steadily in the river. Abdul Khader Sahib wanted to have a look at the flood water and also to have a bath. He wound a towel round his waist and was about to step out when Jameela Bibi came near the door and called out to him, 'Listen....' Abdul Khader thought to himself, she wants me to put on a shirt before I go out. Jameela Bibi had begun issuing ordinances about deportment and behaviour soon after they were married and began living together.

Abdul Khader Sahib must dress like a gentleman! He could go out only if he was properly dressed. He must be dignified in his behaviour. He should not stop on the way and talk to riff-raff or his former rowdy friends. Beedi workers, poets, porters, politicians, drivers, rickshaw–pullers—these should not be treated as equals. They needed to have a maid at home. Abdul Khader Sahib must not cook. They must live up to their status.

They should get ahead in life. He had to realise that a woman marries to raise her husband's standard of life...and so on. Similarly Jameela Bibi believed that it was the inalienable right of the wife to keep her husband on the straight and narrow path and to intervene in all matters, physical and spiritual, relating to her man and generally to create confusion in his life. Every woman believes in this. Abdul Khader Sahib did not comment on these examples of a woman's perverted thinking.

What could he say? After all they had not been married a long time. He asked her in all reasonableness, 'My dear Jameela, I'm going to take a bath. Should I put on a shirt for that?'

'Oh!' Jameela Bibi replied as if her heart was in anguish, 'do you ever listen to me?'

'Have I ever gone against your wishes?' So saying, he ran inside, put on his shirt and came out. But his shirt was not buttoned.

Look at the carelessness of these men! She buttoned his shirt for him; all the three buttons.

Abdul Khader Sahib walked away.

Jameela Bibi again called out to him: 'Listen...,'

Abdul Khader Sahib turned round. He thought to himself, God in heaven, now will come the problem of a servant maid! What is one to do? Couldn't one live without a cook? One must learn to do things for oneself. Why can't one cook merely because one has a B.A. degree? Never mind B.A; even if one is an M.A. or a Ph.D. one must know how to cook. If she didn't know, he, Abdul Khader Sahib, could teach her. He had already begun teaching her. He could make anything from tea to biriyani.

'What is it, Jameela?' he asked. 'Is it the problem of the servant?'

'No,' Jameela Bibi pouted as she replied. 'After all, I have passed my B.A. just to be a cook!'

'My darling,' Abdul Khader Sahib replied. 'My pet need not enter the kitchen. I'll look after everything. All right?'

'Oh...you say that every day.'

'My queen, look after the kitchen just one more day. From tomorrow this humble servant of yours ....'

'Empty words! It's your usual trick.'

'Why did you call me now?' He thought that perhaps she wanted him to wear better clothes, comb his hair, or powder himself before going out. But Jameela Bibi said with a great deal of hesitation, coyly and without a trace of annoyance, 'Poovan banana.'

'What poovan banana?' Would these women ever say anything clearly? He asked, 'What are you saying?'

'Poovan bananas! Would you buy me two?'

'*Havoo!* It's poovan bananas you want is it? Greedy for them are you? I'll bring them certainly. They're there in the shop by the riverside. If not I shall take the ferryboat, cross over and get them from the small bazaar two furlongs away from the other bank. I shall get you a whole bunch of poovan bananas.'

'I only want two,' Jameela Bibi said. 'Don't you go loafing around here and there! Come back soon. Don't wait till it's dark. I am afraid to be all alone. Don't forget anything!'

He said, 'No,' and walked along. Listen to these women! Don't go loafing around! Abdul Khader Sahib laughed to himself. All of a sudden he felt a wave of love come over him. Poovan bananas! It was the first thing Jameela had asked of him. God in heaven, what things other women would have demanded of their husbands! Gold, silk, bangles, cars, aeroplanes; even those were easy to get compared to their sillier demands—two strands from the whiskers of a lioness lying in the forest which had just given birth to cubs! And if it was not brought to them they would get angry and say: 'After all, I just wanted two strands of hair from the lion. Isn't it after all just a big cat. So that's how much you love me!' And straightaway they would begin crying. What could the husband do? There was another type. All they wanted would be a lump of snow from one side of the peak of Everest which no one had scaled so far. And if they did not get it their eyes would fill and they would sob: 'Just one small lump of snow and you couldn't get me that. Why don't you kill me?' What could the husband do? Had Jameela Bibi ever demanded such impossible things of him? No. She had just asked for poovan bananas! Abdul Khader Sahib thought to himself, I must have a bath, perform my ablutions and then go and buy a bunch of poovan bananas. And so he reached the river bank.

The river looked like a saffron-coloured ocean. What strong currents! The trees on either bank which one usually saw leaning into the water were not to be seen. They were submerged. All kinds of things were floating down. The river looked frightening.

Abdul Khader Sahib had a bath. That is to say, he took just one dip. The water was icy cold. He forgot to perform his ablutions. He hastily wiped his head and body dry and walked to the riverside shop. When he went there he saw kannan bananas, palankodan bananas, padati bananas, in fact, all kinds of species except the poovan! What was he to do? He got into the ferryboat.

By the time the boat reached mid-river a strong wind began to blow. With that it suddenly turned dark and the skies became threatening. Somehow the ferryman got the boat across to the opposite bank. Abdul Khader Sahib got out and ran in the direction of the bazaar. By the time he was halfway there it began to rain. He ran for shelter to the nearest shop. The rain poured down. Slowly the lights came on in the shops. He waited for the rain to stop. There were strong winds also. He did not realise how time passed. He chatted with old companions and acquaintances sheltering in the shop veranda. Suddenly he realised it was nearing eight ! He felt quite upset.

Jameela Bibi was all alone and would get frightened. He left
the shop he was in and asked for poovan pananas. They were
not available anywhere! What should he do? He was
thoroughly disappointed. Finally he bought a dozen oranges.
Weren't oranges better than bananas? They were more
expensive and contained more vitamins. He had the oranges
packed in a paper parcel and set out for home. It was dark and
it was drizzling. There were no lights anywhere. It looked as if
poovan bananas and the rain were in deep conspiracy. Abdul
Khader Sahib reached the ferry. There was no one there. He
looked into the darkness and called out for the ferryman. He
shouted more than ten times. Who was there to hear him? It
was to no avail except that his throat became sore with
shouting. He made up his mind—come what may he would
swim across. He took off his shirt. He wrapped up the oranges
in the towel and put them on his head. He tied the ends of the
towel firmly round his chin. He tied his shirt and dhoti into a
bundle and put them on top of the oranges. What would she
be doing now? He thought to himself, look, Jameela, if I had
not married you I could have slept somewhere else tonight.
Look at the way male freedom has gone! I am going to jump
into the river and swim. God in heaven, you have to save me.
Abdul Khader Sahib walked upstream for a furlong. The river
was flowing westward. If he walked a furlong towards the east
to swim, there was a chance of the current taking him down
one furlong to the other bank. Or would he be taken further
down?

Abdul Khader Sahib stepped bravely into the river. Suppose
he drowned? But would not even that be for the sake of
Jameela Bibi? The water came up to his waist. He could not get
a foothold. He began swimming with his head above the water.
He moved forward, working his hands and feet. But in the
darkness, with the swift current, which way was forward and
which way was backwards? He could not decide. He moved
on, mainly on conjecture. He did not know whether he had
reached mid-river or whether he was approaching the other
bank. His arms and legs began to feel his fatigue. Suddenly he

caught hold of something. The current was dragging him on
forcefully but he would not let go. He gulped down two or
three mouthfuls of water. Finally Abdul Khader Sahib realised
that he had caught hold of a bamboo cluster. Avoiding the
thorns and the sharp twigs he managed to set foot on the other
bank. He sat down on the ground shivering; shivering with
cold and with fear at what he had escaped. What was the use
of sitting there? Abdul Khader Sahib walked through the
thorny bushes and bramble. He was totally nude! He had lost
his shirt and dhoti. He had not lost the towel and the oranges
as they had been tied round his head. Abdul Khader Sahib
broke off the shoot of a tree with tiny branches and used it as a
walking stick. He was passing through a banana grove. There
was a flash of lightning. He saw his surroundings for a brief
moment. He recognised a house and realised where he was. He
was a furlong down the river from his house.

He passed the house he had seen and crossed the canal by a
rough coconut-palm bridge, tripping and stumbling on the
way. A dog barked. Then another. Soon all the dogs in the
neighbourhood took up the refrain. He thought to himself,
these dogs are barking as if they are the guardians of morality
in the world! What could he do? He walked across many paths
large and small, crossed many streams and finally reached
home. Good God! There was a light there. His dear Jameela
had not gone to sleep. Here was a wife who loved her
husband! 'Jameela, open the door.' No, he did not say that. He
first draped the towel round his waist. He stepped onto the
veranda and looked in through the window. Although he was
shivering in the cold Abdul Khader Sahib could not help
laughing. What a lovely scene!

A lighted lamp stood on the table. There were two big plates
near it, covered with two other plates; four or five smaller
plates around them, all covered. They contained rice and
various curries. The wife sat there waiting for her husband.
She held a murderous-looking hacksaw in her hand. She
looked tired as she dozed with her head on the table.

He also noticed other things. The front door was closed and

latched from the inside. Even then suppose some thief pushed open the door by force from the outside? So a big table had been dragged up close to the door to form a barricade. As if that was not protection enough a small stone had been placed on top of the table! Wasn't all this enough?

Abdul Khader Sahib thought to himself, how wise women can be! He was about to wake up Jameela Bibi when he espied another remarkable thing—light flooded the backyard through the open kitchen door! He went to the back to take a closer look. She had forgotten to close the kitchen door while taking so many other safety precautions! Abdul Khader Sahib realised that all the thieves in the world could march in through the kitchen door. He went in. Noiselessly he closed the kitchen door and latched it from the inside. He put the stick which was still in his hand in a corner of the kitchen and went into the dressing room. There were small cuts and scratches all over his body. Blood oozed out of some of them. He said to himself, Jameela, look how much blood I have shed for you! He took the tin of fragrant talcum powder which she used and sprinkled it all over his body. Then he put on some clothes and combed his hair. He left the oranges in the dressing room and was about to wake up Jameela Bibi when he remembered that he had not said his evening prayers, neither *Maghrib* nor *Isha*. He decided he would finish saying these. He went into the adjoining bathroom, did the ceremonial ablution, came back and said his prayers. He thanked the Almighty God for having saved his life for the sake of Jameela Bibi. He then put the oranges on two plates and placed them on the table. He called out: 'O, Queen!'

Jameela Bibi woke up, startled. She opened her eyes with fear, gripping the hacksaw more firmly.

'Please do not hack down this man before you!' said Abdul Khader Sahib. 'This is no thief. The person standing before you is the humble and foolish Abdul Khader!'

'You have come back after loafing all over, have you?' She looked at the front door. 'How did you come in?'

Abdul Khader Sahib said, 'Before this young man all doors

open of their own accord and all hearts—'

'Don't be silly! How did you get in?'

He said, 'Through the kitchen!'

She asked, 'You must have opened the latch from the outside with a stick. Suppose some thief had seen you doing it? Now they will also enter that way! How can I live with peace of mind in this house now?'

Abdul Khader Sahib retorted: 'You fool, the door was not closed!'

Jameela Bibi said, 'Talk with better manners. I like that—the door was not closed!'

God in heaven, Abdul Khader Sahib thought to himself, is it possible to make a woman admit that she has made a mistake? He asked her, 'Have you said your prayers?'

'Yes, I have,' she said and got up. Then she saw the oranges. Her face reddened. What a fruit to bring! Who could eat the foul things? Jameela Bibi looked at the oranges with eyes that blazed fire, enough to burn them up. But she made no comment.

Abdul Khader Sahib said, 'There are no poovan bananas anywhere.'

Jameela Bibi did not reply. That awful stuff he had brought! What could she possibly say?

She brought water and both of them washed their hands. They ate.

'The curry is good,' Abdul Khader Sahib said. Actually all the curries tasted bad. There was no salt in some and some were too spicy. But was it proper to find fault with his newly wedded wife?

She made a happy announcement: 'I am going to sleep!'

He said, 'Eat the oranges before you go to sleep. I could not get poovan bananas anywhere. I swam through the river to bring these oranges.'

She said, 'Don't tell me lies. I don't like oranges. If you have brought them, you can eat them.'

She stood up with her nose in the air, went to the bed and fell on it.

Abdul Khader Sahib peeled the oranges. He filled a plate

with the segments. Then he called: 'Jameela....

'I don't want it!'

'You don't want it?' Abdul Khader Sahib thought to himself, I should have given the woman half a dozen blows immediately after the wedding ceremony. 'Jameela! Get up and come here now!'

'I'm feeling sleepy.'

'Is that so?' He got up and went to her and said softly, 'Jameela, I've brought these after going through great danger. Look, suppose I had drowned in the river?'

Jameela Bibi continued to lie on the bed and pressed her face into the pillow.

'Jameela!'

Jameela turned her face slighty. 'What I wanted were poovan bananas!'

'There are no poovan bananas anywhere in the village. Tomorrow I shall bring poovan banana saplings from somewhere.'

'Oh, shall I eat them when they grow and bear fruit?'

'Well, eat these oranges. They are full of vitamins.'

'I don't want them.'

'You have to eat them.'

Jameela Bibi sat up in bed. Imperiously, and in typical ladylike fashion, she asked, 'Do you think you can feed them to me by force?'

Right, Abdul Khader Sahib thought to himself, a good idea! He quietly went into the kitchen, picked up the stick which he had brought from the riverside and cut off a small piece from it. He came into the bedroom with it.

Jameela Bibi saw the stick. She looked on indifferently, as if she wanted to defy the whole world.

He said, 'Get up!'

'I refuse to!'

You refuse?' He went to get the hacksaw.

Jameela Bibi continued to look on indifferently.

'Come,' he called.

'I refuse,' she answered back.

'Is that so?' He gave her two stinging blows on her thigh

with the stick. Then he showed her the hacksaw. 'The next weapon is this. A clean cut.'

She got up, her eyes brimming over.

Those tears.... Abdul Khader Sahib's heart broke when he saw them. What could he say! He was a mere male. How could he be indifferent to a woman's tears? Anyhow Abdul Khader Sahib decided to harden his heart into a ball of granite for a short while. He said, 'Jameela...don't waste your tears! If you want, weep into a jar and collect the tears in it. I'll take a bath in it afterwards. Understand?'

Jameela Bibi asked with a sob in her throat, 'Are you...are you...going to kill me?'

'I—ahem!' he said. 'I am going to kill you, cut you into pieces and make biriyani out of you!' He caught her by the hand and dragged her to stand in front of the orange segments. 'Pick them up and eat them,' Abdul Khader Sahib ordered.

Jameela Bibi pretended not to hear him. She looked on as if ready once again to defy the world.

'So you won't listen to your husband?' He lifted the stick and gave her six whacks which fell whistling on her posterior.

She picked up one segment and ate it slowly.

'No, eat more of them!' He spoke in a low roar, pointing at the hacksaw. 'Do you see that? It'll get rid of you for good. Eat!'

She started eating the segments rapidly.

He said, 'Remove the seeds and eat them slowly!'

So Jameela Bibi, tears streaming from her eyes, picked up the segments, removed the seeds and started eating them.

Abdul Khader Sahib decided that other unresolved disputes between them should be settled right then. He asked, 'What's my relationship to you?'

She replied, 'Who knows?'

'Look at this hacksaw! What is my relationship to you?'

'Husband.'

He said, 'Do you see this hacksaw? Will you try to reform me hereafter? Say "no" quickly. See the knife?'

'No.'

He asked, 'What are you eating?'

'Oranges!'

Whack came a blow on her behind.

'See this knife? Say you are eating poovan bananas.'

'Poovan bananas!'

'Do you want a cook? Say "no". Can you see the knife?'

'No.'

'Are you a fashionable woman? See the knife...? You are my woman, aren't you?'

'Yes.'

'Can I talk with motor drivers, poets, politicians, and beedi workers? See the knife? Say "I can"...repeat it!'

'You can, you can.'

'What are you eating?'

'Poovan bananas.'

'My darling!'

Abdul Khader Sahib dropped the stick and the knife and caught Jameela Bibi in a close embrace and kissed her. There were marks of the beating on her thighs and backside. His heart broke when he felt them.

He asked, 'Was it very painful, my darling?'

She sighed deeply and said, 'N – no!'

III

And so that night passed. The day came. The floods rose and subsided many times in the river. Jameela Bibi gave birth to nine children. Many changes took place in the world. There were two world wars. New ideas took over. Mankind progressed in many directions. Both Abdul Khader Sahib and Jameela grew very old. Their hair turned grey and they lost their teeth. They became hunched, decrepit old people who had many grandchildren. Even then they sometimes thought of the old days. Abdul Khader Sahib would laugh and ask Jameela Bibi, 'O Queen, once when you wanted poovan bananas, what did I bring you, swimming the river?'

Jameela Bibi would laugh and reply, 'Poovan bananas!'

He would ask, 'What did they look like?'

She would reply, 'Round, like oranges!'

'Ha – ha – ha,' he would laugh and ask again, 'what did I bring?'

She would say again, 'Poovan bananas!'

Original title 'Poovan Pazham'; from the collection Viddikalude Swargam *(1948).*

A Man

You have no definite plans. You are wandering around far away from home. You have no money with you; you do not know the local language. You can speak English and Hindustani. But very few people know either of these languages. This can land you in many predicaments; many adventures can befall you.

You find yourself caught in a dangerous situation. A total stranger rescues you. Even after years pass by you will sometimes remember the man and wonder why he did so.

Let us say it is I, not you, who remembers the man.

I am now narrating an experience which I had. I have some vague notions about human beings, including myself. There are around me good men and thieves, those who suffer from various infectious diseases and from madness—one has to live carefully. The world has more evil than good. We realize this only after we get hurt.

Let me record here that incident which was perhaps quite insignificant.

It was quite a big city in the valley of a mountain, some thousand five hundred miles from home; the inhabitants of which had never been known for the quality of mercy. They were a cruel people. Murder, robbery, pick-pocketing, these were daily occurrences. By tradition the people were professional soldiers. Some of them went to distant places and lent out money on interest. Many others served as watchmen in banks, mills and large commercial establishments in big cities. Money was highly valued by them. For money they would do anything, even commit murder.

I stayed in that city in a very small, dingy room on a dirty street. I carried on a profession there; teaching English to some migrant labourers from nine-thirty till eleven in the night. I taught them to write addresses in English. Learning to write an address in English was considered great education there. You must have seen people who write addresses at the post office. They were paid anything between one anna and four annas for writing an address.

I taught the skill of writing addresses to people in order to escape the same fate myself and to see if I could save some money.

In those days I would sleep all day and wake up at four in the evening. This was to save the expense of drinking my morning tea or eating the noon meal.

One day I got up at 4 p.m. as usual. I finished my daily chores and stepped out for my tea and a meal. You must understand that I was dressed in a suit. I had a wallet in my coat pocket. I had fourteen rupees in it—my life's savings at the time.

I entered a crowded restaurant. I ate a full meal consisting of chapatis and meat curry. I drank tea as well. The bill came to eleven annas.

I put my hand in my coat pocket to pay it. I began sweating profusely and almost digested in an instant all that I had eaten! The reason was my wallet was not there.

I said, 'Someone has picked my pocket and taken away my wallet.'

It was a very busy restaurant. The owner gave a loud guffaw startling everyone around. He caught me by the lapels of my coat and shaking me, cried, 'This trick won't work here! Put the money down and go...or else I'll gouge your eyes out.'

I looked at the people around me. I did not see even one kind face. They had the look of hungry wolves.

If he said he would gouge my eyes out, he *would* gouge them out!

I said,'Let my coat be here; I'll go and bring some money.'

The restaurant keeper laughed again.

He asked me to take off my coat.

I took off my coat.

He asked me to take off my shirt.

I took off my shirt.

He asked me to take off both my shoes.

I took off both shoes.

Finally he asked me to take off my trousers.

So the idea seemed to be to strip me, gouge out my eyes and send me out naked!

I said, 'I have nothing on underneath!'

Everyone laughed.

The restaurant keeper said, 'I doubt it; you must have something on underneath.'

About fifty people repeated, 'There must be something on underneath.'

My hands refused to move. I saw in my imagination a man standing in the crowd, stark naked and without his eyes. Life was going to end like that. Let it end.... And for all this, I.... Never mind....O creator of the world, my God....I had nothing to say. Everything would end...everything would end to the satisfaction of all....

I began to undo one by one the buttons of my trousers. Then I heard a voice. 'Stop, I shall pay the money!'

Everyone turned in the direction of the voice.

There stood a fair-complexioned man, six foot tall, with a red turban and white trousers. He sported a handle-bar moustache and had blue eyes.

Blue eyes were quite common at this place. He came forward and asked the restaurant keeper, 'How much did you say it was?'

'Eleven annas.'

He paid the amount. He turned to me and said, 'Put on your clothes.'

I put them on.

'Come,' he called me. I went with him. Did I have words to express my gratitude? I told him, 'You have done a great deed.

I have not seen a finer man.'

He laughed.

'What's your name?' he asked. I told him my name and where I came from.

I asked the man his name. He said, 'I have no name.'

I said, 'In that case "Mercy" must be your name.'

He did not laugh at that. He walked on until we reached a deserted bridge.

He looked all round. There was no one. 'Look, you must go away without turning round. If anyone asks you whether you have seen me you must say no.'

I understood.

He took out from his various pockets about five wallets. Five; among them was mine.

'Which of these is yours?'

I pointed to my wallet.

'Open it.'

I opened it. My money was there intact. I put it in my pocket.

He told me, 'Go. May God help you.'

I repeated, 'May...God help you!'

Original title 'Oru Manushyan'; from the collection Pavappattavarude Veshya *(1952).*

Bully Panicker

All the inmates of the police lockup were happy when they heard that Bully Panicker was transferred from the Town Police Station to a village outpost. One of the inmates, Daniel, wished out of sheer mental agony, 'This is your end—the end of the road for you.' This of course he said to himself.

Was it right to put a curse on a government servant? It is true that Daniel only knew about the Government through Bully Panicker. Daniel did not know that this could be wrong. He was not educated. He knew just enough to read and write. He had a wife and three children. He had worked at a job which had helped him earn a living. He had been a compositor in a printing press. Then he was dismissed. So he set out in search of a job and reached a town sixty miles away from his place. He walked in and out of many presses but there were no vacancies. As he went about the town he came across Bully Panicker. He was hauled in, as a vagrant. He was sent to the lockup where Bully Panicker beat him up.

This same Bully Panicker was now on transfer. Not only did the inmates of the lockup feel this way, but even his police colleagues rejoiced at the news.

No one liked Bully Panicker. He would say anything to please the Inspector. He would say anything. He would kow-tow to him and tell tales at the slightest opportunity. Now Bully Panicker was going.

Daniel and his companions looked out through the bars of

the lockup. Now that stout stick of his would remain idle. Bully Panicker used the stick to strike the hours of the day on the gong and he also used it to beat up people.

'I'm going, Writer sir,' said Bully Panicker as he stood in front of the Station Writer's table. He was fair, slim and tall, with curly hair and pious-looking eyes. He looked smilingly at the persons inside the lockup.

The Station Writer signified his assent with a smile.

Bully Panicker, dressed in a white shirt and dhoti, stepped out with a bundle of clothes in his left hand.

'This is his last journey,' Daniel again whispered to himself.

After a few days came disturbing news; Bully Panicker had been found dead, hanging in the police outpost.

Daniel heard the details later. The Inspector and others saw the body as soon as they reached the outpost. It was hanging from the rafter of the building. There was a table nearby, adjoining the wall. It was obvious that he had put the noose round his neck standing on the table.... And so an Information Report was prepared describing it as suicide.

But Daniel felt extremely sorry. Bully Panicker had a wife and five children. Who would look after them now? Didn't Bully Panicker die because of his, Daniel's curse?

Sometimes Daniel would console himself that that cruel end was dictated by Panicker's own overburdened conscience. His fellow prisoners and the policemen said many things in support of this. An innocent woman had been smeared over with chilli paste to make her confess. The sexual organ of a political prisoner had been wrapped round with rags dipped in oil and set afire to make him beg for pardon from the Government. There were many many stories of this kind. Daniel wondered whether all policemen were like Bully Panicker. No one had practised the extreme cruelties he had been capable of. Even then his wife must have loved him. His children too. His wife must have called him 'darling', his children must have called him 'father'. Now the breadwinner of that family was no more. Was that because of his curse?

Daniel could not decide for sure. He continued to be subjected to blows and kicks. He developed itches and scabies.

He was sentenced to one year's rigorous imprisonment. He was moved to the Central Jail.

One night Daniel heard another story about Bully Panicker.

A fat, black man with one eye and a pockmarked face was talking about his exploits and among these he mentioned one incident. He had been convicted to life imprisonment for killing a stage actress and robbing her. He said, 'I have punished everyone who has hurt me. But it is not possible to kill the same person twice.'

Daniel asked, 'Have you ever felt like killing the same person twice over?'

'I did not feel happy about the way I killed one person. Suppose one killed with one blow a man whom one wanted to cut into innumerable bits and kill by degrees wouldn't one feel disappointed? I had hardly touched him. One blow on his face. There he lay dead! No one else was there. I dragged a table near the wall. I took a rope, made a noose and tightened it round his neck. I hung the body from the rafter.'

Daniel asked, 'Who was the man?'

'A policeman. We called him Bully Panicker.'

Original title 'Idiyan Panicker'; from the collection Pavappattavarude Veshya *(1952).*

The Blue Light

This is the story of one of the amazing incidents of my life. No, not just an incident. It is better to call it something out of the ordinary, something supernatural which took place. I have tried to understand it by using scientific logic. But I have not succeeded. Perhaps you may be able to do it—analyse it. I call it an amazing happening...yes, what else can I call it?

This is what happened.

The day, the month and the year do not matter. I was in search of a house. That was nothing new. I am always in search of a house. I never get a house or a room that I like. The place where I stayed I found had a hundred faults. But to whom could I complain? If I didn't like it I could just go away. But go where? And so I lived there full of resentment. How many houses there had been, how many rooms, with which I had been dissatisfied! It wasn't anybody's fault. I did not like them. So I left. Someone else would come in my place and he or she would like it. That is the character of rented houses.

Those were the days when there was a scarcity of rented houses. What could once be rented for ten rupees could not now be got for fifty. And so I wandered about in search of a house and there it was!

It was a small one-storeyed house. Far from the bustle of the town; somewhere near the municipal limit. There was an ancient board—'To Let'.

I liked it on the whole. Upstairs there were two rooms and a balcony. Four rooms on the ground floor, and a bathroom in addition. There was also a kitchen and running tap water. Only there was no electricity. There was a well in front of the kitchen. Nearby, in a corner of the compound, was a lavatory. The well was an old one with a low stone wall round it. There were plenty of trees in the compound which was walled in on all sides. One great advantage was that there were no neighbours. The house abutted on a main road.

I was surprised and delighted. Why hadn't anyone taken this house? I had by luck caught hold of a lovely woman when lovely women were hard to come by. I must hide her with a veil! This was the feeling the house evoked in me. I was excited. I ran about and got busy. I borrowed money. I paid two months' advance rent and obtained the key. In short, I moved into the house. The same day I bought a new hurricane lantern.

I swept and cleaned all the rooms, the kitchen and the bathroom. There was plenty of rubbish all over. And a great deal of dust. I washed and cleaned the rooms once again. Then I took a bath. I felt contented. I went and sat on the wall of the well. I was happy. I could sit and dream. I could walk about in the compound. I had to plan a garden in the front yard. It would be mostly rose bushes; few creepers of jasmine. I wondered whether to appoint a cook—no, that would be a bother. In the morning after I had taken a bath I could go to the tea shop with a thermos flask so that I could bring back tea. I would arrange with a hotel to give me lunch at noon. I could ask them to send me the evening meal. Then I must meet the postman and tell him that I had come to stay here. I must also ask him not to tell anyone that the house was no longer empty.... Nights of lonely beauty, days of lonely beauty; I could write a great deal.... Thinking of all this I looked into the well. I could not see whether it had water. There were plenty of bushes and undergrowth covering the surface. I picked up a stone and dropped it in the well. *Ploom!* There was a splash and an echo. There was water in the well.

It was eleven in the morning.

I had not slept a wink the previous night. I had settled my

account with the hotel in the evening. After this I had met the house owner. I had folded and tied up my canvas bed. I had packed my gramophone and records. I had packed my trunk, my papers, my books, the easy chair, the bookshelf—all my worldly goods. At dawn I had set out with the things in two carts.

I shut the doors of my new house and locked the front door. I stepped onto the road and shut the gate. I put the key in my pocket and walked on with a sense of pride. I thought to myself, with whose song should I inaugurate my house-warming tonight?...I have with me more than a hundred gramophone records; they are in English, Arabic, Hindi, Urdu, Tamil, Bengali. There is nothing in Malayalam. There are some who sing well in Malayalam. One can buy records of their music; but the music score is bad. When will Malayalam have a good music director? Such as Pankaj Mullick or Dilip Kumar Roy? I asked myself, whose record shall I play first tonight? Pankaj Mullick, Dilip Kumar Roy, Saigal, Bing Crosby, Paul Robeson, Abdul Karim Khan, Kanan Devi, Kumari Majumdas Gupta, Khurshid, Juthika Ray, M.S. Subbulakshmi... I thought of ten or twenty names. Finally I decided. There's a song which goes 'Here comes the wanderer.' *Door desh ka rahmewala aya,* it begins. Who sang that? A man or a woman? I couldn't recall. I decided to look it up. I walked on.

First I met the postman and talked to him. When I told him of the house I had occupied he said with a touch of fear, '*Ayyo!* Sir...in that house...a violent death took place there. No one stays there. That's why that house has remained vacant all this time.'

A house where there had been a violent death? I was somewhat taken aback. I asked, 'What kind of violent death?'

'Isn't there a well in the yard?...someone jumped into it. After that there has been no peace or quiet in that house. Many people stayed there. At night the doors would shut with a bang. The water taps would start running....'

Doors would shut with a bang! Water taps would run! Amazing. Both the water taps had shackles and locks. The house owner had told me that people used to jump over the wall and have a bath there, so the taps had been kept locked! I should have asked him why the tap inside the closed bathroom had also been kept locked.... I hadn't thought of it then.

'The ghost will hold you by the throat, strangle you! Didn't anyone tell you this, Sir?'

I thought to myself, splendid...and I have paid two months' rent in advance! What can one do? I told him, 'Oh, that's nothing serious. One magic incantation will take care of it. Anyhow, see that letters and so on reach me there.'

I said this bravely. I am neither courageous nor cowardly. I fear what most people are normally afraid of. So perhaps I should be considered a coward. What would you have done under such circumstances?

I walked on slowly. I wondered what I should do. I never create situations just for the sake of the experience. But when an experience comes your way uninvited what can be done then?

I stepped into a hotel and drank tea. I didn't feel like having a meal. It was as if my belly was on fire. I talked to the hotelkeeper about my food being sent to the house. When he heard the location of the house he too said, 'I'll send you food there during the day, but at night...! The boys will not go there. A woman jumped into that well and drowned. She'd be somewhere around the place! Sir, aren't you afraid of ghosts?'

A good half of my fear left me. It was a woman, was it? I said, 'Oh, that's nothing serious. And I have the right magic incantation!'

I did not know any magic incantation. But then it was a woman, and, as I said, half my fear was gone. From there I went to a bank nearby. I had two or three friends who were clerks there. I told them the news. They were angry with me.'You did a foolish thing. That house is haunted by a ghost. It harms men especially.'

So the ghost hated men. That was nice!

One of them said, 'Couldn't you have talked to one of us before you leased the house?'

I said, 'Who knew about all this then? Let me ask you one thing. Why did that woman jump into the well and kill herself?'

'Love,' another friend replied. 'Her name was Bhargavi. Age twentyone. She passed her B.A. Even before that she was in love with one chap—deeply in love. But he married another girl. On the night of the wedding Bhargavi jumped into the well and killed herself!'

Most of my fear left me. So, was that the reason for her enmity towards men?

I said, 'Bhargavi won't harm me.'

'Why not?'

I said, 'I know a magic incantation!'

'Ah, let's see.... You'll shout and cry in the night!'

I said nothing to that.

I returned to my house. I opened the doors and windows. Then I went down and stood near the well.

'Bhargavi Kutty!' I called out in a low voice. 'We have not met. I have come to stay here. In my opinion I'm a good man; a confirmed bachelor. I've heard a number of complaints about you, Bhargavi. It seems you do not let people stay here. You open the water taps at night. You bang the doors shut. You hold men by the throat and try to strangle them.... These are the kind of things I hear. What should I do now? I've paid two months rent in advance. And I like this place very much.

I want to sit and work here. That is to say, I want to write some stories. Incidentally, let me ask you something. Bhargavi Kutty, do you like stories? If you do I can read out all my stories to you, Bhargavi Kutty. Shall I?...I've no quarrel with you, Bhargavi Kutty. The reason being that nothing has happened between us.... I dropped a stone into the well thoughtlessly. Nothing like that will happen again. Forgive me. Do you hear me, Bhargavi Kutty? I have with me a very good gramophone. And some two hundred excellent songs. Are you fond of music?'

Having said this much, I kept quiet. To whom was I talking?...to an open-mouthed well ready to swallow anything?—to the trees, the house, the atmosphere, the earth, the sky...to whom? Was I talking to my disturbed mind? I said to myself, I am talking to a creature of my mind. Bhargavi.

I had not seen her. A young woman who had been twentyone years old. She had loved a man deeply. She had wanted to live as the wife of this man, as his life-long companion. She had dreamt of her life with him. But that dream...yes, it remained just a dream. She became disillusioned, felt unwanted ....

'Bhargavi Kutty!' I said, 'you should not have acted that way. Don't think I am blaming you. The man you cared for did not love you enough. He loved another woman more. He married her. So life became bitter to you. Quite so. But life is not full of such bitterness. Let that go. As far as you are concerned history will not repeat itself.

Bhargavi Kutty, don't think I am blaming you. Did you really die for love? Love is the dawn of an eternal life. Silly girl that you were, you knew nothing about life. That is what this enmity of yours to men proves. You knew just one man. Let us agree that that particular man harmed you. But was it right for you to look at all men through tinted glasses? If you had not committed suicided but had lived on you would have realised that your attitude was wrong. There would have been men who would have called you a goddess and worshipped you. But as I said, in your case history will not repeat itself.

Anyhow, you must not harm me. This is not a challenge. This is a request. If you strangle me to death tonight there will be no one to ask you why—not that one can take revenge on you. There will be no one to do it for I have no one.

Bhargavi Kutty, do you now understand my situation? We are both staying here. That is to say, I intend staying here. The well and house belong to me by right. Let that be. You may use the four rooms on the ground floor and the well and we shall share equally the kitchen and the bathroom. Do you like this arrangement?'

I was satisfied. Nothing happened.

It was night. I went to eat my meal and returned with the thermos flask full of tea. I switched on my electric torch and lighted the hurricane lantern. The room was steeped in yellow light.

I went downstairs with my torch. I stood still in the darkness for some time. My object was to lock the water taps.

I opened all the windows. Then I went near the well and the kitchen. I decided that the water taps would not be locked.

I shut the doors and secured them and went upstairs. I drank some tea. I lit a beedi and sat on the chair for a little while. I was about to start writing when I felt as though someone stood behind my chair...Bhargavi!

I said, 'I dislike anyone looking on when I am writing.'

I turned round...wasn't anyone there?

Somehow I did not have the inclination to continue writing. I got up and paced back and forth across the two rooms. There was no breeze. Outside, even the leaves on the trees did not stir. When I looked out through the window...there was a light!

I could not make out whether the light was blue or red or yellow....I saw it only for an instant.

Oh, that's an illusion, I told myself. I could not swear that I had seen the light or that I had not seen it. But then, if I had not seen it, how could I have imagined it?

I paced up and down for a long time. I stood near the window for a while. I saw nothing different. I tried to read but I could not concentrate. I thought I might as well sleep early and made my bed. I put out the lamp. I suddenly felt like listening to some records.

I lighted the lamp again. I opened up the gramophone. I fixed a new needle to the sound box. I wound up the machine.

Whose song should I play? The world was silent. But there was a hum all round. The humming resounded through my ears. I did not feel afraid. But there was a thrill, a vibration, which went through me. There hung suspended in the air a frightening silence which I wanted to shatter into a hundred thousand bits. Whose song would do that? I searched among the records and finally picked up one by the black American singer Paul Robeson. He sang through the machine. The sweet sonorous, manly voice sang, 'Joshua fought the battle of Jericho.'

That was followed by Pankaj Mullick:'*Tu dar na Surabhi...*' (Surabhi, you have nothing to fear...).

After that the soft, melodious, feminine voice of M.S. Subbulakshmi: '*Katinile varum geetam...*' (The song wafted by in the breeze ...).

M.S. Subbulakshmi's song came to an end.

After the three songs I felt a sense of peace. I sat in the stillness for some time. Then I decided to call on the great Saigal. He sang in that low voice full of sweetness and pathos. '*Soja Rajakumari*...' (Sleep princess; go to sleep and have beautiful dreams).

That song too came to an end.

'That's all; we will resume tomorrow,' I said, and closed the gramophone. I put out the lamp, lit a beedi and lay down. Next to me was the electric torch and my watch.

I had closed the door to the balcony before I lay down. It must have been about ten o'clock. I lay listening.

I could hear nothing but the soft *tik-tik* of the watch. The minutes and hours moved on. There was no fear. What I felt in my mind was a cool...a cool alertness. This was nothing new for me. In my twenty years of solitary life I have had many experiences the meaning of which I have not been able to fathom. And so my attention shuttled between the past and the present. In between I listened...for knocks on the door...the noise of running water from the pipes. Would I feel the pressure of being strangled? I listened till three o'clock.

I heard nothing. I experienced nothing. Absolute calm. I slept. I had no dreams. I got up the next morning at nine.

Nothing had happened!

'Bhargavi Kutty, many thanks...I understand one thing now. People are finding fault with you, Bhargavi Kutty, for no reason at all! Let them say what they like, don't you think so?'

Days and nights passed thus. Most nights when I was tired of writing I would put on records. Before each song I would announce the name of the singer and the meaning of the song. I would say, 'The next song is by the Bengali singer Pankaj Mullick. It is a sad song which evokes memories of days gone by. Listen to it carefully. '*Guzar gaya woh zamana kaise... kaise* ...' (How those days have gone by...vanished...).

Or else I would say, 'The next song is by Bing Crosby, "In the moonlight", which means—you're a graduate, excuse me.'

I would say all these things to myself. Two and a half

months passed thus. I nurtured and brought into being a garden. Whenever flowers bloomed I would announce that they were for Bhargavi Kutty. During this time I wrote a short novel. Many of my friends visited me. Many of them stayed the night with me. Before they went to sleep I would quietly go down and speak in a low tone into the darkness. 'Look Bhargavi Kutty, some of my friends are staying here tonight. Please don't strangle them to death. If anything like that happens the police will catch me. Please be careful...good night!'

Ordinarily, before I left the house I would say, 'Bhargavi Kutty, look after the house. If any thief comes you can strangle him to death. But don't leave the dead body here. You must take the corpse some three miles away! Otherwise we will be in trouble.'

At night when I returned after the late cinema show I would call out: 'It's me.'

All this was during the first few months of my stay. As time passed I tended to forget Bhargavi. That is to say, I did not talk to her much. I would occasionally remember her, that was all.

On this earth...since the beginning of man in this world... countless, hundreds of thousands of men and women have died. They have become one with the earth, with the dust of the earth. We all know this. Bhargavi survived as a memory of them all; that is how I thought of her.

Then something happened one night.

It must have been about ten o'clock. I had been writing a story since nine. It was a highly emotional piece. I was writing feverishly. I felt that the light was gradually dimming.

I took up the lamp and shook it. There was no kerosene at all; even then I thought I could write one more page. This was not a clearly thought-out intention. My entire attention was on the story I was writing. When the light dimmed what would one's natural reaction be? To find out if there was enough oil, as I had done. Then I turned up the wick. I went on writing. Again the light became dimmer. Again I turned up the wick. I continued writing. Again the light dimmed. Again I turned up the wick. As this went on the wick of the lamp became a glowing object four inches long and half an inch wide.

I switched on the electric torch and lowered the wick of the lantern completely. I need hardly say that the lamp went out.

I asked myself, 'How does one get a light?'

I needed to get kerosene. I remembered that I could go to the bank. Those clerks stayed in a portion of the building. I could borrow some kerosene from their stove. I picked up the torch and the empty kerosene bottle, locked the door, went downstairs and closed the front door. I stepped outside, closed the gate and walked along the road. There was a misty moonlight. The sky was overcast.

I walked fast.

I reached the front of the bank building, looked up and called one of the clerks by name. After I had called twice or thrice, one of them came down and opened the side gate. We walked along the side of the building and climbed up the back stairs. Here I found that the three of them had been playing cards.

When I told them about the kerosene one of them laughed and asked me, 'Couldn't you have asked that Bhargavi to fetch you kerosene?'

I said nothing though I too laughed. While one of them was taking some kerosene out of the stove it started raining.

I said, 'You must give me an umbrella also.'

They said, 'Never mind an umbrella, we don't even have a bare stick to make up one. Let's play cards. You can go when the rain stops.'

And so I played cards. My partner and I lost three rounds which was mainly because I could not concentrate. My mind was on the story I was writing. It stopped raining at about one o'clock. I picked up the torch and the bottle of kerosene. The clerks got ready to go to bed. When I went down the stairs and reached the road they switched off the light.

There was no movement on the road, nor any light. I walked on. There was no light anywhere. I turned the corner and approached my house. In the dim moonlight the whole world appeared steeped in misty wonder. I do not know what thoughts passed through my mind. Perhaps I thought of nothing in particular. I walked along the deserted and silent road with the torch switched on.

I reached the house, opened the gate and went in. I opened the front door, entered and closed it. I had no reason to think that anything out of the ordinary had happened upstairs. But I must mention one thing—my mind was full of a strange sadness for no reason whatsoever. I wanted to weep. I can laugh easily. But I find it difficult to weep. No tear, not even a drop usually comes out of my eyes. When I wanted to weep I would feel a strange sense of divinity. I felt it then.

I went up the stairs in that frame of mind. And then...an unusual sight met my eyes. My subconscious recorded it. This is what had happened. When I had closed the door and left, the lamp had gone out completely for want of oil. The room had been dark. After that it had rained for a while. About three hours had passed. But now there was light inside the room. It could be seen through the chinks in the door.... This was the light my eyes had seen and my subconscious had registered. But this, this mystery, was not recognised by my conscious self.

As usual I took out my key. Then I focused my torchlight on the padlock. The lock gleamed like silver...or is it more correct to say that the lock smiled in the light?

I opened the door and went in; then I saw everything. That is to say, my entire being realised with a start what was happening. I did not tremble in fear. I stood there stunned. I felt a kind of warmth go through me and I sweated.

The entire room and its white walls were illuminated with a blue light. The light came from the lamp...two inches of blue flame....I stood there struck with amazement.

Who had lit the lamp which had gone out for want of kerosene? Where did this blue light come from?

Original title 'Neela Velicham';from the collection Pavappattavarude Veshya *(1952).*

A Little Old Love Story

This event happened some twenty years ago. I remember it as if it were yesterday. I have often wondered what has happened to the smartness and courage of those days. There was only one force; the impulse of youth with no second thoughts. One plunged into action and went the way the heart directed.... O age of beauty and blind faith, I bow before you!

We lived in hunger, perpetual hunger. Hunger for everything, thirst for everything, We were angry with someone and something unknown, furiously angry. We basked in the beautiful glow of idealism. Everything would turn out right. We would refashion the world. We would wash the universe in blood and make it clean and new! We were atheists. We were revolutionaries. I was the leader of a group which would not hesitate to kill. O age of terrorism with dagger and gun held aloft, I bow before you!

Fire and brimstone flowed from the tip of my pen. Annihilation was the ideal of life. There were some three hundred young men imbued with these ideals; we ran a newspaper of which I was the editor.

The newspaper office was a room hardly bigger than a matchbox.

We stayed there. Night and day we spent thinking; and we wrote. Night and day we held discussions. Night and day we made plans.

What I laid down was taken as the gospel truth. I was held

in high respect and was the undisputed leader. In my heart I felt a sense of inadequacy, of something wanting. Also a kind of suffocation, with a tinge of sadness.

All this was not suited to terrorist activities. And yet I sometimes had a tendency to sing sad songs. Two varieties of emotions battled in my heart. I had an overpowering feeling of breathlessness.

When I felt suffocated I would walk out into the yard. I would stand near the wall and look at the wide world. One day as I was standing thus I saw a beautiful young girl.

What a sight...!

It did not take me many moments to fall in love. O lovely goddess made for love, I bow before you.

I stood there looking at her with a song in my heart. It was an act of worship.

She was not aware of all this; she did not see me.

My seeing her was an accident. I happened to be standing in a particular place and looking in a particular direction. And I saw her.

Suddenly it seemed to me to become a holy spot the place where I stood and looked at her.

I stood with my elbows on the wall and my fingers on my head looking east. On the other side of the wall was a grove of banana trees. The grove was bordered by a low wall. Beyond that was the main road which ran north to south. On either side of the road were double-storeyed buildings.

On my left there was a dirty canal which ran east to west dividing the town into two. There were high walls on either side of the canal. There had been a coconut tree on the other side of the canal. They had built the wall very close to the tree. Later the coconut tree was cut down. It left a gap in the wall.

I saw her through the gap. A fair, well-built beauty. Her breasts tied down inside her blouse stood out firm and round. She had her hair loose on her shoulders as she stood there dreaming.

What is she dreaming of, so sweetly? Can't she see me? Why doesn't she look my way?

I stood and coughed. Not once, not even ten times; it was

more like a roar of coughs.

It was, useless. She did not hear them. Why doesn't she hear me?

From then on life was a succession of coughs. Go stand at the holy spot, look through the gap in the wall. Is she about anywhere? If she was, I would start coughing immediately. I would stand there well prepared with an array of different coughs in stock. Sometimes she would appear in a flash, like lightning. Immediately a series of staccato coughs would be let out in quick succession! With no result. She did not hear the sound of my coughing. And she did not look in my direction.

A month and a half went by thus; by which time I had learnt something of that house as well of the neighbouring one. There was nothing exciting about them. They were respectable householders living respectably.

The object of my worship was a servant maid!

What did it matter. Does love make petty distinctions between the hut and the palace? Love was eternal. Love was divine!

However she had not seen me; I had not appeared on the horizon of her existence.

I stood there with my store of coughs. Finally I became frustrated. All my coughs had finally sputtered out. My world became dark.

Wonder of wonders—she had seen me! The moonlike one had sent forth soothing, life-giving rays. She looked at me; I looked at her. She smiled at me. I could not smile. Was not a smile a sign of weakness? But new life flowed into me. I had unearthed a treasure. My goddess had deigned to acknowledge my presence. I was blessed.

My sorrow disappeared. I plunged with increased vigour into my activities.

Every day we would see each other. She would smile at me. I too learnt to smile a little.

The love-filled days went by.

One evening at dusk there was a light drizzle of rain. Dressed in a sleeveless vest and shorts I was standing on my side of the canal looking through the gap in the wall. At my waist I had an unsheathed dagger. A terrorist must always be armed with a deadly weapon, mustn't he?

I was waiting for my loved one. The people going in and out of our lodge could see me. When someone came I would pretend to kneel and urinate. And so kneeling and standing up I waited there for some time. Suddenly the gap in the wall was covered with white.

I became hot all over. My heart thumped...my mouth went dry. I heard a magically sweet voice, 'Why do you stand in the rain?'

'Oh, it's nothing.'

Emotion-filled moments sped by. People passed along the road which was lit which electric lamps unaware of all this. In the canal somewhere a frog had been seized by a snake. I heard the frog croak in agony. The darkness was deepening. We could see less and less. She asked, 'Have you gone?'

'No. Shall I come over there?'

'What for?'

'For nothing.'

'No.'

'Yes! I'll come!'

'We have a dog!'

'It doesn't matter!'

'They'll be coming here to have their meal.'

'It doesn't matter! I'll come.'

'*Ayyo*! No.'

She ran off. The gap in the wall became black again.

I sat on top of the wall. Light from the road fell onto the canal and onto the top of the wall. I tried to step into the canal slowly; my legs wouldn't reach the ground. I reached down with my feet and let go of my hold on the wall. There was knee-deep mud and the water was waist high. It felt as if there were plenty of thorny brambles and glass pieces underneath. My feet became heavy with mud, as if stones were tied to it. I crept forward. I reached the middle of the canal. I stood in the clear light. I could not move a step forward. I stood stuck in the mud. People could see me. I had to move forward. Somehow I moved on; I inched my way to the other side of the canal. I looked up and was stunned.

A wall rose out of the water—a wall which seemed to touch the skies! What was to be done? How would I climb the wall? Suppose I turned back? No, I had to climb up. There was a branch of banyan growing on the wall, beyond arm's reach.

I leapt to catch hold of the banyan branch. The next thing I was aware of was that I was sitting on top of the wall.

'Oh!' I heard her cry of surprise.

But I was still far away from her. I could not jump down. In the distance there was a half-wall on the western side by the house. That was a low wall. I walked along the top of the wall like a cat. I managed to jump into the yard of the neighbouring house. I saw a cattle shed there. As I skirted it dry leaves crackled under my feet.

I planted my steps warily on the ground till I reached the half-wall.

She came quietly to the other side of the wall.

I slowly put my arms across and lifted her by the shoulders on to the top of the wall. Her blouse rubbed against the sharp edge of a stone and tore with a ripping noise.

Then my love gave me two stinging slaps on my face in this manner.

She said, '*Ayyo*.... They'll be coming over here for their food. Go away!' When she said that her foul and stinking breath hit my face and nose like well-aimed slaps. My head sank under the stench.

I moved away as much as I could. A number of twigs snapped under my feet. A dog barked.

She again said, 'Go away,' jumped off the wall and walked away.

Then the dogs started barking. Were there so many of them?

I walked slowly and climbed the half-wall. From there I got onto the high wall. I moved forward. Suddenly the wall and the yard were in blazing light.

The only screen in front of me was a wispy banana leaf. The leaf would be blown aside in the wind. I would stand exposed in the light!

At that moment I saw some of my comrades going towards my room. They could have seen me easily. But they did not look up. How could they suspect me?

Two or three women and two men came into the yard below talking among themselves. The youngest of them stepped forward and came towards where I was squatting on the wall. He was coming to catch me! He must have seen me. What a disgrace!

'What are you doing there, you rascal?' he would ask me as he seized me!

A crowd would gather. 'Oh, isn't this the editor of that fiery paper?'

O God, whatever I have said about you till now is wrong. Please save me from this situation. Let him not see me!

I took my dagger in my hand. If he gets hold of me... I'll cut my throat! O God, destroy his eyesight, destroy his sight for a little while!

My comrades were calling for me loudly. They wanted to meet their leader! God almighty...please do not disgrace me!

The young man who had stepped out into the yard and come towards me, knelt and urinated. He then got up and went away.

I felt drained of all strength. Something had died within me.

I do not remember clearly what happened afterwards. I vaguely remember having jumped into the canal, cutting myself all over and, encased in mud, appearing before my comrades after scaling the wall.

They were aghast when they saw me. They thought that their leader had returned after some great exploit! They did not guess that I had fought a victorious battle with love. So help me God!

I soaped myself all over and had a bath. I changed my clothes, combed my hair and sat on my usual chair. I described to my disciples all that had happened.

At the end of it all, they said, 'We must move from here immediately.'

We moved.

In the silence of the night we moved out of the abode of love. And so...and so....O age of love which did not take away self-respect, I bow my head to you!

Original title 'Oru Pazhaya Kochu Premakatha'; from the collection Viswa Vikyathamaya Mooku *(1956).*

The World-Renowned Nose

It is sensational news. A nose has became a topic of controversy among intellectuals and political thinkers. A world-renowned nose!

I record here the true story of that nose.

The owner of that world-renowned nose had completed twentyfour years of age when the story began. No one knew him before that. Does the twenty-fourth year in a person's life have any special significance? Who knows? If one looks through the recorded pages of world history one finds that the twenty-fourth year had a significance in many great lives. Students of history need hardly be told this.

The hero of our story was a cook, a kitchen worker if you like. He was not particularly intelligent. He could not read and write. His world was confined to the kitchen. He was totally indifferent to happenings outside the kitchen. Why should he pay attention to them? He could eat to his satisfaction; take as much snuff as he wanted, sleep, work. His daily routine was confined to these activities.

He did not know the names of the months of the year. When it was time for him to receive his salary his mother would come and collect it. If he wanted snuff the old woman herself would buy it for him. He lived a contented life till he reached his twenty-fourth year. Then an amazing thing happened!

His nose grew slightly in length. It passed his mouth and reached the level of his chin.

The nose began to grow in length every day. Was it possible to hide this? Within a month the nose reached his navel. Did he feel uncomfortable? Not in the least! He could breathe freely. He could inhale snuff. He could distinguish between smells. There was no inconvenience worth talking about.

However because of his nose the poor cook was dismissed from his work.

What was the reason?

No group came forward with the battle cry, 'Take back the dismissed employee.' Political parties shut their eyes to this piece of blatant injustice.

'Why was this man dismissed?' No lover of humanity came forward with this query.

The poor cook!

No one needed to tell him why he had lost his job. The reason was that the people living in the house where he worked could find no peace or quiet because of him. People came visiting night and day to see the long-nosed one and his nose. Photographers pestered them. News reporters became a nuisance. A number of things were pilfered from the house.

As the dismissed cook sat starving in his lowly hut he was convinced of one thing—his nose had acquired great publicity!

People from distant lands came to see him. They stood stunned with surprise at his long nose. Some touched it too. But no one asked, 'Have you eaten today? Why do you look so weak?' There was money in the hut not even to buy a small packet of snuff. Was he a wild animal to be kept starving? He might be a fool, but he was a human being. One day he called his old mother aside and told her in a whisper, 'Get these horrid people out and shut the door!'

The mother promptly sent them all out and closed the door.

Good fortune came to the mother and son from that day. People began to bribe the mother to see the son's nose! Some upholders of justice protested against this corruption. But the Government did not take any action. Many protested against the inaction of the Government and joined revolutionary parties out to sabotage the Government!

The income of the long-nosed one grew day by day. Need one say more? In six years the poor cook became a millionaire.

He acted in films thrice. What vast audiences were attracted by the Technicolor feature film, 'The Human Submarine'! Six poets wrote epic poems about the noble qualities of the long-nosed one. Nine well-known writers wrote biographies of the long-nosed one and won wealth and acclaim.

His princely abode was also a guest-house open to all. Anyone at any time could get a meal there; and a bit of snuff.

He had two secretaries. Two comely, accomplished women. Both of them loved the long-nosed one. Both of them worshipped him. When two beautiful women love the same man at the same time there is bound to be trouble. Troubles came into the life of the long-nosed one.

Other people also loved the long-nosed one; that long nose reaching down to the navel was considered a sign of greatness. The long-nosed one gave his opinion on important world events. Newspapers published his comments:

'An aeroplane with a speed of 10,000 miles an hour has been built! The long-nosed one commented in this way on the event—!'

'Doctor Bundrose Furasiburose has brought a dead man to life! The long-nosed one made the following speech about it—!'

When people heard that the highest peak in the world had been scaled they asked, 'What does the long-nosed one say about this?'

If the long-nosed one said nothing about an event....*Poo!* It was unimportant. And also the long-nosed one was expected to comment on anything and everything! Art, the watch trade, mesmerism, photography, the soul, publishing houses, the writing of novels, life after death, the conduct of newspapers, hunting.

It was at this time that conspiracies were hatched to capture the long-nosed one. To capture something, taking something by physical conquest, was nothing new. The major part of world history consists of conquests and captures.

What does it mean, to capture? Suppose you plant coconut

seedlings on a piece of barren land. You water the land and manure it. You fence it in. Expectant years slip by and the trees bear fruit. Coconuts hang in proud clusters from the palms. Then someone takes that garden away from you.

First of all it was the Government that made an attempt to capture the long-nosed one. They tried a trick. The Government awarded him the title 'Chief of the Long-Nosed Ones'and gave him a medal. It was the President himself who tied the jewelled gold medal round the neck of the long-nosed one. Then, instead of shaking the long-nosed one by the hand, the President tweaked the tip of the long nose. This was filmed by newsreel cameramen and shown in all the theatres.

By that time the political parties in the country had come forward enthusiastically. Comrade Long-Nose must give leadership to the people's struggle! Comrade Long-Nose indeed! Whose Comrade? Comrade in what? Great God! Poor long-nosed one!

The long-nosed one must join The Party! Which party? There were many parties. How could the long-nosed one join so many different parties at the same time?

The long-nosed one said in his own tongue, 'Why should I join a party or parties? Me, I am too tired.'

Then one of the secretaries said, 'If Comrade Long-Nose likes me he must join my party.'

The long-nosed one said nothing to that.

'Need I join any party?' the long-nosed one asked the other secretary. She guessed what he was aiming at. She replied, 'Why should you?'

By that time one of the political parties had come out with the slogan: 'Our party is the long-nosed one's party, the long-nosed one's party is the people's party!'

Members of other parties were incensed by this. They got at one of the secretaries and made her issue a scathing statement against the long-nosed one: 'The long-nosed one has deceived the people! He has been cheating them all this while. He has made me a partner in this fraud. Let me declare the truth to the public—the long nose is made of rubber!'

What a statement! All the newspapers splashed the news on their front pages. The nose of the long-nosed one is made of rubber! Would the people keep quiet at this? Would they not react in rage? Cables, telephone calls and letters came from all parts of the world! The President was allowed no peace or quiet. 'Destruction to the rubber nose of the long-nosed one! Down with the Long-Nose Party! Long live revolution!'

When the anti– Long-Nose Party put out this statement the opposing party made the other secretary issue a counter-statement: 'Beloved countrymen, citizens! What she has said is a lie. Comrade Long-Nose did not love her and this is her revenge. She was trying to keep for herself the wealth and good name of Comrade Long-Nose. One of her brothers is in the opposite party. Let me reveal the true colours of the members of the other party. I am the faithful secretary of Comrade Long-Nose. I know for a fact that the nose of the comrade is not made of rubber. It is as real as my own heart beating inside me. Long live the members of the party supporting Comrade Long-Nose at this critical time! They have no motives of gain other than the progress of the people. Long live revolution!'

What was to be done? There was confusion in the minds of the people. The leaders of the party against the long-nosed one began finding fault with the President and the Government. 'Stupid Government! They gave the title "Chief of the Long-Nosed Ones" to a deceiver of the people. They gave him a jewelled gold medal. The President is also involved in this fraud. They have betrayed the national interest. The President must resign. The Ministry must resign! The rubber-nosed one must be killed!'

The President reacted angrily. One morning the army and their tanks surrounded the house of the poor long-nosed one. He was arrested and taken away.

There was no news of the long-nosed one for some time. The people forgot about his existence. Then came fresh news with the impact of a nuclear bomb! Do you know what happened? Just when the people had forgotten everything came a brief announcement from the President: 'The trial of the "Chief of the Long-Nosed Ones" will take place on 9 March. Expert doctors who come as representatives of fortyeight countries will examine him. All the newspapers of the world will be represented by their respective correspondents. The proceedings will be filmed for all the world to see. The people must keep calm.'

People are people. They could not keep calm. They came in large numbers into the metropolis. They invaded the hotels. They burnt public conveyances. They set fire to police stations. They destroyed government buildings. There were communal riots. Quite a number of men and women died as martyrs in this fight for the long-nosed one.

9 March, 11 a.m. The square in front of the Presidential Palace was a vast sea of humanity. The loud speakers blared forth: 'People must be disciplined. The examination has begun!'

The doctors surrounded the long-nosed one in the presence of the President and cabinet ministers. One doctor blocked the nostrils of the long-nosed one; he immediately opened his mouth wide. Another doctor took a needle and punctured the tip of his nose. To his amazement a drop of blood appeared at the tip of the nose.

The doctors gave their unanimous verdict: 'The nose is not made of rubber. It is genuine.'

One of the female secretaries kissed the long-nosed one on the tip of the nose.

'Long live Comrade Long-Nose! Long live the "Chief of the Long-Nosed Ones"! Long live the Progressive People's Party of the long-nosed one!' As this shouting and revelry ended, the President thought of another gimmick. He nominated the long-nosed one as a member of parliament! 'The Honourable Long-Nose M.P!' Three universities conferred doctorates on him. 'The Honourable Long Nose D. Litt!' The ignorant populace acclaimed the actions of the equally ignorant Government which ruled over them.

But the parties of which the long-nosed one was not a member formed a United Front and began to proclaim: 'The

Ministry must resign! This is a fraud on the people! It's a rubber nose!'

Look at the way falsehood was being perpetuated! Would there not be confusion of thought? What could the poor intellectual do?

Original title 'Viswa Vikyathamaya Mooku'; from the collection Viswa Vikyathamaya Mooku *(1956).*

The Walls

Has anyone heard this little love story? It's called 'The Walls'. I could have named it 'The Smell of Woman'. But then I thought I would call it 'The Walls'. Listen carefully. The events happened quite some time ago. In what we generally call the past. From the other side of the river of memories; remember I am on this side. From this solitary heart you will now hear a sad song.

High stone walls that seemed to touch the sky. They stood there surrounding the Central Jail (and me). Many buildings inside these walls; many human beings inside these buildings. There wasn't much noise. Most of the prisoners were confined indoors. Some were condemned men who were to be hanged the next day at dawn. There were others who had done their term and would be released the next day. All the same there was an air of calm.

I was walking. It was not a broad road. To my left and right were long high walls. Ahead of me was the warder. Only a few minutes had passed since I had been put into jail uniform and given a number. White cap with black stripes, white shirt , white dhoti. A thick bedspread to lie upon, a black blanket to cover myself with, vessels to eat out of and drink from—each of them had a number. I wasn't a novice. I had been made into a number before. I remembered a book on the study of numbers I had read once. I looked at my number again and added up the digits. Nine. What is the horoscope for nine?

What would happen to me in this jail?

The warder grumbled. 'Can't you walk faster?' I felt like laughing. I never lose an opportunity to laugh. Laughter is God's special gift.

I asked, 'Where are you going in this hurry? Leaving this great universe?'

He didn't answer. He kept on walking. I said, 'Do you have a big business deal to settle after you've locked me up in a hole?'

The issue was somewhat serious. I had been in a police lock - up in a town fifty miles away for some twelve or fourteen months. They wouldn't take up my case. They just kept me locked up. On the advice of the police inspector I started to kick up a row. I starved. That is to say, I did satyagraha and went on a hunger strike! I got my case taken up. I got myself convicted. I had spent my time at the lockup as a member of the family. My right hand from the tip of the index finger to the wrist would be beaten into pulp! That was more or less what some reserve-police constables had told my father and mother. Actually it was not any policeman who had said it but a magistrate. The conceit of the police! This was when my house had been surrounded by the police to arrest me. I was not there then. Finally they caught me. No one beat me up. Quite a few of the policemen became my admirers. I enjoyed the status and dignity of a head constable at the lockup. I wrote a number of police stories when I was in there. Pencil and paper were provided by the Police Inspector. I said goodbye to all of them and left. They sent two police constables with me, who were armed with guns. They had handcuffs in their pockets. It was they who handed me over at the Central Jail. However this is not the serious issue I am talking about. Those two policemen had bought and given me two packets of beedis, a box of matches and a new razor blade. The warder took everything from my pocket with the benign statement: 'All these things are not permitted in jail.' He took off his lofty looking cap and put the things inside it, replaced the cap on his head and marched away as if nothing serious had happened. Let him march, the scoundrel!

Do you know what the razor blade is for ? Not for what you

think. It is used to split matchsticks into two. I have seen great artists who could cut up a matchstick into six. The blade has other uses also. Matchboxes are not easy to get in jail. They cost money. One doesn't have money in jail. But one needs a razor blade to make a chakki. Do you know what a chakki is? How would you know? Let me tell you.

The jail authorities give you a thick bedspread to lie on. You collect its threads to the thickness of two fingers; they should be as long as one's palm. Tie them up two inches from one end. Burn up the loose ends. Great artists tie up the charred ends in a small piece of leather folded up twice or thrice. But wretched amateurs like us could tie it up even in a thick jackfruit tree leaf. Now what we need is a small piece of steel. Where does one get that? It is not only pieces of steel but many other things which are available in jail if one has the money. If one has a steel blade it could be rubbed on cement or granite to produce sparks. When those sparks touch the charred end of the apparatus then one has fire in plenty. The blade has to be embedded in a piece of wood with just one end sticking out. That is a chakki. All this equipment now lay inside the warder's cap.

I remarked, 'Policemen are not bad people!'

Didn't the warder hear? He was walking along, silent. He would sell all those things. The mean fellow must have already earned enough to feed his children and his children's children!

I asked, 'How many children do you have, warder?'

He woke up from his daydream and said, 'Six, five girls and a boy.'

The poor warder. Five girls!

I asked, 'Are the mother and children well?'

'Yes, yes,' the warder said. 'Walk fast.'

The reason for the hurry was evident now!

I asked, 'What'll they do if you die?'

The warder said, 'God will look after them!'

I said, 'I doubt it very much.'

The warder asked, 'Why do you say that?'

I said, 'Knowledge of divine intent! I'll tell you how I came by it. I used to be half a sanyasi. There are no temples in India in which I have not stayed. There are no holy rivers in which I have not bathed. On the mountain peaks, in the valleys, in forests, in deserts, on the seashore—'

'And so?'

'God won't let you go free!'

'I haven't done anything wrong.'

I asked, 'What about the brazen bit of robbery today?'

The warder was taken aback. He asked, 'What robbery?'

I said, 'The warder dies. His soul goes before the resplendent presence of divinity. God asks, "You petty-minded warder...! Where is that poor Basheer's razor blade and box of matches and two packets of beedies?" '

The warder suddenly stopped. I walked on and called out: 'Come, come! Don't you want to put me in my cage and get away?'

The warder stood still. He didn't say a word. He shook with laughter as he took off his cap. He gave me back all my things.

'Good warder,' I said. 'The police inspector told me this morning that Gandhiji was on his death bed. Have you heard anything warder?'

'He has ended his fast by drinking limejuice.'

'Good. May Mohandas Karamchand Gandhi live long!'

We went along, passing through many steel doors.

I asked, 'How many political prisoners do you have here now?'

'Seventeen persons at the place you are going to.'

'That's all. Is it a special place you're taking me to? The Government looks upon this humble individual with a certain degree of concern. Good.'

As we walked on we smelt the most heady perfume in this world.

The smell of woman!

I was completely shaken. Every atom of my being came alive and alert. My nostrils flared. I breathed in the whole world...into myself.

Where is she ?

I looked around. There was no one. Nothing.

Walking on we heard the most beautiful sound in

this world.

The laughter of a woman!

Did the sound and the smell come together? Or did I imagine the one because of the other?

I had forgotten that wonderful species of creation called woman.

The laughter I had heard was real. The smell that came rushing to me was also real.

I am not talking about the smell of soap. Nor of the smell of things that women use like hair oil or medicinal herbs. It was not the smell of a mixture of powder and sweat. It was the veritable smell of woman!

Where did it come from...and that laughter?

I thought of that smell again...I was unable to breathe. My nostrils flared again, as if my heart was going to burst in anxiety.

I asked, 'Where did that laughter come from?'

The warder mocked, 'Aren't you married?'

I said, 'No...but what's the connection between that and my question?'

'Why do you listen to all these things?'

'In the Central Jail...in the neighbourhood of the gallows...one hears the laughter of a woman. I need to get married immediately! Only then can I ask where the laughter is from! Fine reasoning!'

The warder laughed. He said, 'It's from the women's jail. You're going to be next to it. What's your sentence?'

'Two years' rigorous imprisonment and a thousand-rupee fine. If the fine is not paid, another six months' rigorous.'

'There will only be a wall between you and the women's jail.'

We walked on. I held the bedspread and blanket close to my heart.

He opened an iron-barred door and we entered a specially walled-in enclosure. There were many trees, mostly jackfruit. A number of cottages. If one faced the east, on either side in the distance were two high walls. Beyond the wall on the right lay the free wide world. On the left beyond the wall...the women's jail.

Each of these cottages was a lockup surrounded by low walls.

The warder there took charge of me. I bade farewell to the warder who had brought me. He said goodbye and went away. The new warder led me to a cottage. He opened its steel door into a very small room. Outside the room at a little distance was the latrine. There was a water tap near the door. I opened the tap and washed my feet and hands and face and drank some water. With a vessel filled with water and the name of God on my lips I entered the room right foot first.

The warder closed the steel door and locked it with a padlock.

I said, 'This guest hasn't had dinner.'

The warder said, 'You have not been included in today's account. You'll get food from tomorrow.'

I said, 'Then let me out. I'll come in on tomorrow's account!'

The warder asked, 'What's your offence?'

'Writing...treason.'

Apparently stunned the warder said, 'Treason!...God Almighty save us all!'

Above the steel door of the lockup a high-powered electric bulb lit up. The warder left.

I laid out the thick bedspread. I put the vessels in the corner. Both the inside of the lockup and I were in bright light. I was not in today's account...therefore I would starve overnight. I knew how I could get some food. I could create a hubbub shaking that steel door and roaring for the warder. I could bring down the warder and the superintendent and others. Then I would get food. I decided against it. I must after all undergo some sacrifice in the cause of literature! I have been beaten up a great deal for the country. I have been very kindly hit on the chest with the stock of a gun and felled to the ground, gently. I have been dragged along the streets. And I had spent quite a number of terms in jail.

This stay in jail was for the glory of literature! The thought put some pride into me. I drank some water.

I forgot to split a matchstick with the razor blade. I used a whole stick with extravagance and lit my beedi. After taking some five or six puffs I stubbed out the beedi. Prodigality is not good.

I sat down and listened. I could not hear the sound of woman's laughter. I could not smell woman's smell either. Why? I was sitting near the women's jail.

That smell—had it perhaps been my imagination? Once...aeons and ages àgo...when I, as Adam, had woken up in the Garden of Eden and smelt the smell of Eve!...I probably stored that experience in the recesses of my soul...the mirage seen in the desert by the tired and thirsty wanderer...like a mirage it vanished...leaving flaring nostrils...a breaking heart.

Where is that beautiful voice? Where, where is that heady perfume?

I looked out. I could see nothing through the light. Darkness had engulfed the world. But one could not see the darkness distinctly.

I realised one thing. I had not seen darkness till now! Night that steals one's heart and hides everything! Stars in their twinkling millions! Night polished over by moonlight!

You...and you...you...I have not seen you till now.

This is a lie. I have seen them. I have seen them all. But I have paid no heed. Who takes seriously the beauty of the night and the stars?

As I thought I remembered a beautiful night. A tiny village. Beyond that thousands of miles of desert. The time was after sunset like this. I stepped out into the desert. I must have walked about a mile...it was as if white silk had been spread out all round. I was at the centre of the world. Above me was a full moon so low I could touch it with my hand.

A blue sky that looked washed clean.

The full moon and stars.

Stars which shone with extreme brilliance. A million...a million million...stars in their countless numbers.

A silent universe...but...there was something...something... like divine silent music...the infinite melody of passion... everything was immersed in that. I stopped with wonder, in ecstasy. My ecstasy and my wonder turned into tears. I wept. Helplessly I ran weeping.

O creator of these worlds within worlds! Save me. I cannot contain these within myself. This great glory of yours...this great wonderment...I am a tiny living creature. I am weak, powerless, save me.

I became aware of my surroundings only when the warder came the next morning, opened the padlock and shook the door a couple of times. 'Salutations to the world!' I got up. I lit the remnant of my beedi and in grand style went about the early morning chores. I brushed my teeth with the twig of a margosa tree. I had my bath standing under the water tap. I put on the jail uniform, washed the vessels they brought food in and then went to meet the leaders. All of them were leaders. By the time I had visited them all a large vessel of kanji, rice gruel, was brought in. I drank the kanji with plenty of chutney. Actually what I took was kanjo. I'll explain this kanjo recipe. First drink up the water of the kanji. Then mix the chutney with the remaining rice and eat to your heart's content. After that you must wash your hands and mouth and the vessel well. Then drink a little water...life is bliss. After reaching this state of bliss I split a matchstick into two and lit a beedi. I stubbed it out after a few puffs and then went out to see the world. That is to say, to look around the entire jail. I wanted tea leaves and sugar. I had to have some tea even in jail. Black tea was enough. The leaders had neither tea nor sugar. One great leader had secreted away a bottle of Eno's Fruit Salt. Without that he would not be able to start his morning routine. The secret of another important leader was that he had a copy of that great work, Karl Marx's *Capital*. Another leader had two packs of playing cards. He promised to teach me the wonderful game called Bridge.

I avoided the company of the leaders.

A month later I was leading a 'deluxe' life in princely style. There are two bricks in front of my cage. Close by lies a bundle of dried jackfruit tree twigs. Next to it is a pot. All this is for making tea. The leaves and sugar lie in two bundles under the bed as little pillows. Then there is the 'deluxe chakki'; any number of beedies. Writing paper. Pencil. A long knife. This knife had been graciously given by the Jail Superintendent....

He found out that I was an expert in gardening and planting trees and grafting. He had told me to hand back the knife to the warder immediately after I had used it. I forgot to do that. I have made a square front yard to my lockup. On the borders are rose plants with the roses in bloom shedding their sweet smell all round. And with my meals I have fried fish, eggs, liver, a special chutney. This life of affluence starts with the great man who brings my kanji in the morning. He is a 'red cap'. Which means he had killed a human being. He was not sentenced to the gallows. He received rigorous imprisonment for life. He is a fair-complexioned fat man with a round face and smiling eyes.

When I get up in the morning I do some physical exercises. Near my rose garden there was a tall slender jackfruit tree. Its lowermost branch was the size of my thigh. I would do some exercises using it as a bar. By the time I finished all this and had my bath, he (of the red cap and smiling eyes) would have got ready my kanji and special chutney served in two covered vessels. There was no such thing as kanji. It was rice. But was it even rice? There was a little kanji water in the rice. When he first poured out kanji for me he whispered in my ears, 'Go and meet the hospital orderly. He will serve you tea.'

I went and saw him. He was dark and lean with a fine moustache; beautiful white teeth; a lovely smile. He is an old friend of mine; I have lived in his village. He was involved in a dacoity case involving robbery with violence. Besides, two persons had been killed. He was a 'red cap'. He received rigorous imprisonment for life. He became a hospital orderly because of good behaviour and his educational qualifications. I had no trouble thereafter about getting tea, sugar, liver, bread, milk, beedies and so on. Coming to think of it my rose garden was completely transplanted, roots and soil and all, from the hospital backyard. When the leaders saw my garden they also wanted similar ones. I made up small gardens for each of them. The leaders had established lines of communication with the outside world through the warders. Letters were sent out and letters came in. All that cost money. In the nights some packets from over the wall would come and fall inside. In the morning the leaders would pick them up—banana chips, banana candy, lime pickles and so on. Sometimes I would also join in picking up the packets. One day a leader presented me with some lime pickles. Ha, what taste; what a rare treat! And the look on his face as he gave it to me! I felt my debt would not be repaid even if I composed a great poem on it.

I thus lived in peace and amity with my colleagues and my admirers, the 'red caps'. I was in want for nothing. Sometimes I would look towards the women's jail. That enormous devilish wall! I would remember the laughter I had heard and the smell I had smelled. I would scramble up the jackfruit tree near the garden. That would be when the leaders had finished their noonday meal and were enjoying their siesta. I would stand right on top of the tree. In the free world beyond the walls, in the distance, men and women would be walking by unaware of me.

Friends look this way once...! I talk to the women. Turn this way please!

After some time I would climb down the tree. Every male within prison walls would say the same thing. Imagine that every male in jail is thinking the same thoughts as I. Our lonely nights...our thoughts in our loneliness...it is better you do not go deep into our minds. I would stand still in the midst of my rose garden. All around me were flowers shedding perfume. There was beauty. There was sweetness. But something was wanting. What was this?

No. Such thoughts are not good. I walked about. So many walls and doors. There were warders everywhere. It was not possible to do anything in jail without the warders seeing you. There was even a tower from which they could look down.

I walked around that observation tower. I saw something and could not help laughing. It was magnificent...a rogue elephant in chains! No...a man. Black cap. A fair tall well-built young man. Sparkling eyes. With head held high and leaning well back, he walked with difficulty. From his neck two chains came trailing down his back and were clasped round his feet. The chains made him bend backwards. Was he a convict who had tried to jump jail? I went near him. I stood stunned...he was an old classmate of mine!

We looked at each other. Our eyes met. We laughed. We talked of many things; we laughed again. He had set out to meet me secretly.

I asked,'Couldn't you have sent someone?'

'Suppose people came to know that we knew each other... wouldn't it be bad for your reputation?'

'...knew each other? Say I am your friend, you rascal.'

I embraced him and planted a kiss on his cheek. It was as if I had kissed every single inmate of the jail. The news of the kiss spread throughout the jail. The whole prison was thrilled.

This chained being, the possessor of those sparkling eyes, was a martyr of that jail.

He had entered jail as a thief with a sentence running to a year and a half. He carried on a little business in beedis, jaggery and smoked fish. A small incident happened after six months in jail. A warder perpetrated a piece of roguery... something no other warder had done. Please listen to this carefully. Let us call that warder 'the rogue warder'. My classmate did not like the roguery of the rogue warder. All warders had a share in the business that went on in the jail. Quite a number of the inmates of the jail were taken some distance away from the prison campus to break rocks for laying roads. A whole business went on there. And thus my classmate became a big businessman. Many things came into the jail premises in the prisoners' underwear. There is checking at the gate; one has to untie the dhoti and show oneself just for half a minute and you are declared clean! Cap, shirt, dhoti and towel were supplied by the jail authorities. Only those are checked. Nothing is normally found. The underwear is not taken into consideration by the jail! Perhaps it is considered a part of the human body. But that is not the important point here. I was talking about the rogue warder and the roguery he had perpetrated. My classmate struck the rogue warder on the face, cheeks and ears.... The news spread all over the jail. They heard about it not only in the men's jail but in the women's jail too. Everyone was thrilled..... My classmate was tied to a whipping post and given twelve lashes with a whip. His

sentence was raised to three years. His bruises healed. He was
able to walk about again. He naturally wanted to be taken out
to break stones. But the rogue warder was against that.
'You don't know me. You don't know where I come from
either. Here, take this!' With this remark my classmate gave the
warder two well-aimed blows on the neck. To round it off he
gave a mighty blow to the solar plexus, right on the navel.
There was nothing wrong with this. Even outside jail the
rogue warder would have been similarly rewarded for his
roguery. Such was the enormity of what he did. My classmate
was again tied to the whipping post and given twentyfour
lashes. He bore it standing up; he did not faint. His sentence
was increased to six years.

In jail the rogue warder was isolated. He was a marked man
among the inmates. He saw murder in each of their eyes. The
warder resigned, pleading that he had important work of his
own to attend to.

One hears the saying that people should stand united. In jail
the inmates were truly united. Although he was not allowed to
be taken outside to break stones, all the business in the jail was
still organised by my classmate.

And so I lived happily and in comfort. I had all the essential
things in my room. Most people knew that. Often the Assistant
Jailor would come to my lockup. A fair-looking, pleasant
young man in khaki shirt and pants and hat. The convicts
called him Brother Jailor! He did not visit me to inspect the
lockup. He came to chat. He had a small Alsatian dog. It was
called Joker. We talked about its training, exercise, food. I told
him a number of dog stories. Brother Jailor listened to them
with great interest. I made black tea for him. Most people knew
that I had tea and sugar with me. Sometimes a condemned
man who was to be hanged at five in the morning might want
some tea at night. The warder would wake me up and inform
me. I would make some black tea and send it to him. I would
send word to him to be brave. I would say that death could be
faced in two ways; weeping or smiling. Either way one would
die. So it was better to face death with a smile!

I would keep awake on such days. I would go to sleep only

after five. As I dozed off one of the political leaders would come and wake me up; not with any intention to annoy me. They could not have known that I had been keeping vigil over death.

There would be laughter and discussion then, a little township in itself. Arguments, noise, laughter, hubbub. Sometimes the Jail Superintendent came with Brother Jailor. They talked with the political leaders and came to my garden. I am fond of trees and shrubs; I love every single tree and shrub. I have even felt that trees and shrubs understand what I say to them. The Jail Superintendent also felt the same way. We would talk about trees and plants; about tending and manuring them. We would pace up and down talking of these things. In his house the Suprintendent had six big potted rose plants. I had presented him with those. Some of my friends among the 'red caps' did not like my fraternising with the Superintendent. Can't one live here without his favours? Why should one talk and smile and make up to him? Was he not the person who increased the number of lashes at the whipping post to two dozen? Brother Jailor was an infinitely better person!

Do you see the way things are? One has to join one group or another. It is not possible to be impartial and love everyone just as a man!

I generally spent most of my time in my room. Or I would stand and talk to my trees and shrubs. On one such occasion Brother Jailor came and told me that the political prisoners were going to be released!

Everyone was happy. There was laughter and shouting and whistling. Brother Jailor brought out everyone's clothes. The clothes were washed, ironed and put in separate packets. Everyone had haircuts and clean shaves. Along with them I too had my hair cut, whatever there was of it.

We all got ready to leave.

I bade farewell to my jail friends. I said I would write to them. I promised all of them I would send them my books.

And so we waited for the time of departure.

The release orders came.

We were released!

All except one—there were no orders to release this humble writer. It had to be a mistake! Brother Jailor ran to the Jail Suprintendent. He was made to put through a special telephone call for me. The information was correct. I was not to be released. All right. Perhaps I had not been reformed enough.

The political leaders took leave. Eno's Fruit Salt, Karl Marx's *Capital*, two packets of playing cards, a small bottle full of lime pickles, a large tin of banana wafers, a packet of banana candy, ground flakes of raw tobacco, betel leaves, areca nuts, lime —I became the sole surviving heir to all these.

The political leaders left smiling. Everything became silent. All was still; as if I was all alone in that deserted city. When all the sheep were let out to graze, the fattest one had been kept back and tied up. Why? For the butcher's knife obviously. I had a premonition of impending calamity. I could not laugh. I did not feel happy. I felt inert and listless. It was as if my mind experienced neither light nor darkness. I presented Brother Jailor with Karl Marx's *Capital*. I arranged for the banana candy to be distributed among friends in the hospital. I made a special present of the two packets of cards to my classmate. I gave away the betel leaves and nuts to my disciple who brought me my kanji. I distributed the banana wafers among everyone. The balance of half a tin of wafers, the jar of lime pickles and Eno's Fruit Salt remained with me in the lockup. After two days I threw away the Eno's over the jail wall. I lived on.

As I said my heart felt dead within me. What was going to happen to me? We can advise others. One can say face things with courage; with laughter not tears. So it is better to face reality with laughter!

O God, I cannot laugh. I am a very, very small and insignificant human being. A poor little creature. Save me. What am I to do?

Escape! I decided to escape. Between me and the outer world there were two walls. I must tunnel out of one wall and climb over the other. The warder would be sleeping at night.

Let there come a wild night of rain and thunder and lightning.

This was my plan of escape. The walls of my lockup are not very thick. I have tools to tunnel through it. And so I can get out. After this there is the old high wall of the jail itself. It is made of bricks. There is mortar between the bricks. I would acquire some ten or twelve big nails. I would hammer the nails in with the help of granite pieces covered with cloth. And thus I could reach the top of the wall. Then I could make a rope of my blanket, bedspread, dhoti and towel, tie the rope to the nails securely and climb over to the other side to freedom. The plan is sound. I need nails. In a corner of the jail wall any number of buckets used in the latrines lie rusting. The rounded handles of the buckets are there in a heap, almost all in fairly good condition. I picked them all up and straightened them out and kept them as nails. There were about thirty of them. I waited.

Let it come; a wild night of rain and thunder and lightning.

There came such a day.

Some red-capped friends and disciples came along with a warder. They want to make a vegetable garden beside the wall of the women's jail. Would I go?

No; I have no interest in anything. The warmth and the brightness have gone out of life. You go your way. Who wants vegetables anyway? I am waiting for a night of mighty storms and thunder. Don't bother me.

But they wouldn't let me alone. Why do you stay away like a hermit?

I went and helped them. We laid out a garden. A friend showed me something. Below the level of the reddish-looking wall there was a round cement patch looking like a pappad.

In the past it had been a proper hole. It had been the product of the hard toil of many, many loving hands spread over countless hours and days and months.

Imagine! It stayed like that. For days, months, years it stood like that. The inmates of the jail turned obedient, decent.

Through the hole the women could look into the men's jail and the men could look into the women's jail and they could thus see each other....

The smell of woman spread to the men's jail through it. The smell of man spread through it to the women's jail.

This was not a very closely guarded secret. But no one saw, no one heard. It was allowed to pass without comment. One can get on a stage at this spot and make mighty speeches about morality and culture.

But O great soul full of all good qualities! We are human. We have many weaknesses. Show us mercy. Look upon us with divine mercy!

But the rogue warder saw a business opportunity there. He demanded a fee for looking through the hole. An anna or six paise per head.

There are both rich and poor here. What would the poor man do?

My classmate told him, 'Warder, this is not right!'

'Then I will block this hole,' The rogue warder threatened. But he didn't stop there. He actually had it blocked with cement. The cement had not been kneaded with the blood of men and women. But still I bent my head and smelt that cement patch. Did it exude the smell of woman?

That was the reason my classmate received four and a half years of extra time and thirtysix whiplashes. We prepared the vegetable garden with alacrity. But my side of the jail was deserted. There was only me and a sleepy warder.

In the morning people come to water the vegetable garden under the escort of a special warder. I would just walk about. As if I were strolling through the empty streets of a vast ruined city.

The place was dull. There was silence everywhere. As I walked I would stop suddenly. Could the silence thicken and become any heavier? I would whistle to myself. I would talk with the trees and the plants. There were quite a number of squirrels there. I decided to catch one. I would chase one up a tree. Then I would pelt it with stones to bring it down.

And then one day as I walked beside the wall of the women's jail whistling there came a divine call! The most beautiful voice in the world; from across the wall. A question was heard from the women's jail. 'Who is whistling there?'

It was not from the men's jail. I was thrilled. I looked to the left and right. Then I said, 'It's me.'

One had to talk a little loud. She was on the other side of the wall. I was on this side.

She asked,'What's your name?'

I told her that I was a Muslim, that my name was Basheer and that I was a writer. I also described the nature of my offence and my period of imprisonment. She in her turn told me everything about herself.

She was a Hindu, with the beautiful name of Narayani.

Her age was a desirable twentytwo.

She knew how to read and write and had a little education. Her term was fourteen years. She had been here for one year.

I said, 'Narayani, both of us came to the jail about the same time!'

'Is that so?'There was silence for some time. Then Narayani asked, 'Will you give me a rose plant?'

I asked, 'Narayani, how did you know there are rose plants here?'

Narayani said, 'Isn't this supposed to be a jail? Everyone knows. There are no secrets here. Will you give it to me?'

Do you hear what she says? There are no secrets! What do I know about the women's jail? What do I know about the women there?

Narayani asked again, 'Won't you give me a rose plant?'

'Narayani!' I shouted loud enough to uproot my heart. 'I will give Narayani all the rose plants that grow in this garden called earth!'

Narayani laughed. It was as if thousands of golden bells were tinkling. My heart scattered in hundreds of little pieces.

'One is enough. Just one. Can I have it?'

Do you hear that? Would I give her one? What was I to do with Narayani? One should hold her in a close embrace and smother her with kisses. But what else!

'Narayani,' I shouted. 'Stay there. I'll bring one now. Did you hear me?'

Narayani said, 'I heard you.'

I ran. When the squirrels saw me they scuttled up the trees.

I said, 'Why are you running up the trees, you little blighters? Get down and play around here.'

I ran into the rose garden. How wonderful! The flowers stood bathed in the sunlight in full bloom with new-found smiles!

I picked the most beautiful plant with the most branches. I dug it up keeping the earth round the roots and wrapped up the roots and earth in a secure gunny packing. I bound together the leaves and branches. I ran back to the wall.

'Narayani!' I called. No one answered back. Had she gone?

'Narayani!' I called again. There was laughter. Then, 'Yes!'

I asked, 'Where were you when I called you?'

'I was here.'

'Well?'

'I had hidden myself in silence.'

'You sly girl!'

She laughed. She asked, 'Did you bring the rose plant?'

I was silent; because I was busy kissing. I was kissing every rose flower and bud and leaf.

Narayani called my name. ·

I was silent.

I kept on kissing; I kissed each branch and shoot and thorn. Narayani called me again anxiously.

I answered.

Then Narayani said with a trace of annoyance, 'If only I had called on God with the same love!'

I said, 'If you had called on God...?'

There was a sulk in her voice. 'I said, if only I had called on God with the same love!'

'If you had called on God with the same love...?'

She said, 'God would have appeared before me!'

I said, 'Didn't I appear before you?'

'Why didn't you answer when I called you?'

'I was busy kissing.'

'The walls?'

'No!'

'What then?'

'Every flower, every twig, every leaf.'

'Oh God, I feel like crying.'

'Narayani!'

'Yes.'

'Don't untie the knot below. Dig a hole in the ground and plant this with the name of God on your lips. Then fill up the hole with earth and water it. Understand?'

'I understand.'

I said, 'Then here it comes!'

I held the plant by the tied-up branches, swung it and threw it over the wall.

'Did you get it?'

'My God!' Narayani exclaimed with the happiness of having won a kingdom. 'I've got it!'

'You must untie the knots holding the branches.'

'I will,' she said.

'I'm going to pluck the flowers and keep them!'

'Keep them where? Put them in your hair?'

'No.'

'Where then?'

'In my heart...under my blouse!'

They were full of my kisses. I leaned against the wall; I caressed it.

Narayani said, 'Let me plant it and water it. You must always look at the top of the wall. I will hold up a dried twig over it when I come. Will you come when you see it?'

I said, 'I shall come.'

I heard something like a sob. 'My God!'

'What is it, Narayani?'

Narayani said, 'I feel like weeping!'

I asked, 'Why?'

Narayani said half sobbing, 'I – I don't know!'

I said, 'Narayani, go and plant it.'

'I'll hold up a dried twig!'

I said, 'I shall watch out for it.'

'Will you come when you see it?'

'I will.'

I went to my lockup. It was a dirty mess! I shook the

mattress and made up the bed after a long time. I restored some order and charm to my prison. Then I sat down and looked up at the sky above the wall. I could see no dry twig rising. God, had Narayani forgotten me?

There was no dry twig rising above the wall. And so I thought that—Heavens, what a sight!

A dry twig reared up into the sky! I kept still. The twig rose again; I did not move. The twig rose again. I stirred myself. I ran, leaped across to the wall. Numerous squirrels scrambled up the trees in mortal fear and twittered at me in protest.

I called, 'Narayani!'

There was silence from across the wall. I called again. Finally she answered angrily, 'What's it? What do you want?'

'Oh!'

Narayani said, 'Go on! My arms are almost pulled out of their sockets holding up that twig.'

'I'll massage them into shape.'

'Here's one arm. Massage it into proper shape. I have kept it close to the wall.'

'I am massaging this wall. I'm kissing it too.'

'I've pressed my breast close to the wall. I am now kissing the bricks!'

I asked, 'Narayani, how many women are you there?'

Narayani laughed. She said, 'Just me.'

'You little liar! Tell me the truth. How many are you?

'Quite a number of us. All old hags!'

'How many?'

'Eightyseven.'

'How many beautiful girls? How many old ones?'

Narayani said, 'One beauty and eightysix hags!'

I admitted defeat. I asked, 'Don't you have rose plants in your jail?'

'No!' Narayani said, 'There's nothing.... I...are you listening?'

I said, 'I'm listening.'

'Tomorrow...I'll make fried bajra powder. I'll put it in a bag and throw it over to you. You must eat it with jaggery. Will you eat it?'

'I'll eat it.'

'No!' Narayani seemed convinced. 'You'll throw it away.'

'Will I?' I said, 'I'll not waste even a bit.'

Narayani asked, 'What does your face look like?'

'Fair, slightly long. My hair is cropped...balding.'

'...eyes?'

I said,'They are rather like small elephant's eyes.'

Narayani said, 'Mine...mine are large elephant's eyes! Your chest...?'

'It's flat and broad.'

'My breasts are also broad. Your waist...?'

'My waist is narrow, tapering.'

'Do you know what my waist looks like...you wouldn't understand!'

I said, 'Wide like a barrel.'

Narayani let out a stifled yell. She said, 'I would like to tear you to pieces!'

'Narayani.'

'Y – yes.'

'What colour are you?'

'Where?'

'...the colour of your beautiful face.'

'Very fair.'

I called out, 'Narayani!'

'Yes!'

'The smell of woman!.... I smelled it!'

'Now? My God!'

I said, 'Not now. When I entered the jail and came this way!'

'Where did it come from? Could it be mine?'

'I don't know.'

'The smell of a man's body...how would yours smell?'

I said, 'I don't know. Narayani...the smell of your body!'

I swelled my nostrils and inhaled strongly.

'Does it come through?'

I said, 'No!'

Narayani said, 'I can't smell either. This blasted wall!'

I asked, 'Narayani. This wall had a hole once. Have you seen it?'

Narayani said, 'I've seen the place where it has been blocked with cement. I have touched it also. It was blocked before I came here.'

I said, 'I have smelt that part.'

Narayani said, 'A prisoner beat up the warder who blocked it up. He was tied to a whipping post and flogged. Each lash was counted with pain by the women prisoners.'

'He was given thirtysix lashes after being tied to the whipping post. The men also counted them painfully.'

Narayani said, 'What a tragedy!'

I said, 'The man who was flogged was my classmate. We come from the same place.'

'Is that so?'

'It's true.'

And so it was sent across, a round white bag of fried powdered bajra. And fried chillies powdered and mixed with salt were also sent across. Lime pickles were sent in return . followed by a whole tin of banana chips.

Narayani asked, 'The banana chips...may I...may I give everyone a piece?'

I replied, 'Give it to everyone.'

Narayani asked, 'Will you...will you...still love me...me alone?'

'Why do you doubt it, Narayani?'

'Here,' Narayani said, 'there are more beautiful women. I am not much of a beauty.'

I said, 'Nor am I handsome.'

She said, 'I want to see you.'

I said, 'I want to see you too.'

She said, 'Oh my God.... I'll lie weeping all of tonight.'

There came a wild night of wind and rain and thunder. I sit in the barred cage steeped in light. Rain falls like crystal rods. Drops of water are scattered like gravel. By God's mercy, let it rain. O wild wind, blow like a hurricane. But don't uproot any trees. O thunder roar softly, softly. Your deafening peals will frighten the poor women! So be soft, soft.

The day broke. The warder came and put out the light and opened the door. I went outside. A world washed and clean. By that time I came to the conclusion that it may not be such a good thing to escape from the jail. After all the trouble taken to get out, what is one to do?

There would be many more nights of wind and rain and thunder. But it was unethical! I deliberately forgot the place where I had kept those big nails. In short, I made up my mind it was wrong to jump jail.

The wall could not turn into flesh and blood. But I began to wonder if it had not acquired a soul. The wall had seen many things; heard many things.

Smoked fish, fried liver, eggs, bread and many other things went over the wall to the other side.

One day when I looked up there was a big squirrel sitting on top of the wall. He was looking at me.

I said, 'Get away, you sly rogue. Aren't you ashamed of yourself?'

Narayani asked, 'Whom are you scolding?'

I said, 'That squirrel. He's sitting on the wall and listening to us.'

'Let him be,' Narayani said.

'He has come to mock at me. I have driven him away—him and his family.'

I threw some gravel. The squirrel ran away.

Narayani said in protest, 'Look...a pebble fell on my breast!'

'Did it hurt?'

'How can we meet?'

'I can see no way.'

'I will think of you tonight and weep.'

I too thought of her that night.

Many days and nights went by thus.

'I'll try and come to the hospital,' Narayani said one day. 'Is it possible...can you come to the hospital? It's enough if I see you at least from a distance.'

I told her, 'I'll come running and hold you and kiss you. On the face, on the neck, on your breasts, on your belly.'

She asked, 'How will you recognise me?'

I replied, 'When I see your face, I'll know.'

Narayani said, 'There's a black mole on my right cheek. Will you look for it?'

'I would like to kiss that black mole!'

'Don't fail me. There'll be other women with me.'

I said, 'I'll come alone. There'll be no cap on my head ; I'm a little bald and I'll have a rose in my hand.'

'I'll look for it.'

'The hospital orderly is an old friend of mine.'

'I guessed as much.'

'How did you know?'

'The way you sent eggs, liver, bread.... Will you think of me when I die?'

'Do you want more rose plants ? There's plenty here.'

'No. I have made a rose garden with what you gave me. Will you think of me when I am dead?'

'My dear Narayani! It's impossible to say anything of death. Who will die, when and how—God alone can give the answer. I may be the one to die first.'

'No. It'll be me. Will you think of me then?'

'I will.'

Narayani asked, 'How? My God, how will you think of me? You have not even seen me. You have never touched me. How will you think of me?'

'Your mark is everywhere in this wide world!'

Narayani asked with sorrow in her voice, 'Everywhere in this world? Why do you flatter me?'

I said, 'Narayani, it's not flattery. It is the simple truth...oh, walls...walls!'

'I'm going to pluck the flowers and keep them!'

I stood looking at the wall. There was silence on the other side.

After some time Narayani said, 'I want terribly to cry.'

I said, 'No. Do that in the night.'

Narayani said, 'I'll tell you tomorrow when we can meet in the hospital.'

We parted full of excitement. The night came. The lights were put on. The warder came. The lights went off. The door was opened. I went out. Brushing my teeth, exercises, bath—I finished all these quickly.

I bolted my food. I lit a beedi from the chakki; I sat there enjoying the smoke. Brother Jailor dropped in for a chat. Just then, up came a dry twig above the wall in the blue sky. I sweated. I was sitting on pins. At last Brother Jailor went away!

I ran.

'Narayani.'

'Yes.'

'When is it to be?'

Narayani said, 'Today's Monday. On Thursday at eleven in the morning I'll be at the hospital. I have a black mole on the right cheek. Don't forget.'

'I'll remember. I shall hold a rose in my hand.'

'I'll remember.'

Monday, Tuesday, Wednesday—I ate my lunch and dozed off. I woke up and had a bath. As I sat there, Brother Jailor came laughing into my rose garden, picked a few roses, came into the lockup and sat on my bed.

'Do you want some flowers?' Brother Jailor asked me.

I wanted to laugh! I said, 'I am the garden. And the flower.'

'Not the fruit?'

'The fruit also!'

As I looked I could see a dry twig rising over the wall into the blue sky.

Brother Jailor said, 'I have never seen you in your ordinary clothes.'

I said, 'A jibba and dhoti!'

Brother Jailor untied the bundle in which my clothes were kept washed and ironed.

I said, 'They'll get dirty!'

'Please wear these. I just want to see you in them.'

I said, 'They'll get dirty!'

'What if they do? Couldn't we get them washed again?'

'Very well.' I wore my dhoti. I put on the jibba.

'How does it look?' I asked.

'Fine!' Brother Jailor said. 'You can leave Mr Basheer;you are free!'

I was stunned. My eyes went blind. My ears went deaf. I felt a tingling sensation all over. I felt I couldn't understand anything. I asked, 'Why should I be free?...who wants freedom?'

Brother Jailor laughed. He explained, 'Your release has been ordered. You are a free man from this moment. You can go!'

A free man! Who wants freedom?

Brother Jailor said, 'You can collect the money to get back home and go. Have you anything to take with you?'

He rolled up my mattress. Under it were some stories I had written. He folded them and put them into my pocket. He led me by the hand outside the lockup. I went and stood in my rose garden. I plucked a flower and held it in my hands as if in a dream.

Over the wall the dry twig rose into the blue sky.

Brother Jailor closed the door of the lockup.

Very well. Narayani, my good wishes to you.

With the money to get me home, I left through the big gate of the jail into the free wide world.

The enormous jail gate clanged shut with a mighty crash behind me.

I gazed at the rose in my hand and stood on the highway for a long, long time.

Original title 'Mathilukal'; published as a novelette in 1965.

The Snake and the Mirror

'Has a snake ever coiled itself round any part of your body? A full-blooded cobra?' All of us fell silent. The question came from the homeopath. The topic came up when we were discussing snakes. We listened attentively as the doctor continued with his tale.

'It was a hot summer night; about ten o'clock. I had my meal at the restaurant and returned to my room. I heard a whirring noise from above as I opened the door. The sound was a familiar one to me. One could say that the rats and I shared the room. I took out my box of matches and lighted the kerosene lamp on the table.

The house was not electrified; it was a small rented room. I had just set up medical practice and my earnings were meagre. I had about sixty rupees in my suitcase. Along with some shirts and dhotis, I also possessed one solitary black coat which I was then wearing.

I took off my black coat, white shirt and not-so-white vest and hung them up. I opened the two windows in the room. It was an outer room with one wall facing the open yard. It had a tiled roof with long supporting gables that rested on the beam over the wall. There was no ceiling. There was a regular traffic of rats to and from the beam. I made my bed and pulled it close to the wall. I lay down but I could not sleep. I got up and went out to the veranda for a little air, but the Wind God seemed to have taken time off.

I went back into the room and sat down on the chair. I opened the box beneath the table and took out a book, the *Materia Medica*. I opened it at the table on which stood the lamp and a large mirror; a small comb lay beside the mirror.

One feels tempted to look into a mirror when it is near one. I took a look. In those days I was a great admirer of beauty and I believed in making myself look handsome. I was unmarried and I was a doctor. I felt I had to make my presence felt. I picked up the comb and ran it through my hair and adjusted the parting so that it looked straight and neat.

Again I heard that whirring sound from above.

I took a close look at my face in the mirror. I made an important decision—I would shave daily and grow a thin moustache to look more handsome. I was after all a bachelor, and a doctor!

I looked into the mirror and smiled. It was an attractive smile. I made another earth-shaking decision. I would always keep that attractive smile on my face...to look more handsome. I was after all a bachelor, and a doctor too on top of it!

Again came that whirring noise from above.

I got up, lit a beedi and paced up and down the room. Then another lovely thought struck me. I would marry. I would get married to a woman doctor who had plenty of money and a good medical practice. She had to be fat; for a valid reason. If I made some silly mistake and needed to run away she should not be able to run after me and catch me!

With such thoughts in my mind I resumed my seat in the chair in front of the table. There were no more whirring sounds from above. Suddenly there came a dull thud as if a rubber tube had fallen to the ground... surely nothing to worry about. Even so I thought I would turn around and take a look. No sooner had I turned than a fat snake wriggled over the back of the chair and landed on my shoulder. The snake's landing on me and my turning were simultaneous.

I didn't jump. I didn't tremble. I didn't cry out. There was no time to do any such thing. The snake slithered along my shoulder and coiled around my left arm above the elbow. The hood was spread out and its head was hardly three or four inches from my face!

It would not be correct to say merely that I sat there holding my breath. I was turned to stone. But my mind was very active. The door opened into darkness. The room was surrounded by darkness. In the light of the lamp I sat there like a stone image in the flesh, on the chair and in the reflection in the mirror.

I felt then the great presence of the creator of this world and this universe. God was there. Suppose I said something and he did not like it.... I tried in my imagination to write in bright letters outside my little heart the words, 'O God.'

There was some pain in my left arm. It was as if a thick leaden rod...no, a rod made of molten fire...was slowly but powerfully crushing my arm. The arm was beginning to be drained of all strength. What could I do?

At my slightest movement the snake would strike me! Death lurked four inches away. Suppose it struck, what was the medicine I had to take? There were no medicines in the room. I was but a poor, foolish and stupid doctor.... I forgot my danger and smiled feebly at myself.

It seemed as if God appreciated that. The snake turned its head. It looked into the mirror; and saw its reflection. I do not claim that it was the first snake that had ever looked into a mirror. But it was certain that the snake was looking into the mirror. Was it admiring its own beauty? Was it trying to make an important decision about growing a moustache or using eye shadow and mascara or wearing a vermilion spot on its forehead?

I did not know anything for certain. What sex was this snake, was it male or female? I will never know; for the snake unwound itself from my arm and slowly slithered into my lap. From there it crept onto the table and moved towards the mirror. Perhaps it wanted to enjoy its reflection at closer quarters.

I was no mere image cut in granite. I was suddenly a man of flesh and blood. Still holding my breath I got up from the chair. I quietly went out through the door into the veranda. From there I leapt into the yard and ran for all I was worth.'

'Phew!' Each of us heaved a sigh of relief. All of us lit beedies. Somebody asked, 'Doctor, is your wife very fat?'

'No,' the doctor·said. 'God willed otherwise. My life companion is a thin reedy person with the gift of swift-footedness.'

Someone else asked, 'Doctor, when you ran did the snake follow you?'

The doctor replied, 'I ran and ran till I reached a friend's house. Immediately I smeared oil all over myself and took a bath. I changed into fresh clothes. The next morning at about eight-thirty I took my friend and one or two others to my room to move my things from there. But we found we had little to carry. Some thief had removed most of my things. The room had been cleaned out! But not really, the thief had left behind one thing as a final insult!'

'What was that?' I asked.

The doctor said, 'My vest. The dirty one. The fellow had such a sense of cleanliness...! The rascal could have taken it and used it after a rinse in soap and water.'

'Did you see the snake the next day doctor?'

The doctor laughed, 'I've never seen it since. It was a snake which was taken with its own beauty!'

Original title 'Pambum Kannadiyum'; from the collection Oru Bhagavathgeethayum Kure Mulakalum *(1967).*

The Gold Ring

One day the wife took out an old gold ring from her steel
trunk, put it on her finger appraisingly and asked me,
   'Doesn't it look lovely?'
   I asked, 'Where did you get that ancient-looking toy from?'
   'It's pure gold,' the wife said. 'It was given by a Raja to my
mother's mother's mother's mother. '
   I was indignant.
   'Woman, how can you dare to wear it?' I continued, 'By
rights, it's I who should wear this gold ring. You know if I trace
things back several generations, I'd land in Emperor Akbar's
lap. I'm the heir to this gold ring. Those are the facts of history.
Now give it to me. Let me wear it and show it off.'
   'What a hope!' said the wife. 'If you're that anxious, I may
give it you to wear once in a way.'
   'Who wants your charity.'
   'I see. In that case, not at all.' The wife sounded determined.
'I'll not allow anyone to touch this gold ring.'
   'Oh really.'
   'Oh *yes*.'
   'You woman, I'll show you.' I twirled my moustache.
   Dear God. The wife was pregnant. It was a golden
opportunity for the ring to flash on the finger of your humble
servant. The pregnancy was going well. I asked the wife,
'Woman, that child in your womb, is it a boy or a girl?'
   She smiled and asked, 'What do you think?'

I said, 'A boy!'

The wife said, 'But then it's a girl!'

'Do you want to bet?'

The wife said, 'Fifty rupees!'

"Agreed.' I worked it out. 'If it's a boy you must give me the ring on your finger.' The wife looked at the ring and said, 'This must cost at least two hundred rupees. Isn't the gold old? A Raja's ring!'

'True it's a Raja's,' I said. 'Even so, it's old. What will the Raja's footwear be valued at now? What will your old blouse fetch?'

She looked at her ring without much enthusiasm.

I said, 'You won't get ten rupees if you sell this ring for weight. After all, I'm your husband. It's my duty to show you some consideration. That's a man's moral duty. And so I'm prepared to take it for fifty rupees!'

The wife thought for a while and said, 'Oh all right.... If it's a girl, you have to give me fifty rupees.'

I said, 'If it's a boy, what I get is a rusty old ring! Woman, shake hands on that.'

The wife and I shook hands to seal the contract.

As time passed I became anxious. If it turned out to be a girl I'd lose fifty rupees. Was there some way I could escape this? As I thought about it, those five young men came to mind; three were Nayars and two were Thiyyas. They called me Guru. (Currently we are not on talking terms. These days I've lost faith in Hindus. I've made it clear that they need not call me Guru any more.) What happened was that the three Nayars and the two Thiyyas had each taken a ten-rupee bet. The bet was that it was a girl the wife was expecting. I had bet that it was a boy. We shook hands over the contract. Then one of the Hindus said, 'There should be a law against all this. Does the stupid government think of these things? A Muslim can have ten to three hundred wives. The poor Hindu—only one!'

I said, 'I have only one in my custody.'

Another of them, the fat one, said, 'You can marry some more. The Nizam is your kinsman isn't he? He has three hundred.'

'That's true. A sweet prospect. I shall devote serious thought to the matter.'

'Go on with your serious thought,' said Fatty. 'We have our vital veins cut and carry around uterine loops. We've nothing much to look forward to. And here are these Muslims walking in and out of houses taking bets on the outcomes of pregnancies!'

I asked, 'Who asked you to marry at a young age? Couldn't you have waited till you were as old as I was? Besides, why didn't you take bets on the right occassions?'

'Why, that's true!' The Hindus talked among themselves. 'We didn't think of it. We lost a golden opportunity.'

After that I wasn't allowed a moment to myself. I would be deep in pleasant thought, and the Hindus would come and ask, 'Has the baby come? It's a girl, isn't it?'

I would say, 'Hindus have no cause to worry over the matter. The wife is going to give birth to a golden boy! And you Hindus will be the poorer by fifty rupees!'

As days and nights passed in this way, I woke up early one lovely morning with a start. There is a cry from the wife in the next room, a moan... some groaning.

Good!

I said, 'Smile, woman, smile! You're about to see something great. Smile, don't cry.'

The wife was happy that I had been listening. She began to cry out loud.

I said, 'Quiet! What is so great about all this? Millions, literally millions of woman have had babies. These are birth pangs and spasms and we men have clear notions about them. Quiet now. Pay attention to what's happening.'

There were no signs of movement for a while. Then the spasms came in a collective torrent. There were agonised cries in the course of which several saints were called to assist. I called out, 'Listen, if you're calling out to saints, call out the name of "Allama Basheer". Basheer the scholar. No harm will come of it. Now hurry up!'

By now the noise had subsided, it was just muted grunts and moans. Just then the midwife came in, a good-looking woman. She wasn't married and had never given birth to a child. I knew this but all the same I was about to ask her if she would like to bet five rupees with me. As if sensing it she looked angrily at me and asked, 'Will you just shut up? Don't say things to make her laugh. What do you ignorant men know about labour pains.'

After her stern warning, the woman went back hurriedly. I thought I should celebrate her departure by lighting a cigarette, which I did and puffed out a mouthful of smoke. There was a lurking anxiety in my mind. Would it be a boy...a girl? Nonsense, what did it matter. It was enough if it was a safe birth. Which meant I had abandoned all thoughts of monetary loss or gain. As if in answer to the thought I heard the comforting cry of a baby.

I rushed to the door. It was shut and bolted. I roared, 'Let me in!'

The baby answered with another cry! The midwife put out a bulletin condemning all men.

Then, after a while, the door opened. A golden baby. The midwife brought it to me holding it by the legs, head down. I took the baby, held it right side up, gave it a kiss and went to the wife. She lay there bathed in sweat, tired. Her eyes were still half-shut. I laid the baby gently beside her and with equal gentleness eased out the ring from her finger. Thereafter, I gave the wife a gratuitous kiss.

'Woman, I'm happy. Congratulations!' And with that I left the room. I broke off a bit of lime mortar from the wall and polished the ring with it. Then I put it on my finger.

I said to myself, 'Salutations! O King!' I brushed my teeth, shaved and had a bath. I changed into clean clothes, drank some coffee, lit a cigarette and set out in search of the Hindus. I found them and told them the facts. 'The baby has come.'

I looked at the Hindus with a stern and unflinching eye. Not just that. I gave out a full throated victorious laugh. The Hindus looked a little crushed. I said, 'Haven't Hindus and Muslims taken bets with each other from the dawn of history. Who won those bets? The Muslims. Now let's have that money.'

They were quite speechless. Then they gave me fifty rupees. I showed them the ring.

'Look, a royal ring. Pure gold. It belonged to Maharaja Vikramaditya. No, Emperor Ashoka. I mean, it was Haroun-al-Rashid.'   ·

'Where did you get it?' the Hindus asked.

'A family heirloom.'

'Indeed!' said one of them. 'As if we don't know the family. The brigand Kayamkulam Kochunni or the cat burglar Cheeppavaran must have stolen it from some Hindu.'

I bought some tea and refreshments for the Hindus from whom I had taken the money. I also gave them each a Gold Flake cigarette. Now the Hindus wanted to buy tickets in a lottery. The first prize was a beautiful car. I agreed it was a good thing to get a car for a rupee. Each of them bought two or three tickets. They persuaded me to take a ticket in the name of the baby. In their presence I bought bananas, tomatoes, sweet lime, apples, a pineapple, oranges, dates, halwa and along with it a tiny dhoti with a gold border. As ripe mangoes were not available, I bought some sour ones. Then I engaged a porter to carry the things.

I said goodbye to the Hindus challengingly. 'Are there any Hindus prepared to take a bet on the next occasion?' When I reached home both the wife and the baby had been given baths and they had moved to a larger room.

I dragged a large table near the wife's bed and spread out the fruits on it. The wife did not utter a word. I wrapped the gold bordered cloth round the baby. The wife gently removed it, crumpled it and threw it away with a fierce look at me. She lay there with an angry look on her face, as if I had committed a grievous fault. I could not understand this.

'Woman, what do you want now?' I asked. 'Do you want me to get the parijata flower from paradise? If you do, I"ll get you one or two.'

The wife said, 'I must get my gold ring! And fifty rupees!'

I didn't understand, and said so. The wife looked at me. Then she asked in a low voice, 'The baby...our baby—is it a boy boy or a girl?'

'Quite certainly a girl!'

'Ha!' said the wife.

'*Oho!*' I said.

'What happened then?'

'I bought a tiny gold bordered dhoti and made the little girl wear it. We should cover her nudity you know. Decency demands it.'

'*Oho*, decency indeed! All decent men were born thus!'

'That's true.'

'Of course it's true,' the wife said. 'I must get my gold ring and fifty rupees.'

'Woman, now who won the bet? Before the baby came what was your song? Remember? The first darling one should be a boy, it must look like its father. Now when you sang that song what was mine in reply: the first darling must be a girl, she must be like her mother. The duet said that for you it was to be a boy, and for me it was to be a girl.'

'Some stupid duet!' the wife said. I said, 'Another argument. This labour pain is a terrible thing. It's a veritable earthquake, a hurricane of pain. Blinding lightning and thunder along with a heavy downpour. What happens then? In the midst of all that din a woman forgets many things. As you have. There haven't been any witnesses. We haven't put anything in writing. All this is the truth. You've misunderstood it all, that's why you say such things. Is that right for a good woman?'

That was the right approach. It was always good to ask one's wife about the ways a good woman should carry herself. Some doubts had certainly crept into the wife's mind. She raised her hand as if to make peace with me and get me to go. She felt the fruits on the table and took out a sour mango.

'I've been wanting to eat a sour mango for some time. I didn't tell you because it was not in season. Thank you for buying it without my asking.' Then the wife smelt the mango. 'This should be washed,' she said.

As the wife stretched out her hand to grasp the end of a piece of string, I told her, 'Don't eat a sour mango. If you must, ask your mother first. Eat something sweet now.'

The length of string which lay on the bed was a long one. At the other end of it was a sixty-year-old woman. She was sitting deep in thought in a corner of the store-room beyond the kitchen. She was quite deaf. But the wife and she could carry on a discussion about international problems. They'd discuss even Einstein's theories. As for me I didn't know how to say one word to the woman. I said, 'Ask her to take these away and keep them safe. And also to make some raw mango chutney.'

I gave the baby a kiss, and the wife as well, and came out feeling a little anxious about things. I climbed the mango tree in front of the house, sat down on a branch and looked out into the distance.

Were the five Hindus coming this way?

I was there for a while when the mishars, the little red ants, launched their attack. Mishars are the enemies of Muslims and their bite is painful. I got down, wiped them firmly off my body and went and stood in a corner of the compound. There was a scrub jungle there, rather wild but not tall enough to hide behind. Now what?

I went into hiding. I would walk only in the bylanes. When I walked in front of any of the Hindus' houses, I would stoop and hide behind my umbrella. I stayed indoors most of the time. I put a large padlock on the visitors' sitting room. There would be women coming to see the wife and the baby. The Hindus would hear of it all. I contemplated moving into the attic. But the wife would ask why. Was it possible the Hindus knew already? There was no reason why they should have heard. I consoled myself with the thought. One day I had given the baby a bath and was sitting with the wife. It was three in the afternoon. They were making snow-white pathiri, white rice chapatis, in the kitchen. I could smell the delicious mutton curry. Then there was the sound of the outer gate opening. What followed was not an outcry. It was as if five persons were shouting from five corners, 'Is the Guru in?'

It was the Hindus! They'd surrounded the house. What was I to do now?

I told the wife in a low voice, 'Woman, tell them I'm not here. Tell them President Nasser sent for me and that I've left for Egypt. No, just tell them I've gone to Trippunithara. No no, tell them I've gone to Madras.'

A voice came from outside, 'We're coming in. We want to see the mother and the baby.'

'Tell them they can't come in here, woman. Forbid them to come in!' But before I could say that the five fat Hindus entered the room where a respectable Muslim woman was lying on the bed with her new-born baby. Akbar, Hyder Ali, Shah Jehan... God in heaven, I was in a rage!

I looked dangerously at them. They ignored me altogether. One of them had a large bottle of natural honey. They gave it to the wife. She passed it on to me. I opened the bottle and put two ounces in my mouth to taste the stuff. It was good honey. I poured half an ounce into the wife's mouth and put two drops on the baby's tongue. Then I closed the bottle and put it on the table.

One of the Hindus took the infant in his hands. The others crowded round him. They looked at the child carefully, and then pronounced: 'That's right —a baby girl!'

I said nothing. The wife should have obeyed the husband. If only she had wrapped the lovely gold bordered cloth round the baby!

One of the Hindus asked, 'What have you named the little one?'

The wife said, 'Shahina. I think it means princess.'

'Shahina!' the Hindus said. 'Isn't she the daughter of a Badshah, a king. We give the child and the mother our blessings. May the two live long in health and prosperity!' There was a pause, a frosty one, before they added, 'And the father as well!'

From the table they chose five large bananas. They peeled them and started to eat them. I said, 'The Hindus are eating away a Muslim father's flesh slice by slice.'

The Hindus said nothing. They folded up the banana skins neatly, put them on the table and now turned to the apples. They took a rolled-up rush mat lying in the corner, spread it on the floor near the wall and sat down with their backs against it. Then they looked at me. One of the fat Hindus burst out laughing. Then he said to the others, 'Can he deceive my

Nanikutty. When she looked out the other day she saw a man bending over, hiding under an umbrella—that was a modern Muslim father in disguise.'   .

After a pause, the Hindus said in one voice, 'Hmm... it's a baby girl all right.'

There was sudden doubt on the wife's face; as if she had had a revelation. She asked, 'Was there any bet you took?'

The fattest among the Hindus, Nanikutty's husband, said, 'There was a small bet. If the baby was a girl, the Muslim father would give each of us Hindus ten rupees. If it turned out to be a boy, the poor Hindus would give the father fifty rupees!'

'And...?' the wife asked in a surprised voice. She had her eyes fixed on me.

Another fat Hindu said, 'This Muslim father gave us news of the birth of the child and then proceeded to collect fifty rupees from these poor Hindus. That's all!'

The wife was still staring at me. She asked, 'Did he tell you that a boy had been born?'

'Oh no, not at all' the Hindus said. 'It was in his face!'

'What do you mean?' said the wife. She now had some serious doubts.

Nanikutty's fat husband said, 'The Muslim father came to us and laughed loudly and gleefully, and then said the mother cow had calved. He also said that the Hindus had lost. And the Hindus gladly put down fifty rupees in the palm of the Muslim father.'

True the Hindu rogues had given me fifty rupees. But it wasn't with a smile. Why lie?

There was silence. Only the crunching sound of the apples being demolished by the Hindus; the apples belonging to the unfortunate Muslim father!

The wife pointed her finger at the gold ring flashing from my finger and asked, 'Do you see that ring?'

'The royal ring!' said the Hindus. 'Whose finger has it already adorned? Ashoka's? Akbar's? Haroun-al-Rashid's?'

'It was on my finger,' the wife said. 'The father of my mother's mother's mother's mother saved the king from his enemies. As a reward he was given many things including this ring. The moment he (indicating me) heard it, he said it was his by right, he was the true heir.'

'He's the Sultan, isn't he? What happened then?'

The wife said, 'We had a small bet between us. If I gave birth to a boy, I was to give him this ring. If it was a girl, he would give me fifty rupees. Soon after the baby came, when he pulled the ring off my finger, I smiled.'

'Liar!' I cried. 'You certainly didn't smile. You didn't even know. You were lying there tired and bathed in sweat.'

'Can't I smile in my mind?' asked the wife. I told the Hindus, 'Here's some advice free. Never argue with the likes of woman.'

'I see. Charming!' The Hindu with the buck teeth said, 'Let's all stretch ourselves.'

The five Hindus stretched themselves, half on the cement floor, half on the rush mat. I asked, 'What are your intentions?'

The Hindus said, 'Satyagraha! Fast unto death. We've a good stock of slogans. What is due to the Hindus must be given to the Hindus... what is due to the wife here must be given to the wife. *Inquilab Zindabad!*'

Just then Shahina whimpered. I said, 'Daughter, now don't be afraid.'

The Hindus suddenly sat up. Their nostrils twitched and they looked in the direction of the kitchen.

'Oh so there's meat being cooked. Very good! We hereby declare our fast postponed. We shall sit here until death removes us. A sit-down satyagraha!' One of the fat Hindus said, 'If we don't reach home by six-thirty this evening our wives and our fortyseven children will come for us. Then they too will stay here!'

The wife continued to look hard at me. I said, 'Did you hear that? The Hindus each on an average have nine and a quarter children and this stupid Muslim....'

'Marrying ten to three hundred women!'

The poor stupid Muslim said, 'O ye citizens of the world! This round earth came into being millions of years ago and remains the same. But humans multiply. Every day humankind multiples a thousandfold. There is no food to eat. They have no place to lay down their heads. Fields and forestland dwindle. There is scarcity all round. The Muslim saw all this and thought to himself that hereafter two children would suffice. Then the Hindus—'

'It was the Hindus who said this first!'

Another Hindu said, 'I think it was a Christian who said it first.'

I said, 'The truth is the truth, no matter who utters it. The Muslim certainly acted according to it. But the Hindus... did you hear that, woman...each has nine and more.'

The wife slowly stood up. The she looked hard at the Hindus. I said, 'Woman, your body is in a weak condition. You should not beat the Hindus or scratch them. You can always shower abuse on them in a low voice. I will amplify it by becoming your loudspeaker. Nine and odd children! *Foo!*'

One of the Hindus said to the wife, 'He is saying this to provoke dissensions among us. This elderly father has ideas of getting into many more marriage contracts. He's a Sultan, isn't he? And so a harem....'

'I'd like to see him marry them and bring them along!' the wife said. 'I'll stand at the gate with a giant pestle. I'll beat them to death one by one as they come in.'

'Is this the morality of women!' I said with surprise. 'In Sri Krishna's time the wielding of giant pestles was not prevalent.'

As I was saying this the wife was counting with her fingers. 'Tarukutty, Dakshu, Viswalakshmi, Lalita, Nanikutty. Out of them only Nanikutty has three children.'

At this point Fatty, Nanikutty's husband, said, 'How am I responsible for that? Nanikutty had twins the second time.'

'The Hindus can trot out many excuses,' I said. 'They can always bring forth twins at their convenience.'

The wife asked, 'Then where did we arrive at these thirty and thirtysix children?'

I said, 'Well those are the blackmarket children of the Hindus.'

'Blackmarket children?' The wife looked at the Hindus in surprise.

I did not want to give the Hindus time to explain that I meant their sisters' children. I told the wife, 'Woman, give that string one or two yanks. And tell the old hag to give each of the Hindus half a pathiri and some curry, a piece of meat for each of them. The dispute has been settled. We—that is to say I —have decided to give each of the Nayar Hindus five rupees and the Thiyyas four and a half!'

The wife said, 'Everyone will be served as much as they can eat of pathiri and meat curry. Tea as well!'

I said, 'That's right.'

And so everything was going to end happily. But would the Hindus allow that? Two of the Nayar Hindus laughed. One of them said, 'Great! So the lower caste gets half a rupee less. That's most fair!'

Nanikutty's fat husband, who was a Thiyya, became angry.

'Who's the low caste? This elderly Muslim father should give us Thiyyas a sum of forty rupees.'

Would the Nayar Hindus allow that? One of them said, 'In the old days murders have taken place for much less. This Muslim father has to give us Nayars sixty rupees! And by way of interest pathiri and meat to our heart's content.'

Would the wife stand for anything less? She said, 'My darling little Shahina's father has to give me a gold ring and fifty rupees.'

And in this way the wife and the Hindus won. Under the supervisory eye of the Hindus I gave the wife the gold ring and fifty rupees. As for the Hindus they got pathiri and meat curry and tea and cigarattes as well as a hundred rupees. The Hindus heaped accusations on me jointly and severally before they left.

The wife asked, 'Do you want the gold ring to wear, free?'

I said, 'No woman! You...you....'

The baby girl gurgled. 'Gunguru.'

I said, 'That's right, daughter!'

The wife asked, 'What's the little one saying?'

I said, 'That God exists.'

Can anyone be the loser when he has been blessed by God? One day I returned from town and asked the wife, 'Here's money, cash. How much do you want for that silly ring of yours?'

The wife said, 'A hundred and one rupees!'

'Right,' I said. 'Now then, with a smile and with faith in God, take off that ring. Here's the money!'

I counted out a hundred and one rupees from my pocket and gave it to her. The wife took off the ring and gave it to me. I put it on my finger.

'A gold ring. How stylish!'

I took out a bundle of rupee notes, lots of them, and showered them on the baby. The wife muttered in surprise, 'She'll wet them,' picked up the notes and counted them.

'Three hundred and sixtyfive. Where did you get them from?'

'Where? From God. I got a transistor radio from a lottery ticket taken in the daughter's name. The Hindus got nothing. We sold the radio for four hundred and seventyfive. We had tea and things to eat. Now woman, who has won?'

The wife said, 'I have.'

'You?' I asked as I strung the ring on a piece of sewing thread and swung it to and fro. 'O king, even your name has faded into the distant past. We pray for eternal peace for your soul. With your blessing, an insignificant person, me, is going to tie this round the neck of my daughter.'

I tied it round my daughter's neck. The ring flashed brilliantly from her chest.

The baby girl said, 'Gunguru!'

I said, 'Daughter Gunguru.... As time passes and I and my name merge into the infinite millenia of the past, a young woman will say...the father of my mother's mother's mother's mother tied this gold ring round her neck.'

Original title 'Thanka Mothiram', published in a collection Oru Bhagavathgeethayum Kure Mulakalum *(1967).*

Elephant Wool

This is the story of a theft. There was a huge elephant tusker which had killed two mahouts by trampling them underfoot— a hair from his tail was to be stolen. No one was to see it being done; neither my Bappa nor Umma, not even the mahouts. I was to try to bite off a strand of hair from his tail. There was not just one elephant but three of them. One tusker between two cow elephants. What I wanted was one hair from the tusker's tail; not for myself, but for Radhamani. She was the Excise Inspector's daughter and my classmate. She had given me a peacock feather to keep between the pages of my book. Oh yes, I had a nickname then—Elephant Wool. My schoolmates would ask me, 'Where are you off to, Elephant Wool?' Or else, 'Elephant Wool's sum has gone wrong, he got zero marks!' I used to call the elephant's tail elephant wool.

Elephant wool!

This incident happened ages ago. At the beginning of time, so it would seem. I was about eight or nine years old then. My brother Abdul Khader was a year younger than I was. He was the pet, the darling of the family. I had been born after prayers and offerings at many shrines; but even so I could not remain the pet for long. Abdul Khader was lame in one leg, so all sympathy was showered on him. He was a paragon of virtues who could do no wrong. I was answerable for all mischief. I had to receive punishment for things I did not do. But I was a stalwart in my own right. I was adept at swimming, diving, and climbing trees. I was great at whistling. I could emit shrill blasts with just two fingers or even one finger in my mouth.

Abdul Khader did not know these noble arts. But he was slightly better than I was at studies. He called me Elephant Wool.

In those days the first sight that greeted our eyes on waking up was elephants. My Bappa was a timber merchant. He would have trees in the Kadayathur hills cut and brought down the river in rafts. The elephants were required to haul these logs and stack them in the compound near our house. The elephants were tied up in another compound near the house. I would supervise the feeding of the elephants with coconut and palmyra palm fronds. That is to say, I would stand there and watch it being done as if I was the lord and master of the elephants! It was great fun to pick up big pieces of caked mud from the ground and break them with one throw against the bellies of the elephants. I however resisted the temptation to do it. I would watch out for any of my friends throwing caked mud at the elephants. Once I gave Owl Damu permission to do so. He threw a lump of mud at the belly of the tusker and gave me a small ripe mango in return.

Owl Damu was the same age as I. We studied in the same class. Owl Damu had round bulging eyes. His full name was Damodaran. His father Sankaran Kutty was my father's manager. Sankaran Kutty's mother Nangeli was our cook and my Umma's secretary. One day Owl Damu called me Elephant Wool. For that Nangeli chased him all over the place. I helped her to catch him and I held him while she beat him.

He asked, 'Then why do you call me Owl Damu?'

'I won't, from now on.'

'Then give me a ripe banana. Otherwise I'll tell the mahout that you threw a lump of mud at the elephant.'

'Wasn't it you who threw it?'

'Who gave permission after getting a lovely ripe mango from me?'

So I stole a few ripe bananas from home. I gave one to Owl Damu and one to Abdul Khader. I ate one and gave the rest to the mahouts.

I was an almost constant companion to the mahouts. I looked after their needs. They were all Hindus. These men who looked after the elephants and who made the huge beasts obey their commands were the supermen of the world. I respected, no, worshipped them. To be a mahout, that was my ambition. Their magic word of command 'Settiyana'; which came out through the nose, made the elephant move around at their wish. I learnt to say it through the nose with the slight echo—'Settiyana....' I polished the metal hook with which the mahouts used to pull the elephants by their large ears. I dusted their long staffs; their big spear was kept on the veranda of our house and I would not allow anyone to touch it. I got on very well with the mahouts. I would take from the house tender betel leaves, ripe areca nuts and the best tobacco, and give them to the mahouts to make their pan. I would listen with awe and reverence to their talk. Oh, to be a mahout!

Those were the days; how different they were! In those days the sun shone brighter. The moonlight was more enchanting. The flowers were more colourful and smelt sweeter. The birds twitted more musically. The water in the river was more limpid and it contained tastier fish. Oh, how we jumped and frolicked among the birds and the flowers! We, the eight year olds, were the life and soul of the world. The earth revolved around us. In our minds we ignored people older than us as being decrepit. Those younger than us were mere babies and those older just ineffective ancients. We considered boys who were sixteen years' old men. But there was one thing—we respected age.

Time was not very important in those days. Wristwatches were rare. Pocket watches were more common. My Bappa had a heavy gleaming pocket watch. Bappa could tell the time from it as if by magic. He liked people to ask him the time. He would then take the watch out of his watch pocket with a supercilious smile. It was not possible to tell the time immediately after the watch was taken out. One of its sides had to be snapped open first. Bappa would then tell the time. We wondered how it was done! Time, eternal and infinite, had been imprisoned in the machine called the watch. Who had done it? We had no idea. The old men had many things to say about it. We would listen to them, but we did not believe them. We dared not show contempt for them! So we were silent. The sun was our guide to time. The sun was our watch. We would measure our shadows and compute the time.

Although most of us did not have pocket watches, we did have watch pockets, concealed slit pockets beneath the breast pockets of our shirts. Abdul Khader and I had shirts with watch pockets. We also had caps. We went to the Malayalam School. One had to wear a coat and cap to go to the English School. The English School was some five or six miles away. The pupils of the English School would walk along with dignity, clad in coats and hats speaking English and we would gaze upon them in wonder. Abdul Khader and I learnt Arabic. We would also learn English, Bappa had promised us. After we passed the fourth standard in the Malayalam School we would attend the English School. We were told to study hard. Pudusseri Narayana Pilla 'Saar' taught us with great enthusiasm. He beat us sometimes. But even so we liked him. We respected him. There were no strikes in those days, no strikes either by students or by teachers. We had to maintain discipline or we would be punished. Insubordination was punished with beating. If that was not considered sufficient, the boys were asked to stand on the bench. The next step was sending the boy out of the class and making him stand outside the room. I have been told many a time both to stand on the bench and to stand outside the classroom.

In those days we had a subject for study called 'Loyalty'. The Maharaja ruled the State; our beloved ruler, the Maharaja of Travancore. There was also a Maharaja of Cochin. I wonder whether we had heard of Malabar? There was no Kerala then. Travancore, Cochin and Malabar were the Malayalam-speaking regions. Malabar was ruled over by a Governor who was the representative of someone who was the king of an island far away somewhere. He was also the Emperor of India. I did not know all this then. All that I knew was that I had to be loyal to the Maharaja, who was considered God incarnate. The Maharaja was not spoken of casually; he was the Beloved Ruler, the Worshipful Highness. We prayed to God to sustain the rule of the Maharaja over the state as long as the moon and the stars shone. The schools began their classes every day after the masters and pupils had stood with folded hands of supplication and sung the state anthem. It was called 'Vancheesa mangalam' and called upon the Almighty to ensure the perpetual rule of the Ruler of Vanchinadu, the other name for Trávancore, and his victory!

We walked to school and in fact to every other place. There were no buses or cars. The roads were covered with red powdery sand. They were called royal highways. Some people travelled by bullock cart. There were even a few horseback riders. But most people just walked. Only those who paid land tax were considered full-fledged citizens. They alone had voting rights. My Bappa paid land tax.

Bappa went on foot to the hills for having trees felled. It took him some two days to reach the workplace. He had to go through hills and jungle and Owl Damu's father Sankaran Kutty accompanied him. They would take packets of cooked rice to eat on the way. I liked to eat the specially cooked meal. So Sankaran Kutty would leave one packet of the rice at home; Abdul Khader, Owl Damu and I would share it.

In those days our hunger was great. So was our thirst. We had plenty to eat and drink. But all that seemed insufficient. We would gobble up anything edible we saw and drink large quantities of water. With bulging stomachs we would lie down anywhere and go to sleep. It was Umma or Nangeli who would pick us up at night and lay us down on the bed. Abdul Khader and I generally slept with Bappa on his bed. The mattress' was a thick double-lined mat made of fine handwoven screwpine leaves which was spread on a cot. Bappa, Abdul Khader and I lay on that bed, in that order. Umma slept a little distance away on a bed made up on another cot. We thus lived in great comfort. And then one day a terrible event took place. Truth, justice and morality were crushed mercilessly and the way was opened for the destruction of the world. The reason was just bedwetting. Someone was wetting the bed at night!

Who was it? Abdul Khader or I?

There was no clue. Who ought to be punished? Umma and Bappa thought over it deeply. They could not come to a decision.

It was then that truth, justice and morality were butchered. The cruel act took place one evening at dusk. The sun had not set. The sun was looking down at everything through the coconut palm near the western door of our house. None other than the sun was a witness. I was declared guilty. For the first time the world saw me hanging my head in shame!

The scene remains clear in my mind. How could it fade?

It was on the gleaming white spread of sand in front of our house. The eminent judges were sitting on the sand. Everyone was there. My Bappa and his friends, Madhavan Nayar, Krishnan, Ousep Mapila, Sankaran Kutty and the mahouts. Then there was Palasseri Mohamed, the beloved brother-in-law of my Bappa, my uncle. This uncle of mine was a fighter with a wrestler's body and a stentorian voice. In my uncle's lap sat the lame darling of the family, Abdul Khader. The revered elders had drunk strong tea with plenty of milk and sugar and they were now chewing pan mixed with good-quality tobacco. Abdul Khader sipped tea from the glass which my uncle had given him.

Bappa called me into that group. I went before them, though I did not know why. Bappa made me stand close to him. He pulled off my dhoti and made me stand there naked. On my waist was tied a broad silver chain on which hung some silver pendants. They looked dull and lustreless. Bappa said, as if addressing the world at large, 'Do you see this? All the silver has become black and lost its lustre.' He didn't stop there. Bappa killed truth, justice and morality with one stroke. He said, 'This fellow wets his bed at night!'

The skies did not break asunder. Nor did thunder reverberate. Perhaps the sunlight blanched a little and became dimmer. Madhavan Nayar said with a dignified accent: 'Night fever!'

I said, 'It's not me who pisses in bed. It's Abdul Khader!'

Abdul Khader declared: 'It's Ikkaka. Not me!'

Three people sleep on the bed, in the morning the bed is wet.

One of them wet it. Who's that? That was the question! What's the proof that it was me? I said with conviction, 'It's not me.'

But the world would not accept it. The world wanted to wipe out truth, justice and morality. My uncle did it with one terrible shout. 'It's not him, it's you!'

Everyone looked at me. I was branded as the shameful wetter of beds! I looked at the sun. It was motionless. I called my Umma. She did not answer. The world had abandoned me!

They joined together and passed their verdict. There was only one specific cure for 'night fever'—for wetting the bed at night. It was to crawl between the legs of a tusker elephant! Having passed judgement, the group dispersed. I did not swoon at the thought of it. When I looked up I saw the tusker sprinkling sand on its back with its trunk. What fierce-looking sharp white tusks! Cruel eyes devoid of sympathy!

I went to my mother and told her in a frightened voice, 'Umma, did you hear that? It seems I have to crawl between the legs of the tusker.'

'That's because you wet your bed, isn't it?' Umma answered.

Nangeli consoled me, 'My dear, you have "night fever".'

Bappa said,'If you want to stop wetting the bed, you should crawl between the legs of the elephant.'

'Is it all right if I crawl under the cow elephant?'

'No, you must crawl between the legs of the tusker. You're a male.'

Very well. They have passed judgement. I am the person who wets the bed at night. I am the person who should crawl between the legs of the tusker. So be it. If the elephant kills me they would all be happy!

I would become a martyr!

I walked about with my prospective martyrdom looming large before me. But was I allowed to go about in peace without being teased about it constantly?

'Ikkaka is going to crawl between the legs of the tusker. To cure him of "night fever". That's why Ikkaka wets the bed!' Abdul Khader broadcast the news to everyone at school. Owl Damu assisted him in his efforts.

He was now an inseparable companion to Abdul Khader. Damu had been my friend but now he changed sides and loyalties. Abdul Khader must have bribed him with presents. Let my time come. Owl Damu would come to me. I would also have something to give him. What hadn't I given him once— dates, halwa, fried mutton! Ungrateful Damu! Gratitude had disappeared from this world and Owl Damu was mainly responsible!

'Bed-wetter!' They shouted after me. Not just one boy; but the whole lot, in gangs. 'Bed-wetter!'

I went on the warpath and beat up some of them. I could hit out at some; but I got beaten in return. When the fight was over there stood in front of us Pudusseri Narayana Pilla 'Saar', cane in hand. Owl Damu said I had started the fight and Abdul Khader supported him. When Abdul Khader had fallen down into the canal from the coconut palm bridge it was I who had gone down and brought him out. When he had begun swallowing mouthfuls of water and was drowning in the river I had rescued him. More than all that I was his very own elder brother. And he was now prepared to speak against me! Is anything more required to bring destruction to this evil world?

I stayed silent.

Owl Damu and Abdul Khader gave a highly misleading version of my doings. I had hit out at everyone without cause; also, I had 'night fever' and I wet my bed at night. Further, I was to crawl between the legs of the tusker!

'Who said first that he wets his bed?' Pudusseri Narayana Pilla 'Saar' asked.

Abdul Khader replied, 'But he does!'

I said, 'It's not I!'

Pudusseri Narayana Pilla 'Saar' turned to me and asked, 'Wasn't it you who offered to show your arithmetic lesson in return for fried fish?' Yes, that was true. But what connection did it have with what was happening now?

This was what had happened.

Both Abdul Khader and I were bad at arithmetic. We used to get beatings often for getting our sums wrong. After a little while however only Abdul Khader was getting beatings for wrong answers. A Muslim girl who sat next to me started showing me her answers. So I went about in borrowed glory. One night while we were eating our meal I noticed a piece of fried mullet on top of the rice in front of Abdul Khader. I had already finished eating my share of the fish. I asked Umma for one more piece, as mullet was my favourite fish. But she refused. How was I to get a piece of Abdul Khader's fried mullet? He was busy eating the rice.

'Hey you, give me that piece of fish. I shall show you my sums,' I said.

Thinking of all the blows he would get for his incorrect sums, Abdul Khader sadly passed on the piece of fried fish to me. I ate it with relish.

That was all. I forgot the incident. Why should I keep it in mind? I did my sums correctly by looking over my neighbour's shoulder but how was I to advertise this?

The next day I copied the sum as usual and sat quietly. Abdul Khader had not done his sum. But how was I to show him my sum? The whole class would see me doing it. And along with them Pudusseri Narayana Pilla 'Saar' too. I was grateful for the fried mullet; but there was nothing I could do. Those who could not do their sums had to stand up. Among them was Abdul Khader. He was the eleventh pupil, just behind me. Pudusseri Narayana Pilla 'Saar' started caning them, starting from one end of the row. Abdul Khader began to cry loudly even before his turn came.

'You there, Abdul Khader, why are you crying?' the master asked.

Abdul Khader replied sobbing, 'I gave up my fried mullet. Now I have to receive the beating also.'

'Why, what happened?'

'Ikkaka promised to show me his sum and took my fried mullet. He didn't show me and now I have to be caned.'

All this was said quite loudly. All the students of Class One and Class Two heard it. I was quite ashamed. Pudusseri Narayana Pilla 'Saar' gave me two hard blows on my palm. Why? Was it because I had taken and eaten the fried mullet or because I had not shown Abdul Khader the sum? I had no idea. When masters punish children they should state the reason for doing so. He didn't tell me, though.

As I said, justice and morality had been abandoned by the world. Why should Pudusseri Narayana Pilla 'Saar' rake up the incident of the fried mullet now? The point was that I had been called a bed-wetter. That was why the fight took place. Anyhow it was I who had been told to crawl between the legs of the tusker. I explained everything at length but Pudusseri Narayana Pilla 'Saar' said it was not clear to him. Everyone had received just one whack each. But he gave me two. Was there any justice in this? But then, the world is like that. Didn't I tell you, truth, justice and morality have fled from this world?

As we were returning home from school Abdul Khader said in a whisper, 'Bed-wetter!'

You must remember that he was jeering at his own elder brother! Didn't he need to be punished? I gave him one blow! He ran away weeping and complained to Bappa and Uncle. Each of them gave me a clout on the head and twisted my ear for good measure. Was there any justice in all this? I couldn't see any.

And so life went on amid all this injustice. But I did not feel frustrated. I had been chosen to crawl between the legs of the tusker. That was a rare honour indeed. No one in our town had done this great deed. I was going to do it. My classmates looked at me with envy. I was happy. There was a change in my gait and my demeanour; even in my talk. I went around as if I didn't care a bit for the whole world. As the appointed day drew near I began to have some misgivings. And a creeping sense of fear. Would the elephant stamp me to death? I had heard that somewhere far away, a tusker had gored its mahout to death!

The elephant under whose legs I was to crawl had been a wild elephant once. He had roamed about freely in the dense forest. He was caught and tamed. But he had not been tamed properly. If he was asked to turn left by the mahout he would turn right. Or he would stand still and not turn at all. When the mahout pulled him by the ear with his hook he would trumpet with a frightening sound. Even then I had got on his back. The mahout had held me while I did so. The mahout said I was trembling with fear and that I had pissed on the back of the elephant out of sheer terror. That of course was a total lie. But the elephant had heard him say it. Suppose the animal were to hold it against me?

At last the auspicious day dawned. On that day I was to crawl under the legs of the elephant.

The tusker was given a bath and brought to the compound. I also bathed. That is to say, both the elephant and I bathed in the river. They made me wear a brand new dhoti, shirt and cap. My shirt had a watch pocket in which I hid a small raw mango. I did not find time to eat it. I needed salt to eat it with. It could wait. I could eat it after I had crawled under the legs of the animal.

I took a good look at the elephant. He was jet black like a rough spherical mound of granite with four thick pillar-like legs, a fat trunk, thick tail and pointed tusks. His eyes gleamed with villainy and cruelty. I felt as if I were choking. Would the elephant stamp me to death? Or perhaps he would wind his trunk round me and put me into his mouth and chew away for all he was worth. I felt like running away from home. But where could I go? And how?

There were people all round. On one side were my classmates, both boys and girls. Among them was the Muslim girl who used to show me her sums secretly. Radhamani was there. On the other side beyond the elephant were my Bappa and uncle and Madhavan Nayar and Sankaran Kutty and Krishnan and Ousep Mapila. They were sitting on coconut fronds and eating ripe bananas. As usual Abdul Khader was to be found on my uncle's lap. The fellow had a banana in his mouth and one in each hand.

Bappa brought a huge bunch of ripe palangodan bananas and gave away most of it to the elephant, the mahouts and the others. He did not give me any. A quarter of the bunch was left on the ground near Abdul Khader.

I shouted, 'Bappa, you didn't give me any bananas.'

'I've kept them for you here. Come crawling beneath the elephant!'

On my side there were the women. My Umma and her

younger sisters, my Umma's Umma, aunt, Nangeli and the wives of Ousep Mapila, Sankaran Kutty and Krishnan. Among the women was Owl Damu. He was eating a banana with enjoyment and giving advice to me, 'Go on, go quietly under the elephant. Why are you afraid? Am I not here?'

He was the one who had changed sides. He had joined the enemy. But it has been said that one should love one's enemy. I took out the raw mango from the watch pocket of my shirt and gave it to Damu.

'The elephant may stamp me to death. You can eat this mango. Use plenty of salt. It's nice and sour.'

Umma said, 'Don't be afraid, you scamp.'

More than fear I felt greedy for the bananas and disappointed at not getting them. I was standing with the women, on one side of the elephant. My mouth watered for the bananas but I felt afraid. My legs seemed to have been swallowed up by the earth. They would not move. I sweated profusely. All of a sudden my mouth seemed to have dried up. I wanted to urinate. I felt hot and flustered. Was I feeling giddy? Had my eyes lost their power of sight? No. I could see my father and others through a gap between the legs of the elephant as if through a thick black open door. Abdul Khader had finished eating the bananas in his hand. He was pulling out the ones from the bunch on the ground.

I shouted, 'Bappa, he will finish the entire bunch!'

Bappa picked up the bunch and held it out to me. Uncle commanded me in his loud voice, 'Come here, you imp!'

I stood motionless.

Chakki, Krishnan's wife said, 'Go on, go through those legs. Aren't you ashamed, child? You're old enough to get married. And yet you wet your bed!'

'I don't pee in bed. That is Abdul Khader.'

'No, it's you,' Umma said.

I shot back, 'How do you know?'

'Haven't I brought you into this world? After Abdul Khader was born you would feed at my breast on the sly!'

'I've not fed at anyone's breast on the sly!'

'You have been breast-fed by auntie Madhavi Kutty too.'

Owl Damu said, 'So you've fed at my mother's breast! That

explains your spirit. Would any other boy be able to run and catch me?' He turned to his mother. 'How dare you give away my milk to strangers?'

'I've fed at no one's breasts!' I said.

Umma asked, 'After all, didn't I give birth to you?'

'No one has given birth to me.'

'How can that be?

'I came by myself.'

Adam was created by Allah. Adam, the first man, had no Umma or Bappa. Adam was not breast-fed by anyone. I knew about these things.

Umma said, 'I carried you inside me for nine months. When you were born you were a tiny weak baby. I fed you at my breast and looked after you till you grew up healthy. Now you say I didn't give birth to you. That's cheek, indeed!'

'Who is your witness?'

'Your Bappa!'

'Anyhow I don't pee in bed!'

'It is you!'

'It's not me....! The elephant will stamp me to death!'

Nangeli said, 'Son, don't be afraid. Aren't the mahouts there?'

Owl Damu said, 'Why are you afraid? Am I not here?'

I felt like strangling him.

'Son, go on, call out the name of Allah and crawl through!'

I recited the verse with which every chapter in the Koran began— 'In the name of Allah, the beneficient and merciful....' I could see Bappa holding out the bunch of bananas. I felt greedy for the bananas; I also felt afraid of the elephant. I could see Abdul Khader gobbling the bananas. At this rate he would run through the entire bunch. I walked as if in a dream. A vile stench emanated from the elephant. I crawled between the legs of the animal and emerged on the other side as if out of a dark cavern. The elephant made an attempt to urinate on me. The urine came down in a sudden torrent without warning. It just escaped falling on my head!

The spectators applauded. Bappa gathered me into his arms. I wriggled out of his hands and caught hold of the bunch of bananas. I snatched away the bananas from Abdul Khader's hands. Then I gave a fruit each to my classmates. I gave two each to the Muslim girl who had shown me her sums and to Radhamani.

Owl Damu stretched out his hand, 'What about me? Don't I pay land tax?'

I gave him one banana. We gathered all the banana skins in a heap and fed the elephant. That is to say, the mahout fed them to the elephant.

I was the brave chap who had crawled between the legs of an elephant. This was greatness indeed!

And so we all lived on happily. Umma said I did not wet the bed after I had crawled under the elephant's legs. The simple fact was that I no longer slept with Bappa. I slept in Umma's bed. Everything went on fine.

Then one night there was an uproar. It was Bappa striking Abdul Khader left and right. When Umma struck a match and lighted the lamp we found that Abdul Khader had wet the bed!

Who then was the shameless fellow who had been peeing in Bappa's bed all this time? And the innocent who had been getting the blame for it all? Look at the ways of the world! Wasn't it Abdul Khader who ought to have crawled between the legs of the tusker? But Abdul Khader who had both his hands up warding off the blows, cried out, 'I did not do it! Ikkaka must have come and peed on the sly!'

He is not guilty!

Umma remarked, 'He could be right!'

What an unjust world! The innocent are punished. Imagine I was considered the guilty one! Abdul Khader who had passed gallons and gallons of urine in bed was a good boy!

Anyhow there were no clues as to who had really wet the bed. Umma and Bappa had some doubts. They were not sure whether the guilty one was Abdul Khader or I. Anyhow the world at large was divided into two camps. At school Abdul Khader bribed many of the boys and girls and enlisted them on his side. Owl Damu was in the non-aligned camp. He had a theory that neither I nor Abdul Khader had passed urine in bed. It was Bappa who had done it!

When Nangeli heard this she and Sankaran Kutty chased Damu all over the compound striking him left and right.

. Radhamani switched from Abdul Khader's camp to mine. When Abdul Khader gave Radhamani a particularly juicy piece of tamarind she joined his side again. Was it right to change loyalties for just one piece of tamarind? I gave her some toasted cashewnuts and she came back to my side. She didn't stop with that. She enthusiastically proclaimed, 'Abdul Khader is the bed-wetter.'

I was overjoyed.

Radhamani longed for something She told me in confidence, 'I want a hair from the elephant's tail. Will you get it for me?'

If I had an elephant of my own I would have given the entire animal to Radhamani! I told her so.

She replied, 'I don't want an entire elephant. I want one hair from the tail.'

'I'll get it for you!' I said this in front of Owl Damu and Abdul Khader. I had seen Hindu friends of Bappa and Umma using hair from the elephant's tail. They would wear it in rings round their fingers. Some wore it round their wrists also. It was believed that elephant's hair had miraculous properties.

I could easily get elephant's hair from the animal's tail. After all the mahouts were my friends. Even so I thought I would ask Bappa and Umma. They flatly refused. 'You don't need elephant's hair.'

They said this before the mahouts. I did not realise they had changed sides. Owl Damu and Abdul Khader had told tales about me to them. On top of it they gave the mahouts a coconut shell full of toasted cashewnuts.

I approached a mahout. 'I want an elephant's tail.'

The mahouts made fun of me and said, 'The elephant has only one tail. If we cut it off and give it to you, what will the animal do?'

I said, 'I don't want the whole tail. Just one hair. Just one woollen hair!'

The mahouts laughed, 'Elephant wool! As if it is a sheep!'

'One elephant hair!' I begged of them. The mahouts refused to give it to me and said so before that lame-legged Abdul Khader and Owl Damu.

Should they not have got it for me? After all the things I had given them—betel leaves, areca nuts, tender coconuts, tobacco, bananas, halwa and dates. Hadn't I given them the thick strong-smelling cigars which Bappa smoked? Why are these mahouts such an ungrateful iot? I had asked for just one strand of elephant's hair! They refused to get it. I'd show them! I would decide against becoming a mahout when I grew up! That way the mahouts would lose a very useful addition to their company.

I then decided to steal the elephant's hair!

How was I do it?

I thought of it night and day. How was I to steal a hair from the tail of a tusker elephant which was very much alive? As I went about lost in thought...'Elephant Wool!' came the mocking cry of voices in the air. Most of the pupils in the school seemed to be calling me by that name. The lame chap and the owl were the gang leaders. I felt isolated. Even Radhamani joined the ranks of the enemy. Everyone seemed to be calling, 'Elephant Wool! Bed-wetter!' There were some fights and I was caned by Pudusseri Narayana Pilla 'Saar'.

Even at night Abdul Khader would mock me from his bed, 'Elephant Wool! Bed-wetter!'

I'd show them all! I swore in my mind. I'd steal an elephant's hair! What was the best way to do it?

The days passed. One fine morning I walked into my class like a conquering hero. I called together everyone, friend and enemy alike. I looked hard at Owl Damu and the lame Abdul Khader. Then I asked Radhamani, 'Have any of you seen elephant's hair? Have you ever touched it?'

No one from the audience replied. They were silent. I handed over one long elephant hair to Radhamani. Then I looked at the assembled audience and said in utter contempt, 'Bloonko!'

They wanted to know how I had managed to get the elephant's hair. Owl Damu and the lame Abdul Khader also wanted to know how I had managed to get it. They asked me several times. I would not tell my secret; I would not tell the story for a long, long time. I shall do so now.

How could one steal a hair from the tail of a huge tusker elephant! One could pluck a hair from the tail while the animal is tethered to a tree. But suppose the tusker turns round and gores you with its tusk? As I told you I thought over it night

and day. Finally I struck upon an easy plan. The elephants and
all of us bathed in the same river. I had very often joined the
mahouts in massaging the elephants' bodies with smooth
rounded granite stones.

All the people of the village bathed in the river near the
ferry. The elephants were also given their baths there. It was a
broad river and the water was crystal clear. One could see the
clean white sand at the bottom and there was hardly any mud.
On the other side of the river was an ancient toddy shop. All
the swimmers made a beeline for the toddy shop. They were
able to have a bath and drink some toddy as well! Near the
bank of the river three elephants lay in the water. The tusker
lay between the cow elephants. I had to steal a hair from the
tail of the tusker!

At this time a number of people were bathing. Quite a
number were swimming over to the other bank. Some people
were going across in a ferry boat. Among the bathers were
Bappa, my uncle, Sankaran Kutty, Krishnan, Padmanabhan
Nayar and Ousep Mapila. Owl Damu and I took off our dhotis
and plunged into the river. Owl Damu was cleaned of mud
and dirt by his father. Bappa scrubbed me clean in the water
before letting me play around in the river. I dived and swam
underwater for a while. I surfaced and looked around. The
coast was clear. No one was watching me. This was the time. I
dived again and went towards the spot where the elephants
were lying down. I slowly raised my head above the water and
located the tusker. I dived again and gently caught hold of the
tusker's tail. It was quite rough. I thought I could bite off one
strand of hair. I could not get a proper hold with my teeth. I
tugged hard at the tail and bit deep into it. I pulled at it once
again. That was the last thing I was able to do before the
confusion that followed.

The elephant stood up with a gurgling cry. I let go of the tail
and surfaced. It turned round and saw me. I dived again. I
swam as fast as I could underwater, putting as much distance
as possible between myself and the animal. I was choking,
unable to breathe underwater. But I kept on doggedly till I
came to a dark portion of the river where I came up. I was
below the branches of a silk-cotton tree which slanted over the

river, near the Excise Station.

I looked back.

The tusker had got up and was standing with its trunk and tusks pointing upwards. It was trumpeting and making other frightful noises. The other two elephants were now also standing up and trumpeting loudly. People were running about and there was great confusion. I was stark naked. I climbed onto the bank. I stumbled through pot holes and thorns and caught hold of some creepers hanging from a big tree. I climbed to the top of the tree and hid myself among its luxuriant foliage. Big red ants crept over me and gave me stinging bites. I tried my best to brush them away as I clung on in great fear. I do not know how long I sat there. After some time the noise made by the elephants and the running people seemed to have subsided. It was as if nothing had happened and it had all been a bad dream. All the water on my body had dried up. I was left with the pain of the ant bites. As I sat thus I heard the voice of Bappa. He was calling me loudly by name. I called back, 'Bappa!' and slowly climbed down the tree. Bappa made me wear the towel which he had on him in order to cover my nakedness. He picked out the ants which were still clinging to me. He gently massaged my body and laid his hand on my head.

We went home. I told Umma, 'Umma, I lost my dhoti.'

Umma replied calmly, 'Everyone lost their clothes.'

When the elephants were roused the people around ran for their lives. They forgot their dhotis and even their underwear. Among those who ran away without any clothes were Bappa, Uncle, Padmanabhan Nayar, Krishnan, Sankaran Kutty, Owl Damu and Ousep Mapila. They ran through the pathway, waded through streams and reached our house. On the way Ousep Mapila stumbled over a stone and hurt his knee. The tusker gored one of the cow elephants but not very deeply. The mahouts managed to control the elephants with a great deal of difficulty and finally tethered them.

They said the tusker had gone mad.

This of course was not true. I was responsible for it all. How was I to reveal this? If Bappa came to know of it would he hang me upside down?

I said, 'Bappa, the tusker did not go mad!'
'Then what happened?'
'It was bitten.'
'Who bit it?'
'Bappa! I bit the elephant.'
'You bit that tusker elephant?'
'Yes, I swam underwater and tried to bite off a hair from its tail!'

Bappa laughed. He laughed loud and long. Then he asked me, 'Why did you want elephant's hair?'

I said, 'Bappa, you know that friend of yours, that Excise Inspector. His daughter Radhamani asked for an elephant's hair.'

It was then that Umma started laughing.

'My dear child,' Umma said, 'it was Allah who saved you from great danger.' She turned to Bappa. 'Get him a strand of elephant's hair. Otherwise he will again go and bite that poor tusker!'

Bappa said, 'You rascal! That you should bite that animal!'

'I did not bite it. I was trying to pull out a hair with my teeth.'

'Well, come along. Don't tell this to anyone.'

Bappa took me to the place where the elephants were tethered. One of the cow elephants had a small red gash above the foreleg. The mahout had smeared some paste ground out of herbs on the wound, but blood was still oozing from it. Bappa made the mahout cut off a strand of hair from the tail of the tusker and gave it to me. The tusker looked at me with fury not unmixed with mockery. It made some *phutphut* noises in its stomach. It seemed to say, 'Aren't you the sly thief who tried to bite off hair from my tail?'

Original title 'Anappooda'; from the collection Anappooda *(1975).*

Glossary

Badshah	:	king (Persian, Urdu)
bajra	:	millet - a variety of lentil
Bappa	:	term used by Muslims to denote 'father'
beedi	:	a cheap Indian variant of the cigarette, the outer cover being a special type of leaf
biriyani	:	a specially-cooked dish of rice and meat with plenty of spices prepared for festive occasions
dhoti	:	a white cloth, often with a coloured border, tied round the waist to cover the lower portion of the body
ganja/ganja beedi	:	ganja is the dried leaf of the opium poppy which is used as a drug to be smoked. It is often stuffed inside beedis in place of the tobacco
halwa	:	an Indian sweet made from flour and certain fruits cooked in plenty of oil
Isha	:	the Muslim night prayer - can be performed any time after sunset and before dawn - usually performed between 8 and 9 p.m.
jibba	:	a loose shirt, generally without collar, reaching down to the knees
kannan	:	a variety of edible banana
kutty	:	a Malayalam word meaning 'small', or 'tiny' usually used as a term of endearment; also used as a suffix or prefix to names
Maghrib	:	the Muslim prayer performed at sunset
mangalam	:	denotes an auspicious end or closure to any event or ceremony
Nambudiri	:	the equivalent of brahman, the highest caste in

		the Hindu hierarchy
Nayar	:	the original 'warrior' caste among the Kerala Hindus, actually third in the hierarchy - but a little below the Kshatriyas who were the real warrior caste and the rulers
nilavilakku	:	a brass or bell-metal lamp which has a heavy base; used as an auspicious lamp to be lighted on special occasions to shed light on an idol or the holy scriptures
Nizam	:	the titular head of the ruling family of Hyderabad, now no longer living
padati	:	a variety of edible banana
palangodan	:	a variety of edible banana
poovan	:	a variety of edible banana considered specially tasty and a favourite among many
pujari	:	a priest who performs 'puja' which is the Hindu worship ritual
Thiyya	:	an 'outcaste' - one who did menial jobs, especially plucking coconuts and extracting toddy from palms
Umma	:	term used by Muslims to denote 'mother'